He was a red-blooded man . . .

. . . and there was nothing wrong with wanting, Michael told himself. Touching was when problems began. Coming to a stop, he rested a moment. He had to admit that he did want to touch her. Her skin looked so soft, and that mouth . . . No, he was much better off dating women who expected no more than he was willing to give. Jo Knight was definitely off-limits.

Starting back down the beach, Michael was glad he'd had this talk with himself. Then he saw her. She was walking out of the water, her long hair trailing past her shoulders. The afternoon sun shimmered on her golden skin and the suit molded her body. Her legs seemed endless as she bent to retrieve her shirt. Draping it over her arm, she swung her blue eyes to him as he stopped a foot from her.

"You look all hot and bothered," Jo said, noticing the red splotches on his face. "Maybe you should cool off." Turning, she headed for the house.

His stomach in knots, Michael watched her go. *So much for mind over matter.* Pivoting, he ran into the cooling ocean waves and dived under. . . .

ABOUT THE AUTHOR

According to Patricia Cox, humor was definitely a prerequisite when she had to cope with four children under the age of ten and write a humorous column for the *Detroit News*. Her literary career began, though, at the age of sixteen when she wrote a teenage gossip column in the *Akron Beacon Journal*. Patricia makes her home in Arizona with her husband.

Books by Patricia Cox

HARLEQUIN AMERICAN ROMANCE

217—FOREVER FRIENDS
303—THE FOREVER CHOICE

PATRICIA COX

DAYE AND KNIGHT

Harlequin Books

TORONTO • NEW YORK • LONDON
AMSTERDAM • PARIS • SYDNEY • HAMBURG
STOCKHOLM • ATHENS • TOKYO • MILAN
MADRID • WARSAW • BUDAPEST • AUCKLAND

To Corinne Meyer,
who is always willing to climb out
on that shaky limb with me

Published July 1992

ISBN 0-373-16447-5

DAYE AND KNIGHT

Prologue

Jo Knight leaned closer to the airliner window, gazing down at her first glimpse of the Hawaiian shoreline. The sight was even more lovely than she'd been led to believe.

The water was so clear, so blue, and the frothy waves so white as they skimmed the sand then rushed back out to sea. Several boats with colorful sails—tiny as toys from her viewpoint—dotted the serene ocean. In the distance, she could see towering hotels, swaying palm trees and winding roads twisting through the foliage. Jo wondered if her gaze was encompassing the beachfront cottage she'd rented for two weeks.

A vacation. Even though it was a working vacation, she was looking forward to her time on the beautiful island of Maui.

The plane tilted and Jo could see mountains looking like large green hills from up so high. She wanted to take in everything while she was here, all the fascinating places she'd read about for years. Mount Haleakala where the sunrises were spectacular. The city of Hana with its seven sacred pools. The fishing village of Lahaina.

So romantic. Not that she was looking for romance, Jo reminded herself. Of course, she wouldn't run from it either. Jo Knight believed that there was one special someone for every person on earth, and eventually her someone would find her.

The flight attendant announced that they were preparing to land. Jo fastened her seat belt and sighed. A dream come true, this trip. Perhaps one day she'd write a song about it. Settling back, she watched the shoreline move closer.

Chapter One

The barking seemed to be coming from the front porch. Most likely a stray, Michael Daye thought as he unlocked the suitcase he'd set on the bed. He knew for a fact that the nearest house was at least two miles away, so it couldn't be a neighbor's dog. Removing his suit coat, he walked across the bedroom to hang it in the closet.

Pausing, he realized that the yapping was continuing, and then he heard a thud on the wooden porch. He'd been traveling a long while and had come a great distance for some badly needed peace and quiet. His plane had landed a scant hour ago on Maui, where he'd rented a car and driven to his aunt's beachfront home in Wailea Canyon, and already someone had found him even in this isolated spot. With a frown, Michael went to check it out.

Swinging open the door, he saw a small, shaggy dog with gray fringes of hair hanging in his eyes, growling alongside very feminine feet wearing white sandals. His eyes traveled up a pair of impossibly long, shapely legs past white shorts, a dazzling blue top and on to an oval face wearing a puzzled expression. The woman shook back her long blond hair, and lowered eyes as blue as her shirt to check the paper she held in her hand.

"What are you doing in my house?" she asked.

"You've obviously come to the wrong address," Michael answered, trying to replace his annoyance with patience. "This house belongs to my aunt, and I'll be staying here for the next two weeks." He glanced past her and saw no car or taxi in sight. "You shouldn't have let your cab go, but I can call you another."

"Just a minute," she said, angling back to again check the address on the pink stucco wall. "This is the right house." Digging around in her large canvas tote, she found the key and held it up. "Noel Kramer gave me his key this morning when he dropped me off at the airport. Noel must be your cousin, right?"

He certainly was, a thirty-year-old beach bum who'd never held a job longer than six months. Michael cleared his throat impatiently. "Yes, but—"

"We're exchanging, you see," she went on, "swapping, so to speak. He's staying at my place in Los Angeles while I bunk out in his mother's beach house for a couple of weeks. I've got a gig here, you see."

He noticed that she had a wild orchid stuck incongruously behind one ear. "A gig?" he asked as the dog stopped barking and ran past him into the house, obviously convinced that the discussion had ended and Michael was the intruder.

"Musician's term for job." Hoisting high her guitar case as if to prove her claim, she shoved past him holding a pet carrier in her other hand. She surveyed the living room briefly, nodded with satisfaction, then set down the case and carrier.

Staring after her, Michael shoved his hands into his pockets, more stunned than angry. "Look, there's undoubtedly been a misunderstanding of dates here." Aiming for the reasonable tone that worked so well in business meetings, he stepped closer to the woman who was stooping down and murmuring to whatever animal was in the carrier. "I'm an architect from California, and I'm working on a very involved project with a pressing deadline. That's why I requested the use of Aunt Charlotte's house. It's quiet here and I can work uninterrupted and—"

"Where in California?" she asked, not even looking up.

"San Francisco. And I've sublet my apartment to this young man from our Seattle office who's just gotten married. For his honeymoon, so I can't possibly go back on my word." That had probably been a mistake, Michael thought, not for the first time. But Tim was so earnest, so starry-eyed, so *young*. Ah, well, it was only for two weeks. "So you see, you'll have to leave."

Ignoring that, she opened the wire door of the carrier and a huge white cat tiptoed out, sniffed the carpet somewhat disdainfully, then leaped right into a shocked Michael's arms.

The woman laughed. "Say, you've got good reflexes."

"I don't like cats," Michael confessed. He held the furry thing as far from his face as he could, but the silly cat was slithering up his chest.

"They're actually smarter than dogs." Turning, she wandered the room, checking out the large stone fireplace and the louvered doors, opening them to look out at a magnificent view of the ocean. "Wow, this is even more beautiful than Noel said it was." The dog, having toured the entire house, scooted past her and onto the bricked patio. "Heinz, take it easy," she yelled after him.

"Heinz?" Michael questioned.

"Mmm. As in 57 varieties. We're a little uncertain as to his ancestry."

The cat was now busily licking his neck. Michael had about had it. "Look, will you take this... this animal?"

She walked to him, smiling. "Isn't that sweet, he likes you. Floppy doesn't lick just anyone." Taking the cat, she hugged him to her.

"I'm flattered." Michael removed a white handkerchief from his back pocket and wiped his damp neck. Just then, the dog raced back inside and whipped past him, heading for *his* bedroom, long ears flying as he ran, nearly tripping over his oversize feet. "Do you usually travel with all your pets?" he asked wearily.

Setting Floppy down on the floor so he, too, could explore, she shook her head. "Heavens, no. I left my other two cats and my parakeet with Noel. They're not good travelers. They get motion sick, you see."

He got the picture and it wasn't a pretty one. This had gone on long enough. "Look, whatever your name is, I—"

"JoAnn Knight." She stuck her hand out, her expression friendly. "My friends call me Jo."

Friends. No, he didn't want to be friends with this woman and her menagerie, but years of manners came through and he shook her hand. "Michael Daye." She had soft skin. Very soft. And her eyes were the bluest he'd ever seen. But all that aside, she was interfering in his life. "As I was about to say, I'll be glad to phone around and find you a condo or an apartment you can rent."

Jo folded her arms across her chest and quietly but firmly shook her head.

He'd take peace at any price. "I realize this was an honest misunderstanding, so I'll pay for your stay at another location. Do you want to phone or shall I?"

She frowned at his shirtfront. "Do you know you're wearing a tie? A tie, in Hawaii." She scrunched up her face as she raised her eyes to his. "I think that's against the law here."

He was not amused. "Miss Knight, I—"

"Call me Jo. Look, I think we're making a mountain out of a molehill here. What's wrong with sharing? We both agreed to the arrangement in good faith, as did Noel and your Aunt Charlotte. You need the isolation of the house and so do I. I promised Christy and I can't let her down."

He was having trouble following her. "Christy?"

"My friend, Christy Hanes. She's a fourth-grade teacher at a school not far from here."

Michael glanced over at her guitar case, wondering if he'd missed something. "I thought you said something about a gig?"

Jo shrugged. "Gig, job, whatever. See, I tell children's stories and read from books. I sing and play the guitar, mostly songs I write, at schools, library reading groups, that sort of thing. To get kids interested in reading. I'm connected with the national literacy program."

A singer? Guitar music? Noise and confusion. No, that wouldn't do. Michael ran an unsteady hand through his short hair, feeling as if he were losing ground rapidly. "A worthy cause, I'm sure, but I *must* have quiet in order to concentrate on my work."

No sooner were the words out of his mouth than the dog emerged from the bedroom and barreled toward him. Caught by surprise, Michael tried to sidestep as the small gray ball of fur ran between his legs, nearly upsetting him. The music was bad enough. But the animals! No, this was too much.

"I know the man who built this house," Michael began, trying valiantly to keep a lid on his temper. "He's got several more along the coast for rent." He walked to the end table and picked up the phone. "We'll get you one of the newer ones. You'll love it. My treat."

"Sorry, Mike, but I can't take your money, and my expense allowance didn't include a rental fee since I told my employer I had the use of this place without charge."

Michael set down the phone and squared his shoulders. "My name is Michael. No one calls me Mike."

They should, Jo thought, studying him. Lord, what an uptight man. Michael sounded much too formal, especially if they were to share a house for two weeks.

Despite his conservative wardrobe, the man was a knockout. His hair was dark and thick, though he wore it a tad too short for Jo's taste. She had a sudden urge to muss its perfection. And to yank off his tie. Shoulders, seemingly a yard wide, stretched the white linen fabric of his shirt. His chest was broad, tapering to a trim waist, and his suit pants hugged muscular thighs, the kind that caused a woman to speculate, to fantasize. Yes, he definitely had potential.

"Okay, Michael it is, but I still won't take your money." With that, she stepped onto the porch and quickly dragged in her two large suitcases. "We promise not to get in your way," she said sweetly as Heinz began to chase Floppy through the archway that led into the dining room.

Enough was enough. Michael picked up the phone and dialed Charlotte. Desperate men did desperate things, he thought, knowing that calling her could net him the jackpot or wipe him out, depending on his aunt's mood.

Charlotte was not only the black sheep of the family, she was as kooky and irreverent as his father was staid and proper. She was also filthy rich, quite eccentric and looked somewhat like a recycled Auntie Mame. She'd shed husband number four only last year, the divorce becoming final on her sixty-fifth birthday. Despite all that, from the top of her red hair to the tips of her painted toenails, Michael adored her.

But, moments later as he stood explaining his dilemma to her and grinding his teeth at her hearty laugh, he realized she also exasperated him regularly.

"My dear Michael," Charlotte went on, "this may be just the thing to put a spring in your step and a gleam in your eye."

Michael clamped a hand on the back of his neck as he dragged the phone across the room, turning away from the woman who was listening and waiting. "Aunt Charlotte, I thought I'd explained that I have a commitment to get these sketches finished and—"

"Yes, yes, a commitment. I know, dear boy. But if you're a tad late, what can they do to you? You own the company, right?"

"I have a partner who would be quite annoyed if I lagged on this, and rightly so." He heard the sound of inhaling, and pictured her seated on her chaise lounge, smoking through her long, Chinese-red cigarette holder. He tried to relax. "I think you should talk with Noel. This is most inconvenient. Perhaps he'd like to call Miss Knight, or fly in and find her other accommodations."

"Oh, I doubt that, dear boy," Charlotte said, blowing smoke. "He's very wrapped up in someone and gone into hiding with her. And you're lucky he didn't give *her* the key. She keeps a pet snake under her bed."

Lucky. Yes, he certainly felt lucky. Obviously Charlotte was in one of her ditzy moods and not about to relent. Michael didn't lose many battles of will, so he supposed there wasn't much he could do about this loss except *try* to be gracious. "All right then. I'll call you when I get back."

"I might see you sooner. I've just heard from a friend who docks his schooner in Lahaina. He's invited me to go sailing." Charlotte chuckled low in her throat. "Simon's a handsome devil. We met at the racetrack last fall."

He couldn't help but smile. There was no one like her. Shaking his head, he hung up and turned around.

The smile changed him radically, Jo thought. While moments ago he'd looked stiff and annoyed, he now looked enormously appealing. There was a hint of humor in his gray eyes that totally disarmed her. And something else. A sudden sensual awareness that had her heart beating like a trip hammer.

How could she resist a man who was obviously nuts about his Aunt Charlotte, even though she'd not given in to him?

Michael tried to rearrange his face into a scowl, but lost that battle, too. "I don't think you understand. You won't relish your stay. I really don't like being disturbed when I work."

"No kidding?" She removed the orchid from her hair and stroked its soft petals. "Imagine, I found this growing wild alongside the drive." She looked back up at him. "Maybe you're in the wrong line of work. I think people should enjoy what they do."

Just what he needed. Advice from a latter-day flower child who made up songs to sing to children. "I'll give that some thought."

"What is this big project you're working on?"

He bent to shoo away the cat who was back and testing his nails out on Michael's pant leg. "Urban renewal. A shopping plaza south of Union Square."

"I know the area." Though she lived in L.A., she had friends in San Francisco and often drove up the coast. "You're lucky to have gotten such a plum to design."

There was that word again. "Luck had nothing to do with it. Hard work, a good reputation and the right bid." Why was he wasting time explaining himself to her? He turned aside as Floppy leaped onto the dining room hutch in two neat bounds, settled on the top and turned to stare back at them through the archway. "You don't seem to have very good control over your animals." As if to underline the thought, Heinz went to the hutch and stood barking up at the cat.

Jo picked up the dog, quieting him. "Oh, relax, will you?" she said to Michael. "My brothers will be here on the weekend and they're very good with animals. Of course, by then, you'll be used to Heinz and Floppy.''

"Brothers?"

"Yes, three of them. Jerry's sixteen, Jason's twelve and Jon's eight. My mother has a thing for *J*s. Nice boys. You'll love them.'' Oblivious to his glare, she rubbed noses with Heinz.

No, he would *not* love the boys. He wouldn't even *meet* the boys. "There isn't enough room here for one brother, much less three.'' Michael loosened his tie. Was it his imagination or was it awfully warm in here? "All right, you win. You can stay. But no brothers.''

"Okay.'' Tossing him a radiant smile, she set down the dog and picked up her canvas tote. This probably wasn't the best time to explain that her parents had jokingly said that they might fly over with the boys while she was here, but nothing was definite.

She was looking decidedly smug, enough to make Michael suddenly suspicious. "I think you tricked me. I'll bet you don't even have three brothers.''

"I most certainly do.'' She pointed to the phone. "Shall I phone them?''

He couldn't take the chance. "No, no.'' He rubbed his forehead, wondering if his sudden headache was caused by the humidity or by the unexpected turn of events. "You've left the doors open and I've got the air-conditioning on.''

"Air-conditioning? When you can have the sea breezes?'' She looked at him incredulously. "I know you've probably been to Hawaii umpteen times and this is my first visit, but truly, you've got to taste the islands, smell them, feel the sunshine. Or else . . . well, why not just stay in California?''

Why, indeed. Heaving a defeated sigh, Michael walked to the thermostat and turned off the air-conditioning. Turning back, he noticed that she'd strolled over and entered his bedroom. He followed and saw her gazing out the high window. "This is my room," he told her quietly.

She turned and he became aware of the late-afternoon sunlight behind her head shimmering in her hair, turning the strands golden. "Now, Mike," Jo began. "That is, *Michael*, let's be fair. Let's check both bedrooms and see what we have here."

Quickly she marched to the next room and, after a few moments, met him back in the living room. "They're both about the same size, each with a private bath. But one has an ocean view and one a view of the pool." She dug a coin out of her canvas tote. "The only fair thing to do is flip."

He had never done anything so ludicrous in his life. But the sooner he got this over with, the sooner he could get unpacked. "Heads," he said resignedly.

She tossed, then sent him an apologetic look. "Sorry, it's tails. Perhaps we ought to lay down a few ground rules while we're at it. Cohabitation policies, so to speak. So you won't be upset," she said, smiling sweetly.

Michael folded his arms across his chest. "Such as?"

"For starters, I swim seven to seven-thirty each morning. In the nude. Therefore, I'd appreciate it if you'd keep yourself busy elsewhere during that time."

He congratulated himself that his expression didn't change one iota as his mind took off with that thought. Even wearing a loose top, he could tell she had some interesting curves. And those legs. "Go on."

"Of course, the only fair thing is to split the food bill. I imagine that, if you just arrived as I did, there's no food in the fridge. We can take your car and run up to the market after we unpack. We should also take turns in the kitchen, alternating cooking and cleanup." She eyed him suspiciously. A steak-and-potatoes man, she'd wager. "But first, we need to discuss and agree on the menu in advance. I mean, for all I know, you're a sushi freak." She nearly laughed out loud at the look of shocked distaste that appeared on his face.

"Hardly." Raw fish seemed more her style. Along with tofu and pine nuts, most likely. Growing more agitated by the minute but reluctant to let her know, he reached into his shirt pocket and dug out a cigarette. Lighting it, then inhaling deeply, he prayed for strength.

"Oh, no! You smoke!" Grabbing a magazine from the end table, she began fanning the air. "Don't you know what the surgeon general says? How can you do that to your body?" And a mighty nice body it was, too, Jo thought as she ran her eyes over his tall frame. A couple of inches over six feet, broad shoulders, slim hips. If only he'd loosen up and change into shorts. At the very least, remove that silly tie.

"It's my only vice," Michael stated, and deliberately took another deep drag.

Yes, it probably was. "Well, it's your funeral. I certainly hope you have lots of insurance." Fanning the smoke, she hastened it toward the open doors.

Actually, he rarely smoked anymore. He'd been working on giving it up gradually for months. He reached for a cigarette only when he was tense. And he certainly was at this moment. Grinding his teeth—another habit he seemed to have acquired in the last half hour—he walked past her and onto the patio, closing the doors behind him.

Michael had the uneasy feeling that he'd just wandered into an unexpected nightmare.

Edgy. Very edgy, Jo thought as she hauled her bags into her bedroom. The man was probably irritable and tense from too much smoking. She'd read where nicotine could do that to a person.

Humming, she pulled clothes from her bag and hung them in the closet. She paused to smile at Floppy and Heinz who'd jumped on her bed and were having a playful scuffle. Stepping to the window, she admired the tall birds of paradise blooming in the yard and sea gulls dipping low over the rippling water.

Jo had the marvelous feeling that she'd just wandered into a beautiful dream.

HE WAS POUTING and he knew it. It wasn't like him, Michael acknowledged, not very pleased with himself.

The truth was he seldom had reason to sulk because things usually went his way. At the offices of Daye and Stromberg, he and Eric were equal partners, evenly matched in talent and experience, balancing the work load while remaining friends from their early teens to the present. At home he lived as he pleased, alone in a high-rise apartment that was spacious, convenient and kept spotless by Martha, who'd worked for him for six years. In his relationships, he saw to it that he dated women who were attractive, career oriented and who had about as much interest in a long-term arrangement as he did. Which was none whatsoever.

The key to leading a stress-free life was in avoiding complications, Michael felt. And he had, for the most part. Until Jo Knight and her assorted pets had barged into his life earlier today.

Surreptitiously glancing at her across the glass-topped wrought iron table in the kitchen, he had to admit that her dinner menu—she had won that toss, too—was delicious. Cold lobster salad, hard rolls, iced tea. And a bowl of fresh fruit on the sideboard. He never ate fruit, but the lobster was good.

The problem was that he'd been rushing around for days getting ready for his trip, had eaten a cardboard lunch on the plane and he'd been looking forward to a juicy steak, medium rare. Somehow he'd let her talk him out of buying beef and settling for fish.

"This isn't bad," he told her as he sat back to take a sip of tea.

Not exactly lavish with his compliments, but she would take the few he threw her way, Jo decided. "Thank you." They'd debated throughout the aisles of the market about junk food versus health food and she wasn't anxious to resume the discussion. But she couldn't resist one last prod. "You'll probably sleep better after a light dinner."

"I never have trouble sleeping." Which wasn't exactly the truth, but close enough.

Jo took her plate to the sink and brought back the dish of pineapple she'd sliced earlier. "All that fat can clog your pores and you won't be able to sweat. How will your body cool off?"

Her logic escaped him, but Michael decided not to comment.

"Actually, I worry that my voice will change if I eat foods that are harmful." She stuck a sliver of pineapple in her mouth.

He watched the juice gather on her lips, then her tongue slipped out and captured every last drop. Fascinated, he saw her eyes close in appreciation. She was the kind of person who savored her food, making a sensuous feast out of a simple meal. Michael found himself reaching for a piece of pineapple.

"How did you get into your, uh, career?" he asked. That seemed a safe enough subject, one that shouldn't lead them into a debate.

Jo wiped her fingers on her napkin. "I kind of drifted into it. My father taught me to play the guitar when I was quite young."

"What does your father do?"

"He's in insurance." She didn't bother to explain that Jarrett Knight owned one of the largest insurance agencies in California. "Anyhow, about five years ago, when my brother Jon was only three, he was diagnosed as hyperactive."

Thank goodness he'd put a halt to her brothers' visit. Silently Michael reached for another chunk of pineapple, completely forgetting that he didn't like fruit.

"Jon was driving us all crazy with his boundless energy, even on medication. So I started reading to him and telling him stories, making some up as I went along, the wilder the better, to keep his interest. Then, I put together little songs that fit into the story and sang them while I played the guitar."

"And Jon quieted down?"

"Surprisingly he did. And my other brothers began to listen, too. Then one of my mother's friends asked if I'd come to her child's birthday party. Pretty soon, someone on the school board got wind of what I was doing and invited me to work with their remedial reading classes, using their books and songs I wrote to go with the stories.'' She wasn't aware her voice had softened and her eyes had warmed as she remembered. ''Those kids were so cute, sitting cross-legged on the classroom floor, watching so intently.''

''And you got hooked?''

She laughed around a shrug. ''I guess I did. I have a teaching degree, but I find this aspect much more rewarding than a regular curriculum. Especially after I got involved in the literacy program and began working with adults, too. Do you have any idea how many adults can't read? Thousands.''

Michael finished his tea. ''I don't see how your little songs can help them read. I don't mean to belittle what you do but . . .''

''It's okay.'' Jo wasn't offended. She'd heard the same thing often from others. But they'd changed their opinions when the students had become avid readers. ''Because I make it fun, with silly rhymes and nonsensical phrases. Yet they stick in peoples' minds and they want to know more.''

''Sort of a Dr. Seuss set to music.''

She smiled. ''Yes, exactly. Is there a child in your family that you read to?''

''Occasionally. My sister's son Shawn is five.''

''That's a wonderful age. They're like little sponges soaking up information. Do you see much of him?''

''No. Deborah's husband is a professional ice skater and they travel a great deal. I don't know how Shawn's going to get his schooling. They never should have had a child. Never should have married, actually." He got up to clear his dishes.

Jo frowned. "Why do you say that?"

"They're total opposites. Deborah's quiet and introverted and hates the traveling. Kerry's gregarious and outgoing, loves people and hasn't read a book since high school." He opened the dishwasher and bent to stack plates inside.

Jo cleared the rest of the table automatically, her mind on their conversation. How sad that Michael should feel that way. "Haven't you ever heard that opposites attract? Wouldn't it be boring if we were all alike? My brothers and I are all different, as are our parents. Certainly, I'd hate to live with someone who agreed with me on everything."

Michael closed the dishwasher door and turned to look at her. She was either very young, very naive or both. "How old are you?"

"Twenty-six."

"When you get a little older you'll realize that opposites attracting is a fallacy invented by authors and songwriters."

The corners of her mouth twitched. "How old are you, grandpa?"

"Thirty-three, and I've seen how disastrous a union of opposites can be."

Jo was unconvinced. "You're forgetting something. Deborah and Kerry may be opposites, but if they love each other, that doesn't matter."

"It does to Shawn. The children are caught in the middle."

So that's where he was coming from. Only Jo thought it might very well be about more than just his nephew. "I think you're wrong. Love changes everything."

He looked at her as if speaking to a slow student. "I'll bet you still believe in the tooth fairy, too." He smiled, but his eyes stayed serious.

"Yes, and Santa Claus and the Easter Bunny. You're a card-carrying cynic, Mike."

"Michael."

"And perhaps stuffy?" He'd changed clothes—actually taken off his tie—and now wore cotton drawstring pants and a sports shirt. He looked casual and relaxed, though his words weren't. And he looked very male, his bare arms strong and hard as an athlete's. His hands were large and tanned. Jo wondered how they'd feel touching her bare skin.

Uncertain where that thought had come from, she gave him a nervous smile. "I'm sorry. I shouldn't have said that."

"Apology accepted."

She couldn't keep the dismay from her voice. "Are you always so...so polite? So correct?"

His face flushed. "Is something wrong with having good manners?"

"No, nothing." If it wasn't overdone.

Michael turned to leave. "I've got to set up so I can get to work early tomorrow. I'll be using the dining room table."

"Sure, fine." Jo left the kitchen as Heinz came racing inside, a small piece of driftwood between his teeth. She bent to remove it and glanced outside. It was dusk, a lovely time of night, and she felt unaccountably restless. Jet lag, she supposed.

She walked into the dining room where Michael was unpacking his leather briefcase. "You wouldn't want to go for a swim, would you?" she asked.

"No, thanks."

"How about a walk on the beach? I'll bet it's fabulous outside right now."

Michael shook his head. "You go ahead."

Walking on the beach alone, even with Heinz tagging along, held little appeal. Jo wasn't quite sure why, since she lived alone and often did all manner of things by herself. Probably tired, she thought as she brushed back her hair. Absently she leaned over as Michael spread out a rolled-up blueprint.

Honeysuckle, he decided. The scent of honeysuckle was stronger when she was near. He'd thought the aroma had been coming from plants alongside the house, drifting in through the open windows. But no, the smell was coming from Jo and tangling around his senses. He took a step back.

She studied the notation in the corner of the blueprint. E. Michael Daye, Jr. She looked up and her eyes collided with his. "What does the *E* stand for?"

Coloring slightly, he placed a slide rule on the corner of the blueprint. "A family name."

She was enjoying his discomfort. He might even give her a human reaction here. "Come on, what is it?"

He sighed resignedly. "Eugene."

"There," she said with a grin, "that wasn't so hard, was it?"

Leaving him, she wandered onto the patio. The man was pompous and stuffy, but at least he knew it. Actually, he was a challenge. He definitely needed to be drawn out of his shell a bit. And she was just the woman who could do it.

Why had he told her his first name? Michael asked himself as he slammed a book onto the table. Now, instead of Mike, she'd probably be calling him Eugene the rest of this long, torturous stay. Or she would—

"Oh!" Jo cried out. "Mike, come out here, quick!"

"What is it?" Dropping his briefcase, Michael rushed around the living room, hurriedly grabbing a thick magazine. Probably a small snake or a tarantula had crept onto the patio. At the very least, a field mouse. "What's wrong?"

Jo stood by the waist-high brick ledge calmly staring out to sea, her hair shifting in a soft summer breeze. "Have you ever in your whole life seen such a gorgeous sunset?"

Michael dropped the magazine. How was he going to get through the next couple of weeks?

Chapter Two

The sound of lapping water woke him. Michael cautiously opened his eyes. Sunlight streamed in through the slatted blinds. Jo had chosen the bedroom facing the sea, so his was the one that looked onto the pool. Through the open window, he could hear her doing laps.

Rolling over, he stretched sleepily. He'd been tired last night but not sleepy, so he'd read until the wee small hours. The time change, probably. Or adjusting to having someone else on the other side of his bedroom wall.

JoAnn Knight. Jo. Placing his hands under his head, he stared at the ceiling thoughtfully. She was certainly different from anyone he knew, or had ever known. He was used to reserved, sophisticated, polished perfection. Jo was more spontaneous, seemingly innocent yet naturally sensual.

He heard a splash and water churning, as if someone were neatly slicing through on the way to the far end. She swam in the nude, she'd said. Dare he creep over and...no! That would be unfair. Besides, he didn't give a tinker's damn about Jo Knight.

Michael turned onto his side and punched down his pillow. Evidently she hadn't been able to sleep last night, either, for he'd heard the soft sounds of her guitar through the thin wall. She hadn't launched into one of her kiddie songs, thank goodness. The music had been low and melancholy, not loud and abrasive as he'd feared, Michael thought as he swung his legs over the side of the bed.

He shaved and took a quick shower, then pulled on a pair of white shorts and was about to leave the room when he decided he ought to wear a shirt as well. Around his apartment on summer weekends, he often wore only shorts, but he never felt totally at ease half-dressed when others were around. His upbringing, Michael supposed as he shrugged into a shirt and left the room.

WONDERFULLY REFRESHING, Jo thought as she rose from the water and reached for the towel she'd brought out. The water wasn't too warm yet this early in the morning or the sun too hot. Rubbing herself dry, she felt invigorated as she always did after her morning swim.

As a teenager, she'd grown up with a pool in her parents' backyard and had always enjoyed swimming. Last year, her father—a warm and generous man—had given her the down payment for the small house she'd bought just north of L.A. Up a winding hillside road, it faced the distant sea and had a very private fenced pool. Which was when she'd begun her habit of nude swimming.

A quick glance toward the closed blinds of Michael's bedroom window assured her he was probably still asleep. Hurriedly she slipped into her white terry robe and belted it around her slender waist. She inadvertently dribbled water from the ends of her hair onto Floppy who was dozing on a lounge chair. The cat was predictably offended and jumped up to run off in search of a drier napping spot.

Holding the screen door open, Jo paused a moment. Across the room, Michael was crouched down rubbing Heinz's tummy as the dog lay gazing up at him through the furry curtain of his wispy hair. Unless she was hearing things as well as seeing things, Michael was talking softly to her dog. Not as cold and indifferent as he liked to pretend, now was he?

She let the screen door bang shut behind her.

Michael jumped to his feet almost guiltily. "Oh, hi." Caught, he felt flustered. "I . . . I dropped something." He turned from her and reached into the cupboard for a coffee cup. Yesterday she'd had his face reddening. Today she had him stammering. Squaring his shoulders, he poured coffee.

Heinz scurried over to greet Jo, and she bent to pat his head absently. Why was Michael looking contrite over being seen petting a dog? What a strange man he was, she decided as she joined him at the counter and held out her cup.

Michael poured for her. "I'm surprised you drink coffee. No lecture on caffeine and how it harms your body?"

His voice held a kidding note. First he indicates he likes the dog, then he razzes her. All in less than twenty-four hours. My, my. Jo looked up at him. "It's my only vice," she said.

Looking doubtful, he set down the pot and turned to her. She was enough to give a man pause, he couldn't help thinking. Her wet hair framed a morning-fresh, oval face. This close, he noticed a light sprinkling of freckles on her nose, giving her a more youthful look than yesterday. Her lips were full and inviting, but those incredible blue eyes were suddenly wary and watchful.

It was impossible, he knew, yet instead of chlorine he smelled honeysuckle, warm and fragrant. His imagination stripped off the bulky robe and . . .

Michael cleared his throat and took a step back. "Yes, well, everyone's got a weakness or two, I suppose." And if he didn't get the hell out of the room, his was going to be abundantly clear to both of them. "Got to get to work." Turning, he marched out of the kitchen.

Jo sipped her coffee and smiled. She wasn't the most experienced woman in the world, but just now, there'd been a look in his eyes that a girl of twelve could have read clearly.

"Hey, get off of there!"

The commanding voice coming from the dining room sounded highly irritated. Jo went to check it out. Sitting on the center of a pile of blueprints, Floppy stared up at Michael, his yellow eyes challenging. Jo reached to pick him up, but the cagey cat leaped off the table, sending papers and blueprints flying onto the floor. "I'm sorry," she told him, bending to retrieve his things.

"As I said yesterday, you don't seem to be able to control your animals." Michael scooped up his blueprints, well aware his voice was sharp. He rarely gave in to anger and wasn't actually mad now. But dealing with Jo when he was just slightly annoyed was a whole lot easier than when he wanted to reach out and touch her hair to see if it was really as silky as it seemed.

Contrite, she gathered papers. "I'll keep them out of your way today, I promise." Such a minor thing. Why was he so upset?

Sidestepping to take his papers from her, still stooped, he saw something that stopped him in mid-motion. "What is that on your foot?"

Jo glanced down, then wiggled her toes, the nails painted a bright pink. "It's a toe ring."

"A toe ring," he repeated. Michael stood. "Why would anyone want to wear a ring on their toe?"

She rose and set the stack of papers on the table. "For fun. Don't you ever do something just for fun?"

"Fun." He was beginning to sound like a parrot, he realized, yet she truly baffled him. She had no rings on her fingers, but wore one on her toe.

"It's not a foreign word to you, is it, Mike? And it's not a four-letter word, either." Turning on her bare heel, she walked to her room and firmly closed the door.

E. Michael Daye, Jr. had to be the most uptight man she'd ever met.

HOLDING THE LAST NOTE a beat longer, Jo listened to the final chords of the song. Pleased with her progress, she set aside her guitar and reached for her pad to write down the last couple of measures. Fortunately she had a good memory, but she still always jotted down the words once they were set in her mind. Later, when the song was completed, she'd copy the notes on scale sheets for her files.

Leaning back against the rough bark of the tall palm tree, she took a deep breath and decided that rain was on its way. And that might present a problem. Jo had been outside with her two pets since dressing after her morning swim, leaving Michael huddled over his blueprints in the dining room. She'd made progress on her songs, though she'd have probably fared better inside without the distraction of the breathtaking scenery. But she'd promised him that she and the animals would stay out of his way, and they had.

But the rain would soon drive them in and then what? She could probably close Floppy into her bedroom where he'd contentedly snooze away the balance of the afternoon on her bed. But Heinz wasn't used to being locked up, having the run of her L.A. backyard through a doggie door she'd had installed. He would whine or cry if she shut him away, which would likely upset Michael more than letting him roam free.

Nuts! Why was he acting like the owner of a china shop where the bull has just sauntered in? How terrible had it been that they'd had to pick up a few of his precious papers? What kind of a household had he grown up in that he was so easily ruffled?

Brushing back her hair that the wind insisted on rearranging, Jo sighed. Michael sure wasn't a bit like his cousin. She'd met Noel one afternoon when she'd been sitting on what she'd thought was a deserted stretch of California's beach. She'd been composing, lost in her music, and hadn't noticed him until he'd appeared alongside her, dripping wet and carrying his surfboard.

Noel was talkative, friendly and fun, every bit as big as Michael, but with sun-bleached hair and an enviable tan. He'd plopped down beside her in the sand, and by the time they'd parted, she felt she knew him fairly well. She'd thought him nice enough, if a bit shallow and irresponsible. Quite a contrast to his cousin.

She imagined that Michael had grown up among dedicated but humorless people. So unlike her own family where laughter was as constant as California sunshine. She lived only ten miles from her folks and visited frequently because she honestly enjoyed her parents and brothers. The Knight family was a close one, and Jo knew that one day that was the life she wanted.

There was nothing like being raised in the loving atmosphere of a good marriage. Her mother had miscarried several times after Jo had been born and, though Jo had been young, she'd witnessed her parents' heartbreak. And then shared their joy when the boys had come along. A career was fine, and Jo truly loved her work, but real happiness was having someone of your own and children to love.

That was what she'd always wanted—someone of her own to love. She'd often envied the quiet ease of her parents' union, knowing how rare a thing they had. She would settle for no less.

A man of passion and strength, depth and sensitivity. She knew there was such a male somewhere. One who would understand her needs and moods as easily as he could make her care for him.

Meanwhile, Jo thought as she picked up her guitar again, she was content to wait. She was certain she'd know when the right man came along.

MICHAEL GLANCED at his watch and frowned. Five in the afternoon and he wasn't really ready to quit work for the day. The preliminary sketches were going well, but there was a great deal he needed to accomplish in the allotted time. Unfortunately he'd had only a candy bar for lunch, and it was his turn to cook dinner. Fighting a frown, he removed his horn-rimmed glasses, straightened his work area and went into the kitchen.

Truth be known, he'd just as soon "call the Colonel," but he'd agreed to discuss all menus with Jo. When she'd breezed in to make her lunch, he'd offered to drive to the store and get a couple of steaks. Flashing a patient smile, she'd whipped out a coin and flipped it. He'd lost again. Maybe he should check that damn coin.

Michael smelled the rain before he heard it falling softly on the oleander bushes outside the kitchen window. Then he heard the front door open and Heinz came racing in, followed by Jo carrying a damp cat and her guitar case. Wonderful. All four of them trapped inside from the rain all evening, which meant additional distractions to his work. Savagely he stripped the broccoli stalks under running water, fantasizing about what he would do to Noel when he returned to California.

Stormy, Jo thought as she glanced in at Michael, and she didn't mean the weather. Since he was still grumpy, she went into her bathroom to shower.

He was a pretty good cook, if he said so himself, Michael decided as he removed the fish from the broiler, though he rarely cooked for anyone but himself. He'd grated cheese for topping the broccoli and put together his special dressing for the salad. He'd even heated the rolls and poured them each a glass of white wine. He slid a fillet on each plate, then nodded in satisfaction.

Turning to call Jo, he saw she was already standing in the doorway. She wore a black cotton jumpsuit that hugged her lovingly. He watched her wiggle her bare toes, looking a shade uncertain. He wasn't going to pout through another dinner. Besides, it was difficult staying annoyed with someone who looked and smelled as good as Jo did. Michael smiled and pulled out her chair.

Jo sat down. His mood shifts were unnerving, she thought as she unfolded her napkin. "You ought to do it more often," she told him.

Michael seated himself and passed the rolls. "We agreed that we'd take turns cooking."

"I don't mean cook. I mean smile."

"Oh." He busied himself with the butter.

He was back to wearing that puzzled frown. She searched for a subject that might cheer him. "Tell me about your Aunt Charlotte."

Involuntarily, Michael smiled. "She's an original. She's my father's sister, but they're nothing alike. Her hair is red—at least it was the last time I saw her— though it could be most any color by now. Aunt Charlotte bores easily."

"And your father doesn't?"

He shook his head, finishing a mouthful of salad. "My father has at least twenty suits, all gray. Does that tell you anything?"

It certainly did. And lots of ties, probably, all conservative. "The mahimahi is excellent, by the way." She saw him look up, then try not to look pleased. It would seem he wasn't as self-assured as he pretended. "Does Aunt Charlotte live near you?"

"No. She's remodeled this old three-story Victorian house on Nob Hill. Her first husband was twenty years older than Charlotte, made his money bootlegging, then invested in oil. He died soon after Noel was born, leaving her a very wealthy woman. She's very loyal to old Henry. After every divorce, she takes his name back." Michael found himself chuckling.

"How many divorces has she had?"

"Three. But she's stayed friends with all of her exes. It's impossible to stay angry with Aunt Charlotte." Michael paused, his fork in midair. "She works at being a character, I think. She could afford to buy most anything, but she goes to secondhand shops for her clothes—sequined dresses with fringes, big, floppy hats, earrings that dangle all the way down to her shoulders."

Jo smiled at the mental picture. "She sounds like she'd be fun."

He sobered, hearing the word she'd flung at him this morning. He'd never thought about it in quite those terms, but Charlotte *was* fun. He had no doubt that the two of them would get along famously. He gazed across the table at Jo. "Her eyes are blue, only not as blue as yours. And your eyelashes are thicker. Lots thicker."

Jo swallowed, wondering if his comment was an intentional compliment or merely an observation. "I hope I can meet her one day."

With no small effort, Michael pulled his gaze from her and resumed eating. "How long have you known Noel?"

"About a year."

"And you let him stay in your home for two weeks?"

She looked up, amused. "Why, shouldn't I have? Is he a thief? Do you think he'll trash the place? I don't have much furniture and no heirlooms."

"Are you one of Noel's girls?" he asked quietly.

She took a sip of wine before answering. "I think of myself more as a woman than a girl. And I belong to no one but myself. Does that answer your question?"

Michael nodded, feeling flustered. "I'm sorry. That was out of line. It's just that—"

"That Noel goes through a lot of girls. And women. I know. I have never been nor shall I be one of them. I like Noel, as a casual friend." And why would he care? she wondered. "And who is this fellow you loaned your apartment to, an old and dear friend?"

She had him on that one. "Not exactly. Tim Ryan's one of our newest architects, only joined the firm a year ago. He'd asked me to recommend a reasonable hotel in San Francisco for his honeymoon. I know he doesn't make much money yet, and I was going to be gone anyway." It had been an impulse, something Michael rarely gave in to. Mentioning it out loud made the gesture sound silly. He went back to finishing his dinner.

So he was human. And sentimental, even romantic. But embarrassed by something he apparently thought of as a weak moment. "I think it was wonderful of you. A honeymoon's something you never forget."

His head came up. "Have you been married?"

"No."

Michael took a healthy swallow of wine and leaned back. "Then how would you know that?"

"From my parents. My mother told me about their honeymoon and her eyes got all dreamy. They're very much in love."

"After four kids and a bunch of years?" He shook his head in disbelief. "They're an anachronism."

She was getting used to his skepticism. Rising, she cleared the dishes. "Don't look now, but your cynicism is showing again."

Michael carried his plate over. "Better than Pollyannaism."

"That's not a word."

"Maybe not, but it's a viewpoint that's sure to get you hurt."

Jo studied him a moment, realizing they were poles apart in their thinking. She'd never been one to try to persuade someone to change his mind. "Let's not debate. Let's go for a walk."

He glanced pointedly out the window. "It's raining."

"It's a gentle summer shower, not a freezing downpour." Impulsively she grabbed his hand. "Come on, you old stick-in-the-mud. The dishes will wait." Firmly she led him through the house and outside as Heinz bolted happily ahead of them. Once they were on the grass, she began to run toward the beach, pulling Michael along.

He was letting her because he was oddly uncomfortable with her opinion of him. But he still felt foolish. "Where are you taking me?"

"Walking in the rain. You may even find you enjoy it." She smiled to take the sting from her words. At the lawn's edge, she stopped near a big tree loaded with limes and let go of his hand. "Take off your shoes. You can only walk barefoot in sand." To her surprise, he slipped them off without comment. Smiling her approval, she skipped ahead.

Heinz frolicked around her feet, running forward, then dashing back to check on his mistress. Jo picked up a small piece of driftwood and threw it down the beach.

Michael followed, watching her tilt her face up, letting the rain slide down her cheeks as she shook back her hair. The jumpsuit was soon damp and clinging to her body in a way that had his pulse racing. She seemed not to notice as she laughed at nothing at all, then stopped and waited for him to catch up.

She'd been right, it was a warm rain, dampening rather than soaking them. Gray clouds slid through a darkening sky, and the sound of the surf was all that could be heard. Hardly a breeze stirred the huge palm trees bordering the beach in the early twilight.

"Isn't it exhilarating?" Jo asked, slightly breathless.

"I suppose," he said, his eyes on her. Raindrops glistening in her hair. Michael wasn't in the least poetic, yet he found the sight of her reminded him of half-forgotten lines from a poem he'd read years ago in college.

Such enthusiasm. What, she wondered, did it take to excite him? Not one to give up easily, she grabbed his hand and pulled him into the edge of a foamy wave and looked down to watch the water swirl around their ankles. Would he turn and leave if his pant legs got wet? she speculated as she watched him gaze out to sea.

What was he thinking? His face in the faded light was so serious, the hand she held very still in her own. She squeezed his fingers and waited till he turned to look at her. "It's all so vast, isn't it? No matter which direction we look, there isn't a soul to see. It feels as if we're the only two people on earth."

Michael stared at her for a long moment, then shook his head as if to clear it. What was he doing standing here in the rain with a girl who was as vastly different from him as a person could be? She was beautiful, but she was confusing his emotions, the ones he preferred to keep under control.

He wasn't the sort of man who walked barefoot on beaches. He was a businessman with obligations and responsibilities, not a beach bum like Noel. Carefree times were for the very young and the foolish. Michael knew he was neither. The wine must have gone straight to his head.

He pulled his hand free. "I've got work to do. I'm going back."

Disappointment flowed through her, astonishing her with its force. For a moment there, she'd thought he was lightening up, but he'd slipped back into his rigid stance. "All right."

"Are you coming?"

"Not just yet." She turned to walk away.

He felt curiously hesitant. "I don't like leaving you alone out here."

"Heinz is with me. I'll be fine." She kept on walking, her back straight.

Undecided, he stood looking after her. Finally he turned and started back, wondering where he'd left his cigarettes.

Jo strolled on, her enthusiasm gone, but she was determined to not let Michael see. What was wrong with him? All she'd wanted was to walk on the beach, to talk a little, to enjoy. She sighed deeply. That was the thing. He didn't know how to enjoy. Or, for some reason she hadn't discovered yet, he felt guilty whenever he enjoyed anything too much.

Heinz brought the stick back and she threw it again. Never mind, she told herself. She'd come to Maui to work, not to reform a tense jerk who was about as much fun as an afternoon spent watching the grass grow. Tomorrow she'd call Christy and meet her at the school to set up the program.

And to the devil with E. Michael Daye, Jr.

"YOU WERE WONDERFUL," Christy Hanes said as she slipped her arm around Jo's waist and hugged her. The diminutive teacher was just under five feet tall, which put her nose to nose with some of her fourth-grade students, a fact that didn't bother her in the least.

Walking to the school parking lot, Jo got a better grip on her guitar case and smiled. "Thanks. They were really receptive, weren't they?" She'd done a sample story time for Christy's class, which had been attended by the principal and several teachers already involved in a similar project. Everyone had been enthusiastic about her methods and had offered to help in any way they could for the assembly program Jo was planning for next week on the last full day of school.

"I knew they would be," Christy went on. "Of course, I've been talking you up to anyone who'd listen ever since I asked you to come." She stopped, looking up at her friend. "I wish I could have gotten you more than that small honorarium but..."

"Not to worry." The government grant funding her work had recently received a large private donation that helped cover most expenses. Some of her out-of-state trips, like this one, were mostly labors of love, for she knew that Christy's school and many others had only a meager budget available. "I wouldn't have come if I hadn't wanted to. Seeing you is a real bonus."

"What's it been, three years?"

"Right, when we stood up together in Diane and Steve's wedding in San Diego." All three of the women had been college roommates and had reunited for the happy occasion. But a year later, tragedy had struck and Diane's new husband had been killed in an auto accident. "Have you heard from her lately?"

Christy nodded as they resumed walking. "An occasional letter. She's still not over Steve's death."

"I know. She wrote me recently saying she wished she hadn't put off getting pregnant. At least she'd have his baby." Jo stopped alongside a gray Chrysler. "And what about you? How are things going with Pete?"

Christy's pixie face brightened. "I'm still working the plan. He hasn't popped the question yet. But he will."

Christy had been dating Peter White, the only son and heir to his father's export-import business, since moving to Hawaii three years ago. Her letters to Jo were filled with glowing reports on their relationship. "Do you love him?"

Christy sent her a tolerant look as she ran a hand through her short brown curls. "You always did have stars in your eyes. If I've told you once, I've told you a dozen times: love doesn't have anything to do with the most successful marriages. I'm good for Pete and he knows it. I'll be an asset, not a liability. I can run his household efficiently, I'm good at entertaining his business associates and I'm great in bed. What more can the man want?''

Jo tried to keep her voice unemotional. ''You don't think that sounds a little cold and calculating?''

''Oh, come on, Jo. Falling in love only invites heartbreak. The Orientals have the right approach. A practical marriage beneficial to both parties. Where did falling in love get Diane? Heartbreak, right?''

''She couldn't prevent her husband from dying.''

''But she'd be recovered by now if she hadn't been so sappy over him.'' Christy stuck her hands into the pockets of her striped slacks and looked up at her friend. ''Take my advice and find a nice guy who makes a good living and will treat you well. If he falls for you, all the better. But don't you buy into that nonsense. My mother used to say, 'the one who loves the strongest gets hurt the deepest.' ''

''I'll keep that in mind.'' Jo wished she didn't feel such a wave of sadness since hearing Christy's views on love and marriage. She'd hoped her friend had outgrown her cynicism, but she hadn't. Jo opened the car door and placed her guitar on the seat.

Christy's wide green eyes belatedly took in the big car. ''Well, well. Nice car.''

''It's a rental and belongs to a friend.'' Jo got behind the wheel. Perhaps because of the cool way he'd dismissed her last night, Michael had offered her the use of his car this morning when she'd mentioned she was going to meet Christy. Then he'd slipped on his glasses and returned to his blueprints at the dining room table, not even looking up when she'd left.

Closing the door, Christy leaned on the window ledge. ''You've only been here two days. What friend?''

"There was a mix-up with the owner, so this fellow and I are renting the same house." She started the engine, not wanting to go into more of an explanation.

But Christy wasn't so easily subdued. "Uh, huh. Is he fat, bald and seventy, or is he six-feet tall and drop-dead gorgeous?"

Jo laughed. "You'd advise me to go with the first choice if he had money and a future."

"Only if you're thinking marriage. The other ones are to amuse yourself with until Mr. Right shows up. So, give. Is he attractive?"

"In a preppy sort of way."

"Go for it, kid. Put on a bikini, flash those big blue eyes and climb onto his lap."

Jo shook her head, picturing Michael's face if she were to do just that. "He'd have a coronary." She shifted into drive. "See you next week."

Stepping back, Christy nodded. "If you can manage dinner before then, call me."

With a wave, Jo drove off. Even the view from the coastal road did nothing to cheer her as her mind kept replaying Christy's words.

Was she the last person on earth who believed in love and forever after? Jo wondered.

THE HOUSE WAS EMPTY and eerily quiet. Jo tossed her things on her bed where Floppy, his nap interrupted again, sent her a reproachful look. She felt hot and sticky after her afternoon outing. Changing into her bathing suit, she shrugged into a long shirt, deciding that a swim would feel good. She wandered through the other rooms and could find no trace of Michael or Heinz. An unlikely twosome to be off together, she thought as she went outside.

Coming around the side of the house that faced the sea, she saw a figure down the beach lying on the sand. A small dog was chasing sea gulls nearby. As she cleared the grassy area, Heinz must have picked up her scent for he came racing toward her. "Hi, boy," she said, grabbing him up into a fierce hug. His joyous welcome was always something she looked forward to.

Walking on, squinting against the sun's rays, she noticed that the man was indeed Michael, but he wasn't simply lying down. He had something in his arms and was lifting it rhythmically overhead. She strolled within a couple of feet and stopped. "What are you doing?"

"Weight lifting," he answered, then grunted as he heaved the heavy object up over his head, his arms stiff.

"But that's a log."

"Yes, well, it really isn't practical, packing weights on an overseas trip by plane."

"You mean you work out with barbells and all that?" Pretty funny. He preferred junk food but worked out.

"Yes." Only ten more to go, he thought. The log had been the closest thing he could find and it was a heavy sucker. But he'd been sitting at the dining room table for long hours and had decided he needed some exercise.

Jo set Heinz down and stood watching Michael resume his lifting. He wore only cutoffs riding low on his slim hips. His chest was wide and more muscular than she'd have guessed, his shoulders looking broader without his shirt. He had the beginning of a tan, which meant he had to spend some time in the California sun. His face glistened as he heaved the log upward.

"You know, you have a terrific body," she said matter-of-factly.

Michael dropped the log. It fell behind his head with a heavy thud.

Scrambling to his feet, he ran the back of his hand over his damp forehead, taken aback by the compliment. "Uh, thanks." Placing his hands on his hips, he took several deep breaths, cooling down after his exertion, watching her all the while.

He hadn't meant to hurt her feelings last night, but he'd guessed by her cool manner this morning that he had. He was still convinced that they were very ill-suited to share a house for two weeks, but there was no call for him to be rude. Michael had always prided himself on being polite and considerate.

Well, most of the time.

Jo had decided after last night that perhaps she should stop inviting him to join her in things—like swimming and walks—and go about her business. Removing her shirt, she tossed it onto the sand, turned her back on those gray eyes that were studying her so intently, and ran into the sea.

Her suit was one-piece, black and cut high on her thighs, but still conservative by most standards. Why, then, did it seem more provocative than many skimpy suits he'd seen? He watched her arch and dive into a high wave, then disappear. In moments her head bobbed up and he saw her stroking cleanly through the water, heading out.

Michael strolled to where the waves washed over his feet, rolling his shoulders to relieve the kinks. She was a beautifully built woman with a lovely face and wonderful hair. She was good natured, if a bit stubborn. She loved music and animals and children. She would marry and bake cookies and have babies. She was meant for that kind of life.

But Michael wasn't.

He set out jogging in the opposite direction, away from the house. Always back home, when his thoughts kept him from concentrating or when his mind was tired from too many hours working, he would go for a run. In the park near his apartment and along certain streets. As his feet hit the damp sand and he moved into his stride, he began to feel better.

Physical outlet for pent-up energy, that was the best remedy. It's only natural that a woman as attractive as Jo would distract his mind and disturb his body. After all, he was a red-blooded man in his prime. Nothing wrong with wanting. Touching was when problems began.

Coming to a stop, Michael turned to rest a moment. He had to admit that he did want to touch her. Her skin looked so soft and her hair was so shiny. And that mouth...

But he wouldn't. Touching led to more, and that's when women like Jo became starry-eyed, expecting declarations and commitments. No, he was much better off with the type of woman he was accustomed to dating. Women who expected no more than he was willing to give. Jo Knight was definitely off-limits.

Starting back, Michael was glad he'd had this talk with himself. He'd get through these next days by working hard, being polite and steering clear of her. He was an intelligent, disciplined man who controlled his life. Mind over matter. He wouldn't think of her and he wouldn't want her. Simple.

Nearing the spot where her shirt lay, he slowed. She was walking out of the water, her long hair trailing wetly down past her shoulders. The afternoon sun shimmered on her golden skin, and the suit molded to her body. Her legs seemed endless as she bent to retrieve her shirt. Draping it over her arm, she swung her vivid blue eyes to him as he stopped a foot from her.

"You look all hot and bothered," Jo said, noticing the red splotches on his face. "Maybe you should cool off." Turning, she headed for the house, Heinz running alongside.

His stomach in knots, Michael watched her go. So much for mind over matter. Pivoting, he ran into the cooling ocean waves and dived under.

Chapter Three

The muscles in his neck hurt, and his shoulders were tense. Michael got up from the dining room table and rolled his head slowly around, trying to relieve cramps caused by too many hours bent over his work. It was definitely time for a break.

He glanced at his watch and saw it was much later in the afternoon than he'd thought. He'd been at it almost nonstop for nearly nine hours. Usually at his office, he'd get up from his drafting table and move around several times a day when he was working on one of these lengthy projects. But he was anxious to finish, thinking that if he completed the sketches early, he'd take a few days to just relax and lie in the sun. He was well aware that he had trouble relaxing and thought he might take another stab at it before returning home.

Straightening his papers, he heard Jo moving around in the kitchen. She was probably preparing dinner since it was her night to cook, though he couldn't smell anything yet. A glass of iced tea would hit the spot, he decided as he left the room.

"Hi," he said, trying to sound friendly as he poured his tea. She'd kept out of his way so well today that he'd hardly seen her at all. "How are the songs going?"

"Fine." Jo removed a large basket from a low cupboard and set it on the counter. She placed a red-checkered cloth inside and spread it over the bottom, draping the excess over the sides.

Michael took a long refreshing sip, then leaned his back against the counter. "What are you doing?"

"Putting together a picnic basket. I've decided it's too nice to eat indoors, so I'm going to have my dinner down on the beach." From the open refrigerator, she placed plastic-wrapped items into her basket. "I've put together enough for your dinner and stacked it on the second shelf."

He saw cheese, a hunk of salami, olives, crackers and several containers. His mouth began to water, and he realized he'd skipped lunch again. He watched her deftly slice bread from a long loaf and place it into a zip bag. "A picnic, eh?"

"The boys and I used to go on them a lot when they were younger. We'd throw all kinds of food into the basket—every person got to pick two items—then, we'd drive to the beach. We'd play volleyball and swim, then chow down. Food always tastes better eaten outside, for some reason. I miss all that."

He pictured the sandy beaches of L.A., always crowded with people, the wind sprinkling sand into the food, nowhere to wash up. "Sounds messy."

She sighed, having expected exactly that reaction. Michael, she was learning, was all too predictable. "Lots of things are messy. Eating cotton candy, bathing a dog, mud wrestling. But they're fun."

He'd never done any of those things, either, and hadn't felt the lack in his life.

"Oh, but I forgot. You're allergic to fun." She pulled out the nearly full bottle of wine and set it on the counter.

She didn't sound disappointed, just resigned. Oddly, instead of anger, he felt embarrassment. "You make me sound stodgy and boring."

Jo shrugged as she took down a glass. "If the shoe fits..."

Michael cleared his throat. "I've never been on a picnic."

She looked at him as if he'd just confessed to a triple ax murder. "Never?"

He rubbed the back of his neck, wondering why he'd told her. "It wasn't the sort of thing my family ever did."

She had a sudden vision of what his boyhood must have been like, raised by older parents as he'd briefly mentioned, staid and proper to a fault. Their idea of childhood activities had probably been an afternoon spent at a museum. A wave of sympathy for him, and for all he'd missed out on, washed over Jo, but she carefully hid it from him. "I never thought to ask because I felt you wanted to work. But would you like to come along?"

The food she'd packed *had* looked inviting. The idea of having dinner here all alone oddly held very little appeal. Maybe eating outdoors wasn't as bad as he'd imagined all these years. He shrugged nonchalantly, trying to look only mildly interested. "I'm at a stopping point, so I suppose I could."

She smiled, reading more from his expression than he'd ever know. "Great." She reached for another glass and opened the refrigerator to add his portion of the dinner to the basket.

Michael finished his tea. "Is there anything I can do?" he asked, uncertain just what her requirements for a picnic were.

"I noticed a plaid blanket in the hall closet. You can get that." Jo checked the contents, then tucked the cloth around the food. Slipping on her sandals, she grabbed the basket and met him at the door. "I've found a terrific spot down the beach a ways. It's got all these black rock formations covered with dark green moss. A wonderful place to watch the sunset."

Rocks slimy with moss. Picturesque on postcards, Michael supposed, but to eat alongside? Still, he'd agreed to go, and he was determined to prove to Jo that he could have fun with the best of them. Draping the blanket over his shoulder, he took the basket from her and put on a smile. "All right, let's go."

JO SPREAD BRIE on whole wheat crackers and handed Michael one. He took it from her and popped it into his mouth, crunching approvingly. She hid her smug smile as she worked open the can of smoked oysters.

She'd not dreamed he'd come with her. But since he had, she wanted badly to show him that picnicking could be a good experience. With a toothpick, she skewered oysters and set them on crackers, watching him from the corner of her eye. They'd strolled companionably down the beach to the spot she'd found, chatting mostly about the scenery, which was always breathtaking. And about Heinz who'd scampered ahead of them.

He'd told her that as a boy, he'd always wanted a dog, but his parents had forbidden pets in their home. Jo had asked him why he hadn't gotten one later when he'd moved out to live on his own. He'd shrugged and said that by then he'd decided they were too much responsibility. She'd thought it best not to argue the point.

Now, Michael sat on the far side of the blanket, his arms propped on his raised knees, staring out at the rolling waves. His hair, usually meticulously combed in place, was blowing about his head, and he seemed content to let it. His facial expression, though not exactly serene, wasn't anxious either, which it was a good deal of the time.

Jo couldn't help wondering as she anchored the glasses in the sand what had made him so intense. Her upbringing had been open and loving and easily explained. Michael's most likely had been more complex. The few glimpses she'd had, had aroused her curiosity. It was difficult to understand someone unless you knew something of their background. "Would you pour the wine, please?" she asked, handing it to him.

Michael took the bottle and eased out the cork. She'd been right again, he thought as he poured. It was actually pleasant out here in early evening.

Not a breeze was stirring, not another soul in sight on either side of them. The lowering sun had streaked the sky with muted pinks, a flush of orange and hazy slashes of purple. The only sound was the tireless swishing of the waves on the white sand and an occasional gull overhead. The warm air was ripe with the scent of flowers—hibiscus, oleander and wild orchid.

And the unmistakable scent of the woman who touched her glass to his while she watched him with eyes bluer than the distant center of the sea. His gaze locked with hers, Michael drank.

A paradox, Jo thought, setting aside her glass. Back at the house, she'd thought of him as a sad little boy who'd never been on a picnic. Suddenly he looked every inch a man whose probing gaze had her pulse fluttering. Unnerved, she reached for a bunch of grapes and searched for a neutral subject. "Earlier you said your family didn't go on picnics. What did you do instead?"

Michael popped a cherry tomato in his mouth thoughtfully. "We studied."

Crossing her legs Indian-style, Jo shifted to face him. "No one can study all the time, least of all children."

"You'd be surprised." Perhaps if he explained his parents to her, she'd realize that he wasn't against frivolous activities, but rather that he'd been exposed to so few. "My parents believe that children should learn something from every pursuit or it's a waste of time."

He saw by her puzzled expression that she found that theory baffling. Michael lay down on his side, propping himself up on an elbow. "You see, my mother was born into a wealthy Hungarian family and was a concert pianist touring the States when my father met her. She'd led a very formal life where she'd been expected to be well groomed and well behaved at all times. My father comes from a three-generation banking family, and he'd been raised much the same. He never questioned his destiny. He went to Harvard, then to work at the bank and eventually took over for his father. He bought a house in the same neighborhood, belonged to the same men's club and became friends with the sons of his father's friends."

"Was he disappointed when you broke the tradition?"

"Some, at first. But architects are acceptable in his view so he eventually came around."

"And your mother went along with all of that?"

He gazed off toward the sky, searching for the right words. "My mother is very beautiful and very talented. She travels more than half the year giving concerts and spends the other half rehearsing. She's more or less self-contained, needing very little outside her music. She never criticizes my father, nor does he say anything disparaging about her. Ever."

Jo felt her heart soften at the thought of a child being raised by such parents. "But surely they love each other. I mean, married all these years."

Michael's eyes narrowed as he watched a gull swoop down to a rising wave. "I don't know as though love ever played a large role in their lives. My mother's family lost everything in the communist takeover and my father sponsored all of them for U.S. citizenship. She's often said how grateful she was for that."

Jo frowned. "You think she married him out of gratitude?"

Michael sat up. "There are worse reasons. Look, I know you think me a cynic, but not everyone believes in undying love and a blissful marriage. My mother enjoys her music, her gardening, her books. My father enjoys his work, lunching at his club and playing cards with his friends. They like their life, as I like mine."

"You do?"

He was growing irritated. "I was trying to explain to you that my folks chose educational activities for us instead of picnics. Outings to museums, to the library, to concerts. So we could learn and be well-rounded. Is there anything wrong with that?''

He was getting defensive, which had not been her intention. "No, of course not." She picked up her wine. Why was it so easy to get into a heated discussion with him? Because they were so different, she supposed.

Michael's irritation dissipated as quickly as it had arisen. Perhaps she was finally getting the message. "The truth is that my mother and father are very different, yet they've managed to coexist for years. But happiness is the price they paid for marrying opposites. And unfortunately, Deborah made the same mistake."

Coexist? Lord, what a way to live. Jo finished her wine and set the glass back into the basket. "Are you so sure people who are different can't fall deeply in love and live together happily by compromising?"

Michael picked up an apple. "Yes, absolutely sure." He bit into the fruit, satisfied that he'd explained himself.

"I disagree." She flopped back on the blanket, stretching out. "My mother's very artistic, loves to paint, to roam around art galleries, to redecorate the house. My father's a businessman who rarely notices when she changes the drapes or paints a wall. He smokes cigars while she campaigns as an environmentalist for clean air." She turned to look at him. "Need I go on?"

"I don't get your point."

No, she was certain he didn't. "Simple, really. Differences don't matter. Feelings matter. If you care enough, differences disappear."

"Not so. Deborah would be much happier with a man who had been raised as she has, enjoyed the same pursuits, had the same goals. Stuffing a square peg in a round hole only brings about frustration."

She lifted her arm above her head, angling so she could see him better. "What sign are you?"

That cliché question that was repeated endlessly each night in singles bars. Michael wasn't in the mood. "What difference does it make?"

Jo wrinkled her forehead thoughtfully. "Gemini. Yes, that's it. Gemini. Am I right?"

He couldn't prevent a look of surprise. "How did you know?"

She grinned. "The twins, constantly trying to decide which way to be."

"On the contrary, I'm very decisive."

In business perhaps. "Geminis also are argumentative, stubborn and sexy."

"I am not."

She laughed at his indignant tone. "You're certainly stubborn. And argumentative." She let the third thought hang in the air between them.

He waited, but she said nothing more. Oddly, he felt offended. "But not sexy?"

Jo met his eyes. "I didn't say that."

Michael's gaze traveled along her long, tanned legs, then moved upward. He admired the way her cotton knit top clung to her curves as she lay on her back. "You certainly are," he commented.

Noticing his thorough inspection, Jo hurriedly sat up, hoping she wouldn't blush. "There it is, right on schedule," she said, thinking a change of subject was in order. The orange sun looked as if it were sinking into the blue sea, slowly, inch by inch. "Incredible."

She was mesmerized by the sunset, yet increasingly aware of the man who'd set the picnic basket aside and scooted forward on the blanket until he was almost touching her. Those long, assessing looks he gave her more and more frequently unsettled her. It was silly, Jo told herself, to allow herself to feel anything other than casual friendship for him. They were diametrically opposed in every way.

Except one. There was a spark between them that was undeniable. Every conversation they had led to either an argument or the realization that no two people less alike had ever shared a moment in time. Yet she longed to lay her head on his shoulder this very instant, to feel his arm tighten around her and hold her close while they shared the beauty of the sunset.

It was circumstances and proximity and the romantic lure of the islands, that was all, Jo told herself. She was certain he was far better at covering his yearnings than she. To prove that to herself, she turned to look at him.

He wasn't watching the sunset. His eyes were on her, and they were dark and aware. Jo swallowed as he raised his hand and touched her hair.

He was jolted to notice that his hand was trembling. "I've been wondering all week if your hair is as soft as it looks."

"Have you?" The contact was casual, but the impact on her senses wasn't.

Michael trailed one finger along her smooth cheek. "And your skin, it's like silk." He saw her eyes darken and her lips part. She seemed to be holding her breath, waiting. He lowered his head in the direction of hers.

Just then, Heinz came lunging toward them, wet from playing in the waves, spraying sand in all directions as he landed on Jo's lap. Averting her eyes from the grainy shower, she grabbed his wiggling little body and stroked to calm him. After a moment, she glanced over at Michael and saw that he was gathering things up and putting them back in the basket, the mood broken.

He'd been going to kiss her, Jo knew. Helping him repack, she didn't know whether to be annoyed at Heinz's untimely interruption or glad that he'd prevented her from a probable mistake.

AS PLANS WENT, it wasn't particularly clever. However, there was no harm in trying, Jo thought as she settled in the corner of the couch with her guitar.

Walking back from their picnic, she'd felt in a mellow mood. So she'd asked Michael if he'd like to cut his workday short tomorrow and drive up to see the crater known as the House of the Sun on Mount Haleakala. At the store, she'd picked up a brochure that boldly claimed that the view from that mountain was the most spectacular in all of Maui.

Strolling along beside her, he'd rejected her suggestion, explaining that he'd already been there, and besides, he had far too much work to complete. Though disappointed, she'd accepted his refusal. But years of practice on three brothers had taught Jo that there were many ways to skin a cat.

As Michael browsed through one of his thick books at the dining room table, she struck a few chords, tuning her guitar. Floppy was out night roaming and Heinz was snoozing at the opposite end of the couch. It was a quiet, peaceful evening, the silence broken only by her music. Tightening a string, she plucked and listened, then plucked again.

Of course, she could go to Haleakala alone. She could ask to borrow Michael's car or rent one of her own. She could even ask Christy to join her, knowing her friend could probably get a substitute to cover for her for one day. But the truth was, she wanted to go with Michael and the reason was simple.

Her curiosity was aroused. She'd known other men. Had even cared for a few. But not in that heart-stopping way that could no more be ignored than it can be faked. It wasn't that she'd fallen for him, she told herself. But there was definitely something between them. Something that made her want to peel away his protective layers and discover the man behind the carefully erected facade.

With nimble fingers, she ran through the scale, her musician's ear listening for discordant notes. Time. She needed some time alone with him away from his work and hers. Time for him to remember the moment on the blanket with her when he'd leaned closer, intending to kiss her.

Jo glanced over at him and saw he'd set aside the book and was now shuffling through his drawings, studying them from several angles, frowning. Slightly louder, she began working her way through the scales again. She'd felt something on the beach tonight. Anticipation, excitement, curiosity. Since then, she badly wanted to test her theory, the one her mother had spoken of years ago.

Perhaps if she stayed visible, if he came to the conclusion that she might even stay indoors tomorrow, causing his work to suffer, he might change his mind and go with her. Perhaps. Strumming on the strings, Jo bent to her task.

Across the room, Michael was fuming inside. There'd be no point letting her know. After all, what could he say? *That noise is driving me crazy. I can't work unless it's quiet. Go sit out in the dark under a tree.* Hardly.

He slammed a book on top of another, knowing he was finished working for tonight, and whipped off his glasses. He knew exactly what she was doing and why. She wanted him to drive her up that silly mountain and stand around looking at clouds. Childish. Interruptive. Nonproductive. He wasn't going and that was that.

Let her go herself or call a friend. He hadn't come here to be a tour escort. Besides, one mountain was pretty much like another. Well, Haleakala *was* pretty spectacular. He rolled up a blueprint and stuck it into a tube. More than anything, he was annoyed that she was trying to coerce him into going by disturbing his work. What if she decided to hang around inside all day tomorrow? He'd pick her up and haul her outside himself, that's what. Her and her animals.

It was blackmail, that's what it was, pure and simple. Straightening a pile of papers, he glared at her. She looked innocent enough as she played the notes repetitively. She'd showered and changed into a pink, one-piece cover-up, long and loosely belted at the waist. And, as always, he could make out the faint scent of honeysuckle all the way across the room.

Sensing his eyes on her, Jo shifted so her back was to him. And she picked up the tempo. Roused, Heinz jumped off the couch and scooted into the bedroom, evidently having had enough of the disconnected notes. Michael saw her hair lift in a light breeze coming in through the open patio doors. It had felt every bit as soft as he'd imagined. And her skin...

All right, so he was attracted to her. Leaning back, Michael admitted that much to himself. So what would it hurt if he took a half day off and went with her? He had been pushing pretty hard since arriving. And she was fun to be with. Fun. A word that was beginning to haunt him.

Some people, Jo included, simply didn't understand that to him, work was fun. Nothing and no one had ever made him feel as good as wandering around one of his completed buildings, seeing *something* where before there had been only empty space. The women he knew were nice diversions and a few were even friends. But he'd never met one who could absorb, fascinate or excite him the way seeing one of his sketches taking shape could.

Disciplined since childhood, no woman had ever been able to distract him so thoroughly as to keep him awake nights. Until recently. A disciplined man could deal with attraction, then get on with his life, Michael reminded himself.

Quickly, before he could change his mind, he rose and walked over to her, placing a hand on the base of the guitar and effectively halting her playing. When she looked up at him with those huge blue eyes, Michael had a fleeting moment of questioning the wisdom of his decision.

"Something wrong?" Jo asked sweetly.

"All right, we'll go," Michael said, fighting to keep from clenching his teeth together.

"Go? Oh, you mean to Haleakala? Are you sure? I wouldn't want to keep you from working."

In a pig's eye, she wouldn't. He forced a saccharine smile. "No problem. I *want* to go."

She swung around, smiling. "Terrific, Mike."

He had stopped trying to convince her to call him Michael. That, too, had been a losing battle. "The very best view is at sunrise. And it's quite a drive so we have to leave early."

Jo stood and found he was nearer than she'd realized. He was easily a head taller, with shoulders that seemed a yard wide. She took a step back. "No problem. Name the hour and I'll be ready."

Amazing how agreeable she could be, once she got her way. "Five."

She didn't blink an eye. "All right. I'll make us a thermos of coffee to take along."

"Coffee? I thought you'd want to take a cooler of beer."

Jo's eyebrows shot up. She didn't even like beer. "You want to start drinking at five a.m.?"

"Come on, Jo. Don't you like to have fun?" He felt his lips twitch, then gave in to the smile. "Just kidding. See you in the morning."

Jo watched him walk to his bedroom and go inside. If she'd dared, she'd have given out with a victory whoop. The first part of her plan had worked, she thought, picking up her guitar and heading for her room. And he'd even joked and smiled. Things were moving right along.

Now for phase two of her plan.

THE DRIVE UP the narrow, winding road in the first faint light of dawn was slightly harrowing, Jo thought as she scooted away from the door. It was locked, but the drop on her side of the car was sheer and straight down several thousand feet. Gorgeous scenery, but a little nerve-racking.

"I'd pour you some coffee, but I think it might spill on these loops," she told Michael, shifting her eyes to the road ahead. It was easier on the stomach than contemplating the side view.

"I can wait till we get to the top." Michael peered through the window. "Looks like we've timed it just about right."

"I'd hate to be on this route at night. There are no streetlights. Maybe they don't have electricity this high up."

"Sure they do. There's an observatory near the rim manned by national-park people."

Despite the car's cooling system, Jo had the feeling that the air inside was more rarefied as they climbed. "The brochure says that at the topmost peak, it's over ten thousand feet."

"You can go eye to eye with an eagle," he suggested, a little surprised she was so enthralled. "Haven't you done any mountain climbing in California?"

"No. I've hiked, but not up very high. My family likes water activities more, swimming and snorkeling. Ground-level pastimes." She glanced over at him. "And who have you been up here with?"

"An assortment of gorgeous women, each of whom persuaded me to drive her by some devious plot or another," he answered, sending her a pointed look.

"I did not." When she saw his eyes narrow at her again, she gave in. "Well, maybe a little. Keep your eyes on the road, will you?" They sailed smoothly around another hairpin turn. The clouds alongside were thicker now, the sky lightening by fractional degrees as they climbed. "I can't imagine that too many people will be up here at this hour."

"You'd be surprised. This is a big tourist attraction." He maneuvered the heavy Chrysler around another quick turn, causing Jo to strain against her seat belt.

In moments, the movement of the car around a curve had her scooting back. All the jostling had her stomach slightly queasy. And now, out her side window, a rocky mountain wall whizzed by, seemingly close enough to touch. Jo closed her eyes.

"Almost there," Michael said, noticing her discomfort. "Hang on."

Ten minutes later when she stepped out of the car, Jo took in a deep breath and immediately felt better knowing her feet were planted on solid ground. Looking around, she saw that there were several cars parked in the roped off area and more arriving. Taking Michael's offered hand, she climbed the few steps up to the rim and saw why people got up so early to drive up this mountain.

The view left her speechless. Wispy clouds and thick cottony puffs floated all around their heads. The sun wasn't quite up yet, but the sky was streaked with golden shafts. The air was clean and so pure it almost hurt to breathe.

"Come on over this way." Michael led Jo around the side along the crater's rim, away from the people lining up along the other railing, to a more private section. Standing behind her, he felt her shiver in the cool breeze and slid his hands along her arms, easing her into the warmth of his body.

"Look, over there. An airplane, and it's almost parallel to us. Can you imagine?" Jo's voice was husky with excitement as she looked down several thousand feet to the crater's floor that seemed to go on for miles and miles. Richly colored cinder cones dotted the side walls, and along the outer walls of the volcano could be seen ravines and gullies sloping down to the sea. The distant ocean blended with the pale blue skyline, disappearing in a shimmering haze. Jo felt her throat tighten with emotion.

"There it is," Michael said, pointing ahead, then bringing his arm back to wrap around her again.

Shades of yellow spread upward from the horizon, rising with a burst of gold and peach and amber, haloing the clouds as the sun rose slowly. The blue of the sea and sky had seemingly disappeared, replaced by a glowing light that touched everything and everyone. Gradually the shapes and shades became more clearly defined again as the ball of yellow flame soared upward. A bird glided by, so close Jo could feel the flutter of its wings.

Michael's voice was a mere whisper close to her ear. "The guidebook says that legend has it that the demigod, Maui, captured the sun up here and held it captive to give his people more daylight hours."

Moved, she turned to thank him for bringing her here. But the words died in her throat. His eyes were pewter gray and serious. Her hands came to rest on his chest, and she felt the uneven beat of his heart beneath her fingers. Her own pulse was erratic. Phase two, she thought as his head lowered to hers.

He'd turned away from this on the beach, Michael thought. But no more. Her wide, wary eyes searched his, filled with questions. As his were. It was time to find out.

His mouth was hesitant and softer than she'd imagined. His hands moved to her back, holding her lightly as his lips brushed back and forth across hers. He seemed to be holding back, experimenting. Then his tongue slipped inside her mouth and touched hers. On a sigh, she drifted closer, opening to him.

It was then that she saw them from behind her closed eyelids. Fireworks. Bright, beautiful, stunning. The colors burst inside her head, and Jo felt her senses begin to swim. Dazed, she pulled back from him.

Michael frowned, puzzled. Her eyes were filled with confusion and a sort of disbelief. "What is it?"

She was thinking of another time, a Fourth of July evening, the first time her mother had taken her to see the fireworks. She'd been awed by the beauty of the myriad sparkling colors lighting up the sky. "Do you see that, Jo?" her mother had asked. "When the right man comes along—the man you will love with all your heart—when he holds you, when he kisses you, that's how you'll feel inside." She'd always remembered and always believed.

"Nothing is wrong," she told him. "Must be the altitude." But she needed to know for sure. "Could we do that again, please?"

He wanted nothing more. Michael gathered her close again and took her mouth.

This time was different. His mouth was hot and hungry now, making her feel as if she were being touched by the molten sun that had risen behind her in the sky. She'd speculated that Michael Daye's kiss would be lukewarm and very proper, without fire, without excitement. She'd been wrong.

Hard arms crushed her to him more intimately as his mouth moved over hers and his tongue took possession of hers. Awash on a sea of unexpected feelings, Jo's hands slid up to his shoulders and tangled in his hair as she pulled him down to her.

Michael felt a flush of heat, a flash of desperation. When he heard her soft surprised moan, he deepened the kiss, struggling with a stunning need—to never let her go, to explore every glorious inch of her, to find out where this could go. Even as he knew the inevitable answer.

At last he lifted his head, blinking as if to clear his vision. This time, her eyes were no longer confused or uncertain. He saw a lingering astonishment, pleasure and finally acceptance.

Stepping back, Jo gave herself a moment to resume breathing normally. She hadn't been mistaken and neither had her mother.

Not once, but twice. Fireworks.

Chapter Four

Jo's unmistakable laugh rang out in the still morning air, followed by a deep, masculine chuckle.

Seated at the dining room table, Michael's head shot up as he strained to listen. Who was she outside laughing with?

Frowning, he set aside his unfinished sketch and wandered to the front window. He could see no one. Opening the door, he stepped onto the porch. He wasn't jealous, he told himself. Just curious.

Wearing shorts and a long, oversize shirt, Jo was crouched on the ground in front of the flower beds at the far end along with Aunt Charlotte's gardener. Michael remembered seeing the man come around to prune trees and spray for bugs a couple of times before when he'd stayed at the house. Roberto or Ernesto, something like that.

Cramming his hands in his pants pockets, he watched from behind the pillar. Jo was helping the man weed the flower bed, and they were chatting like old friends. She had to have only met him this morning. What on earth could she find in common with the gardener?

He saw Jo toss back her hair and shift to sit on her haunches. Perhaps it was a love of flowers, Michael thought as he leaned against the post. Last night at dinner, she'd told him a funny story about one of her uncles who was a florist. She'd told other stories, warm and touching, about her brothers and parents.

He'd never known that kind of life, that kind of familial caring. His own family barely got together for a dinner during the holidays. He'd blamed it on diverse schedules and busy life-styles, but perhaps it was more than that. Perhaps it had to do with relating to one another.

Jo, however, had no trouble relating, he thought as he watched her stand up and dust off her hands, deep in a discussion with the gardener. The man also stood, his back to Michael. In his hand was a flower, which he presented to Jo with a little bow. The smile she gave him lighted up her face.

Michael sighed. Despite his best efforts to fight it, she was muddling his mind. In all fairness, he couldn't blame Jo. Each morning after her swim, she took her dog, her cat and her guitar outdoors. She'd settle down by the pool, on the beach or under a palm tree. As he'd sit inside working, the gentle tones of her music would drift to him. Sometimes sweet, sometimes stirring. His hand would pause and his mind would be out there with her instead of concentrating on his sketches.

It was getting steadily worse. Instead of designs, he saw an oval face with shining blue eyes and an incredible mouth. Instead of thinking about his plans, he thought of the sunrise he'd witnessed with Jo, of the kisses they'd shared. Instead of moving to the next drawing, he would turn to gaze out the window, day-dreaming like a schoolboy.

At dinner he would lose track of their conversation as he admired the way the sun streaming in the window highlighted her hair. At night he would lie in his solitary bed listening to her turning over on the other side of the wall, then spend the next hour fantasizing about what she was wearing. Or not wearing. He would get up in the morning, cross and irritable. At this rate, he wouldn't finish his project until next year.

What, he wondered, was he going to do about JoAnn Knight?

Sensing Michael's presence, Jo looked up and met his eyes. She said a few words to the gardener, then walked over to him. Her face was damp, her hair windblown, her clothes smudged with grass stains. Michael thought she looked wonderful.

''Ernesto's been telling me about his nephew who went para-sailing on a beach not far from here,'' Jo said, gazing up at him as she toyed with the hibiscus. She'd been pleasantly surprised to find Michael outside and, on the walk over, she'd decided to issue him another challenge. ''It sounds like fun. You want to try it?''

He thought she looked braced for his refusal, even though he'd shocked her last night by suggesting they go for a stroll on the beach. It had been a test, actually, to prove to her that he enjoyed fun activities, and to prove to himself that he could walk in the moonlight with her and not touch her. Yet she still didn't think he would jump to do something spontaneous.

''Sure. Let's go.'' Michael saw the astonishment in her eyes, then the pleasure. He wished it didn't warm him.

"Well, *all right,*" Jo said, jumping onto the porch before he could change his mind. "Have you ever done it before?"

"No." And he wasn't sure he'd do it now. But he would at least go. After all, he wasn't getting any work done anyhow.

"Better put your suit on under your clothes. You could get dunked in the drink." Jo hurried inside.

Hearing a victory tone in her voice, Michael wondered if he'd been neatly maneuvered again.

"JUST SIT HERE... that's right... and I'll belt you in the seat... and you hold on to these straps. Got it?"

"Got it." Jo wiggled around until she felt comfortable.

The very tanned, very muscular man who'd said his name was Chad stepped back from her with a smile that revealed a mouthful of dazzling white teeth. He had sun-bleached shoulder-length hair and wore tight white bathing trunks. Michael watched him reach over and remove a section of Jo's long hair that had gotten caught under her shoulder straps, his hand lingering longer than necessary. She wore only a white bathing suit, one-piece like her black one, yet it had Chad nearly drooling. Michael struggled not to grind his teeth. "You're sure you want to do this?"

Jo smiled up at him. "Absolutely." She turned back to Chad. "Ready when you are."

"I thought you had a tendency to get motion sick," Michael threw out, hoping that thought would deter her.

They'd arrived an hour ago and sat on the beach watching the speedboat pull a long line of para-sailors off from the sandy launching pad one by one. The boat would start out and the harnessed passenger would quickly ascend into the cloudless sky. They seemed to float over the sea, going so far and so high that they'd become mere specks in the distance. Finally Jo had leaped up, eager to try.

"I *won't* get sick," she told him with a frown.

"She's safe as a baby in a cradle with us, buddy," the tanned Adonis said to Michael. He waved to his partner in the speedboat. "Take her away, Kirk."

Michael stepped back. How could anyone trust a bronze beach bum named Chad and his lifeguard-type buddy, Kirk? He watched the powerboat shift into gear, then pull away. Harnessed in her seat, Jo lifted off, gradually rising as the boat picked up speed. Then she was sailing higher and higher. Hands on his hips, Michael squinted up at the sky.

"Never lost one yet, buddy," Chad said. "We took a pregnant woman up last week. She loved it."

Michael didn't answer, too busy watching Jo as the boat whipped her out along the shoreline.

Chad followed his gaze a long moment. "Quite a looker. She yours?"

Michael shifted cool gray eyes to the man's perfect face. "Why do you want to know?"

Chat shrugged. "So I know whether to make a move or not."

"I wouldn't if I were you." His voice was as cool as his gaze.

Chad nodded good-naturedly. "Gotcha, buddy." He strolled over to the launch area where the next customer was waiting impatiently.

It wasn't that he was jealous. He had no claim on Jo, Michael reminded himself. But she was young, and he was only doing her a favor by saving her from getting involved with a shiftless surfer who spent his days strapping people into harnesses and his nights undoubtedly chasing "lookers."

Wandering over to the landing pad, Michael kept his eyes on Jo as the boat began to circle around. He had to admit the flight looked interesting. It would probably be very quiet up there, and the air would be almost as pure as up on Mount Haleakala.

It wasn't that he was afraid to go up. It was more that he thought the whole idea a little undignified and pretty frivolous. When he'd voiced that opinion to Jo, she'd sent him one of those long, baffled looks that told him she not only didn't understand him, but couldn't fathom why he'd feel that the ride was somewhat silly.

Michael wiggled his toes in the warm sand. The fact was he'd so seldom been exposed to impractical choices that he'd gotten into the habit of choosing only constructive pastimes. He rarely watched television unless he could learn something from a documentary. Though he attended an occasional movie, for the most part, he considered films a waste of time. He read a great deal, mostly nonfiction. He told himself he used his time wisely.

The boat was heading back now, though she was still way up there. Brushing back his hair, Michael faced an unpleasant possibility. Maybe he *was* a wee bit stodgy. If he was, it was because he'd chosen to be. It wasn't a cardinal sin. One man's boredom was another man's pleasure. He *liked* his life the way it was. Why, then, was he questioning everything lately?

Because, despite his comfortable existence, he'd come to realize recently that his life did lack something. Excitement. Watching Jo coming in for her landing, he ruefully admitted to himself that, before meeting her, he couldn't actually recall the last time he'd truly been excited. About anything. About anyone.

With her, he felt exhilarated, though it often disturbed him. Like on Haleakala when he'd kissed her until they were both breathless. Or the quiet elation of just strolling on a moonlit beach with her. She made even grocery shopping an adventure. Dangerous thinking.

They were opposites to the extreme. Like his parents. Like Kerry and Deborah. People didn't break out of lifetime molds in the course of a vacation week and change forever. He felt certain that once he returned to San Francisco and his world, he'd be the same conservative man he'd always been. And yet . . .

Who was to say he couldn't deviate from the norm a little during this time away from that life? He could lighten up, as Jo was always reminding him. Take a few calculated risks, try new things, laugh and enjoy and have fun. Temporarily, to be sure. But why not?

She was coming toward him. He could see her face clearly now and it was radiant. Closer and closer, almost at ground-level, aiming straight for the landing pad. Amazing how good old Kirk driving the boat could maneuver her right to the spot Chad had indicated. Feet hitting the sand now. And she ran with it, gradually slowing, until she was in his arms.

"Oh, Mike," Jo said as he hugged her to him. "It was the most fantastic feeling." She drew back as he bent to unbelt her. "It's the way birds must feel. Free and unencumbered."

Chad came running over. "So, how was it?"

"Wonderful," Jo answered, shrugging out of the harness.

"Great. Glad you enjoyed it." Chad waved to the man waiting. "You're next."

Jo's arm slid around Michael's waist as he walked her over to where they'd spread their towels. "I'm so glad I went up."

Michael glanced over his shoulder. Only two others waiting. What could it hurt? He dropped to the sand and drew her down. "Maybe I'll try it."

She turned to him, beaming. "Oh, yes. You'll love it."

AND HE DID. Both times.

He also loved the way she looked at him when he described how he'd felt while free-floating in an endless sky. She didn't look smug because she'd managed to get him out on a public beach and caused him to want to do something out of the ordinary. Instead her eyes, as he'd tried to put his feelings into words, had filled with tenderness, as if they'd shared a special moment.

Verbalizing his feelings had never come easily to Michael. But, with Jo, he found he wanted to try. "I imagine that's how parachutists feel."

"Yes, and free-fallers. Chad was telling me he's tried free-falling."

Michael had seen her sitting alongside Chad on the sand as he'd headed in to land. "I'm surprised he can afford it."

Was that a hint of jealousy in his voice? Couldn't be. She wrinkled her brow at him. "He's a law student. He and Kirk make enough during the summer months to carry them through the rest of the year. Not too shabby, I'd say, and fun besides.''

A law student, not a drifter. Okay, so he'd been wrong about Chad. He still didn't like him ogling Jo.

''I'm so glad you enjoyed it.'' She'd known he was capable of appreciating things if he'd just be more adventurous.

''It reminded me of one time when I was about nine or ten. We had a pool in our backyard with a diving board. But I got the notion I'd like to jump off the cabana roof. I think I was going through my Batman stage.''

Seated across the table from him, Jo smiled at the mental picture of a young caped crusader. They'd left the beach at dusk and driven to an out-of-the-way seafood restaurant with wood plank flooring and nautical decor. Starved after their day at the beach, they'd each devoured a lobster, and Michael hadn't once mentioned how messy a meal it was. Instead he'd been chatty and enthusiastic. ''And did you?''

''I sure did. At least I was bright enough to leap into the deep end. I bribed Deborah to be my lookout.'' Michael removed his paper bib, smiling at the memory. ''The first time I dived, it was great, sailing into the water from up so high, then barreling down to the bottom and shooting back up. I thought I was really something.''

Jo wiped her hands on the thick napkin. ''I wouldn't have guessed you were such a daredevil.''

''Yeah, well, I didn't fare so well the second time. I got cocky and my aim was off. I hit the water wrong and grazed the side of the pool really hard. Broke my left arm and scraped my side. If Deborah hadn't run for help, I might have drowned.''

"You also could have hit your head instead of your arm."

Michael nodded. "That's what my father said. I remember lying in the hospital bed, all bandaged and in pain, and him standing there, intent on making a moral lesson out of a stupid stunt."

"And just what lesson was that?"

He lowered his voice in imitation of his father's deeper tones. "Keep this in mind, son. When you decide to take a risk, consider all the pluses and minuses, and be sure the prize is worth the pain." Michael finished off the last of his frosty beer.

"So today, was taking the risk of para-sailing worth the pain of having to step out of character?"

"Yes. But that's not why I did it."

Her eyes searched his. "Then why?"

"I wanted to share the experience with you." *And I wanted to impress you in front of Chad,* a small voice inside him admitted.

She was sitting back in her chair, separated from him by the width of the table. Yet she felt as if his eyes were caressing her, warming her. "That's nice, Mike. Probably the nicest thing you've ever said to me."

The waiter chose that moment to stop at their table. "Will there be anything else?" he asked.

"Just the check, thanks." Michael reached for his wallet, wondering what had made him share his feelings like that.

HE'D GOTTEN SUNBURNED. Michael peered into the bathroom mirror after his shower and swore softly. He hadn't intended to stay on the beach so long. The weather around San Francisco wasn't sunny enough in early June to have acquired much of a tan, even if he'd had the time to lay out. And he'd been trying to be macho in front of Jo, so he hadn't put on suntan lotion.

There was nothing in the medicine chest. Maybe in the kitchen. Wrapping a towel around his waist, he padded out barefoot to check the cupboards.

He was searching through the last row when he heard a sound behind him and turned to see Jo standing in the archway. She had on that same pink thing, belted loosely around the middle. Her hair was piled on top of her head as if she'd pinned it out of the way for her shower. The scent of honeysuckle was heavy in the suddenly thick air.

Michael cleared his throat and returned to investigating the cupboard. "I'm looking for something for this sunburn," he said by way of explanation.

"I've got medicated cream in my case. I'll get it."

He closed the cabinet door and propped his hands on the counter by the sink as he gazed outside. Moonlight filtered down, shadowing the side yard. He could see fireflies doing their nightly dance and hear crickets chirping nearby. A beautiful night. A peaceful night.

But he was feeling restless.

"Here we go," Jo said as she returned. He turned to take the bottle from her, but she'd already poured cream onto her palm. "I'll do your back and shoulders." Gently she dabbed the healing lotion on him.

She felt him flinch and jerked her hand back. "I'm sorry. Did I hurt you?"

"No. It's just cold." Michael found himself tensing up as she smoothed the cream over one shoulder, then down his back and around to the other shoulder. Her hands were small, fine-boned, yet he felt unexpected strength in her fingers. Her touch was light in deference to his burn, more like a caress than a massage. He became aware that his pulse had suddenly escalated.

"We should have worn shirts today," Jo said, her voice low and soft in the dim, quiet room. He had beautiful skin, clean and smooth, stretched over layers of hard muscles. She'd longed to touch him for days, and now she'd found an excuse. With long strokes, she worked the lotion in.

"I'm surprised you don't burn," he commented, thinking to lighten the tense atmosphere with small talk. "Blondes usually do."

"I guess I've built up a steady tan over the years. But I did get a little too much sun on my face."

He saw a chance to switch positions and turned to find her standing very close. "Then let me return the favor." He took the bottle from her hand, poured a small amount of liquid onto two fingers and leaned toward her face. With his other hand, he tilted up her chin. "Mostly on your nose."

"Yes. Not exactly my best feature."

"What's wrong with your nose?" He dabbed the cream, then spread it onto her cheeks.

"It's too long. And my eyes are too far apart." And her heart was beating wildly in her chest. Could he hear it? Could he see what even the light touch of his fingertips was doing to her? Had her hands on his skin affected him half as much?

Her wide wary eyes were luminous in a splash of moonlight. Michael thought he could be content just looking into them for hours, admiring the various shades of blue, searching their depths for the many emotions they revealed. He moved his hands to frame her face.

"Your nose is just right," he said in a husky whisper, then kissed it lightly. "And your eyes are beautiful." He watched them flutter closed as he kissed each one in turn. When they opened to focus on him, he saw they were filled with unanswered questions and unspoken needs. "I didn't come looking for this, Jo," he told her honestly.

"Neither did I," she whispered.

He brushed his lips over hers while the ache inside him built. "I've always thought of myself as a strong man. But I'm not strong enough to resist you." Helpless to do otherwise, he touched his mouth to hers.

He'd meant to just sample, to savor, to take his time. But the moment her taste exploded on his tongue, he shifted his hands to her back and pressed her to his heated body. He drew in her scent—perfumed cream, honeysuckle and warm woman. He felt her hands on the bare skin of his back, then they moved up to curl around his shoulders as she eased closer.

Lord but he didn't want this, Michael thought through a haze of conflicting emotions. He wanted this more than he'd ever wanted anything before. He couldn't handle an involvement with this kind of woman, not now, not ever. He couldn't bear the thought of not having her. Confusion raced through him along with his heated blood as his hands explored her back and discovered she wore nothing under the pink shift.

This, this is what she'd been wanting. This slow slide into passion, this mindless drift into desire. No, she hadn't been consciously seeking someone, either. But she had found. Oh, what she'd found.

A man who made her blood sing and her heart soar. A man who struggled against his feelings, yet he had so many to share—feelings she was certain he'd never shared with anyone. A man of buried sensitivity, of obvious strength, of hidden passion. A man of possibilities.

And oh, the wonder of his mouth making love to hers, of his hands touching her, spreading fire, arousing needs. Her fingers tightened on his shoulders as she pressed herself shamelessly to his solid frame, wanting more. And still more.

She wasn't your ordinary woman, Michael thought as he shifted to trail kisses along the satin of her throat. At least not the ones he'd known. She was impetuous, outspoken, honest. In her actions, in her emotions. There was no coyness to her, no pretense. She kissed him back as if she burned for him. As he did for her.

Even as he told himself this would never work, he wound his arms more tightly around her. Even as he acknowledged again how different, how unlike, they were in every way, he turned to take her mouth still another time. Even as he reminded himself that disparate individuals made strange bedfellows, he wondered how quickly he could get her into his bed.

Jo felt his hands thrust into her hair and peripherally heard the two combs she'd anchored there fall to the kitchen floor. The fireworks were just as sharp, just as vivid, as that first morning. All her days she'd searched for this—the one man who could light up her life. She knew women who fell in love as quickly and as easily as they changed their clothes, and others who thought of marriage as a financial goal. She also knew she wasn't either of those. She was a one-man woman, and she'd found the special man for her.

But even as she angled her head to give him better access to her already-bruised mouth, she felt strongly that she dare not tell him. E. Michael Daye, Jr. would turn tail and run if he even suspected that she was falling in love with him.

Michael was losing control rapidly, completely. He needed a moment to catch his breath, to regain his pacing. He would pull back and take her hand, lead her into his room and continue this where they could lie down before they crumbled to the kitchen floor like teenagers. He would, in just a minute. After just one more kiss and—

The jarring ring of the phone startled them into jumping apart like guilty children. Breathing heavily, Michael stepped back and rearranged the towel at his waist. "Hold that thought," he told her, then made his way somewhat clumsily to the living room. He cleared his throat and took a deep breath before answering.

"Hello, dear boy. I'm glad I caught you in." His aunt's voice sounded as if she were in the next room.

"Charlotte, is that you?" He knew it was, but he needed to buy a little time as his foggy mind tried to figure out why she'd be calling him.

"Yes. Are you all right, Michael? You sound a little winded."

Winded. Yes, he most certainly was. "Jogging, you know," he lied. There were times . . .

"Of course. I'm calling because I need a favor."

Michael eased a hip onto the arm of the sofa as he brushed back his hair. "Name it." Saying that was dangerous, for Charlotte's requests often bordered on the oddball. But she was the one person he never seemed able to refuse.

"I'll be arriving tomorrow morning. I believe the flight gets in at eleven your time. Would you be a dear and pick me up at the airport, then drive me to Lahaina? Simon wants to pull anchor by evening. It would help me enormously, and we could have a nice visit."

Another day he couldn't work. "Don't you usually rent a car?"

"Oh, bother. I didn't want to tell you, but they've suspended my license again. The police in this city are out to get me, I'm convinced. Every time I leave the house, there's one hiding behind a bush somewhere."

Despite his aggravation at her timing, Michael smiled. Old Leadfoot had done it again. Charlotte drove like a maniac, gathering speeding tickets like some people gathered wildflowers. "I guess I'll have to come to your rescue then." Resigned to another enforced day off, he listened while she gave him the flight number and the exact time. "Fine. I'll see you then."

"I'll be the one in the purple sarong," she said.

"Charlotte, I . . ."

She chuckled. "Only kidding, dear boy. See you."

Michael hung up, then turned around to look at Jo. She was leaning against the dining room arch. She'd straightened her clothes, and her hair hung softly framing her face. But it was her eyes that frightened him. They were soft, dreamy, vulnerable. He ran shaky fingers through his tousled hair.

What had he been thinking of? He couldn't take her to his bed, then blithely send her back to her room. She wasn't a casual fling but a forever woman. He wanted her desperately. But for an interlude not a lifetime. Jo Knight was the stuff dreams were made of. But not *his* dreams. He didn't want to hurt her. But he didn't want to be hurt, either.

He would handle this before he got maneuvered into making promises he knew he wouldn't keep. As different as they were, he would only ruin her life. The thought of having to endure a marriage such as his parents shared sent chills down his spine as he searched for the right words.

"That was Charlotte," he said finally. "She's arriving in the morning and wants me to meet her plane, then drive her to Lahaina where she's joining someone on a boat."

Something was going on inside Michael, Jo decided, and she wasn't sure what. He'd been mere inches away from making love with her, from losing control. Then he'd reined himself in, gathering that protective control around himself like a heavy cloak. He was going to step back, to pretend what they'd just shared in the kitchen had been an ordinary occurrence instead of the fireworks she knew he'd also felt.

"I see," she said, seeing all too clearly. She had her pride, after all. She would not entice or beg or offer herself again. Not until he came to some serious realizations, if he ever would.

Her eyes had cooled, and she'd turned within herself, Michael thought, watching her closely. Thank goodness, she was being sensible. Perhaps she, too, had had second thoughts and sudden misgivings. She'd have to be a dolt not to see how different they were. They'd almost lost their heads in there, but that's all it had been. Physical. For him. If she'd felt more, hoped for more, that would have to be her problem.

"Would you like to come with me?" he asked, trying for a normal tone. "You'd enjoy Aunt Charlotte."

Yes, she would go. And act as if nothing were wrong, as if she hadn't just been jarred senseless. She would not cry, whine or pout. She would simply bide her time and wait for him to see the light. Of course, she might nudge him in the right direction a time or two. Her father had taught her that if she wanted something and knew it was absolutely right for her, to go after it. She believed her father.

Tossing Michael a smile that cost her, she moved to her bedroom door. "Sounds great. What time?"

She was taking this a little too well. Trying not to let his male pride get in the way, he told her. With a nod, she went in and closed the door behind her. Rolling his tense shoulders, Michael sank onto the couch.

He wished he knew what the hell was going on. First she'd run her hands all over him, getting him all hot and bothered. Then she'd kissed him like there was no tomorrow. Her eyes had sent messages he couldn't have misinterpreted. *I want you. I need you. I care.*

Then, when he'd thought she'd protest just a little about not picking up where they'd left off, she'd quickly agreed to go meet his aunt and calmly strolled into her room. As if, minutes ago, she hadn't been seriously considering spending the night in his room, in his arms.

Damn, but he'd like to meet the man who understood women. If there were such men. Rising, Michael marched to his room and slammed the door.

Chapter Five

She hadn't been kidding. Charlotte Kramer stepped from the plane onto the ramp steps wearing a long purple muumuu decorated with huge white flowers. A bouquet of real flowers was stuck in the topknot of her hair, and around her neck hung an orchid lei. She paused at the top somewhat regally and gazed across the tarmac, as if a queen acknowledging the troops who'd come to greet her. Michael shook his head as he watched her finally begin her descent.

"I guess I don't have to ask if that's your aunt," Jo commented, almost laughing aloud at the pained look on his face.

Even among the colorfully clad vacationers walking toward the gate, Charlotte stood out. "Different, isn't she?"

Vive la différence, Jo thought. Michael had at least one relative who couldn't be classified as stuffy, it would seem.

In a swirl of perfume, Charlotte made her entrance and embraced Michael effusively. "My dear boy. Thank you so much for coming." She removed her oversize sunglasses to reveal lively blue eyes that shrewdly examined her nephew. "Don't you feel positively naked without your tie?"

Michael found his face coloring. Wonderful. Now he was with two women who could make him feel awkward. "Actually, I did wear it in, but they made me check it at security."

Charlotte's penciled brows rose in surprise at his little joke. It wasn't that he didn't have a sense of humor, but rather that he so often chose to hide it. In his white slacks and casual blue shirt, he looked almost relaxed, though he hadn't traded his leather loafers in for sandals quite yet. "You do look less tense." She shifted her gaze to the woman standing beside him. "And you must be the reason." She held out a slim hand, her long nails painted a brilliant pink. "Charlotte Kramer."

The smile came naturally as Jo shook the woman's hand warmly and introduced herself. Charlotte was tall and slender, and very striking. "It's good to finally meet you."

Charlotte handed her large straw bag to Michael as they started to walk toward the luggage area. "And you, my dear. Noel's talked about you so much." Her son, for once, had been right on the money. Jo Knight was not only lovely, but there was intelligence in those big eyes, something most of her son's women friends sorely lacked, along with a measure of good sense. "Do you know what the odds are that you'd meet Noel on a California beach, then later bump into his cousin on a Hawaiian beach?"

"Can't say I do," Jo answered as Charlotte took her arm.

"Four thousand to one, my dear." Charlotte turned to grab her nephew by the other arm. "Are you with us, Michael?"

"I wouldn't miss a golden word." Guiding them down the walkway, he looked her over. "Did you fly all the way in that, uh, dress?"

"No. I left San Francisco all girded in some boring little gray suit. I changed on the plane just before landing." She stopped, holding out her arms for inspection. "Do you like it?"

"It's definitely you," Michael answered carefully, knowing his aunt didn't own a boring suit in gray or any other color.

"Your orchids are beautiful," Jo said, liking the woman more each minute.

"Aren't they? This darling man on the plane got them for me. He owns a rum factory in Jamaica and invited me to visit. I believe I will, one day. Are you enjoying the little house, Jo? I should have gotten a larger one, I suppose, but I fell in love with that location. I fancy it as sort of an enchanted cottage. Is your work going well, Michael?" Not waiting for a reply, she inhaled deeply as they reached curbside. "Oh, wonderful. Nowhere else on earth does the air smell so delicious."

Michael glanced at Jo and saw her amused expression. One thing seemed evident. Jo had finally met her match.

As he went to claim Charlotte's luggage, Michael wondered if he ought to remove his aunt's hot-pink shoes and check her feet. It wouldn't surprise him to find she was wearing a toe ring.

"YOUR FIRST VISIT—how wonderful." In the back seat, Charlotte slipped off her shoes and stretched out comfortably as Michael headed for the coastal highway and Lahaina. Ankles only a little swollen, she noted. These long plane rides could be such fun, but her body wasn't quite as resilient as it once had been. Sighing, she patted her hair and concentrated on getting to know the woman angled toward her in the front seat. "Where all have you taken her, Michael?"

"Charlotte, I remind you that this is a working trip for me, not a sight-seeing venture." He kept his eyes on the road. It was a thirty-five-minute drive to Lahaina where he would deposit Charlotte with her new sailing companion. Surely he could handle two chattering women for such a short period. When he wasn't pressed for time—which was seldom—he enjoyed his aunt. But coupled with Jo and her amused expression, they were a formidable twosome.

"Yes, yes, but one can't work *all* the time."

"We did go up to Mount Haleakala," Jo interjected, not wanting Michael to feel guilty. He was already getting that look of barely restrained impatience that he'd worn the first day she'd met him.

"Oh, the sunrise!" Charlotte sighed. "Weren't you moved beyond words?"

Jo risked a glance at Michael's profile and saw his hands tighten on the wheel. "Yes, I was," she answered, thinking that Michael's arms around her had thrilled her more than the sunrise. She noticed a muscle twitch by his eye, but he remained silent.

Charlotte didn't miss the sudden softening of Jo's features before she quickly averted her face. So that's how it was. And it had happened so swiftly, in a week. Ah, but that was often the best way.

"And yesterday we went para-sailing," Jo added.

"*Both* of you?" The picture of Michael para-sailing just wouldn't focus in Charlotte's mind.

Jo's lips twitched as Michael squirmed on his seat. "Mike went up twice."

"I'm not the stick-in-the-mud you seem to think, Charlotte." Lord, did everyone think that of him?

"Incredible view from up there," Charlotte commented.

"You've para-sailed?" Jo asked. She seemed as if she'd try most anything, yet she was in her mid-sixties.

"Oh, many times," she answered, her body relaxed, her mind alert. "I love Maui. We're a bit late this year for whale watching in Lahaina, but you must return to see them one day. Fantastic. And the ride to Hana is breathtaking. Michael, have you seen the tiki torch ceremony at Kaanapali?"

"Uh-huh."

"You know, you two should go there after dropping me. It's just up a ways from Lahaina. Worth seeing, right, my dear?"

She was pushing, but he was good at ignoring such nudges, which she'd been sending his way for years. "For those who believe in legends, I suppose."

"Michael's a bit of a cynic," Charlotte said, disappointment mingling with affection in her voice.

"I've noticed." Jo decided to change the subject. "Have you heard from Noel? Is he enjoying my house?"

"Tremendously." Charlotte placed a cigarette carefully into her red holder, then lit up, inhaling deeply. "I'm so glad he convinced his latest love to leave her snake home during their stay."

Jo swung about, her eyes widening. "Snake?"

"It's a pet, dear, and quite harmless." She really was a pretty thing, Charlotte thought. Spontaneous, energetic. Why on earth couldn't Noel settle down with someone who was obviously fun, yet grounded? Ah, well. Charlotte sighed. She'd long ago decided to accept her son for the errant scalawag he was. "Last year, Noel dated a girl who kept an iguana. In a cage, of course."

Jo heard Michael's chuckle and swallowed hard. Surely Charlotte was jesting. She wouldn't be able to draw in an easy breath until she searched every nook and cranny of her house when she returned. Unnerved, she adjusted the air-conditioning vent so that the cigarette smoke wouldn't bother her.

Charlotte exhaled thoughtfully. There was something crackling between these two and, as she would expect, Michael was fighting it. She'd never known him to get serious about a woman, never known him to bring one to her home or that of his parents. And she'd never known a man who needed a good woman more. She'd have to study this woman and decide why she was different. She certainly was attractive. "You know, you remind me of my second husband, Jo. Doesn't she remind you of Harmon, Michael?"

"Except for the mustache," he said with a straight face.

"No, silly, I mean the eyes. And her hair."

"I think Harmon's was shorter." This time he tossed Jo a quick grin.

Charlotte narrowed her eyes as she studied the back of her nephew's head. Two frivolous remarks in one conversation was decidedly unlike Michael. She loved him dearly, but not even his best friends would label him flippant. Had Jo Knight accomplished the near impossible and helped Michael find his sense of the ridiculous?

Jo punched his arm playfully. "Cute, Mike, cute."

Charlotte opened the ashtray and flipped off an ash. *Mike*, was it? To her knowledge, no one ever called Michael by the abbreviated Mike. Interesting. "What is it you do, my dear?"

"I'm a singer and a storyteller, for children." Swiveling around so she could see Charlotte, Jo told her about her work and her involvement in the literacy program.

"How wonderful to do something you enjoy and yet help people as well." She'd been right. The woman was smart and sensitive to boot. Charlotte frowned thoughtfully. "You wouldn't be related to Jarrett Knight, would you?"

Jo had had a feeling this lady got around. "He's my father."

Charlotte blew out smoke around a big smile. "Jarrett's a marvelous man. We met years ago after my first husband died and I discovered I had all these buildings I needed insured."

Michael glanced toward Jo. "You didn't tell me your father was connected with Southwest Insurance?" The name rang a bell with him, but he wasn't sure why.

Jo shrugged. "You didn't ask."

"Connected with, my eyebrow," Charlotte protested. "Jarrett *is* Southwest Insurance." She smiled at Jo. "So you're Jarrett's daughter." Her eyes grew dreamy. "I remember the first time we met. He's so big and sort of rumpled looking, not paying much attention to matching up his clothes. But you sit down and talk with him and he makes you feel you're the only woman in the world. You get up feeling as if you'd just chatted with Mel Gibson.'' She chuckled at her own whimsy. If Jarrett hadn't been married, well . . .

Jo had heard similar things before. ''Yes, Dad's pretty special.''

With another sigh for what might have been, Charlotte lowered the window and gazed out at the sea. ''Did you know that nine out of ten people prefer living by the ocean as opposed to living in the mountains? On Maui, you can do both.''

''Aunt Charlotte's something of a statistician,'' Michael told Jo as he flipped off the air-conditioning. It really was nicer with the sea breezes.

Gratefully Jo lowered her window, delighted to be rid of the smoke. ''Where do you get your facts, Charlotte?''

''I read, my dear. Endlessly.'' Her throaty laugh bubbled out as if enjoying a private joke. She could smell the salt air and, just ahead, see the masts of huge sailboats in the distance. ''I'm dry as a bone and famished. Let's stop and have lunch.''

Michael checked his watch. With a quick turnaround, as he'd hoped, he could get a few hours of work in this afternoon. ''I should get back to work.''

Charlotte leaned forward. ''Michael, did you know that eighty-seven percent of men who have heart attacks don't know how to relax? And those are the ones under thirty. Over thirty, the number rises dramatically.''

Michael saw Jo snicker behind her hand as she slumped down in her seat. By unspoken agreement, they were ganging up on him. Perhaps he could win with one of them. But two? Never. "All right, where do you want to stop?"

She smiled as she leaned back. That had been easier than she'd thought. "The Banyan Tree, of course. They have the very best mai-tais. Do you drink, Jo? I certainly hope so. I never trust people who don't drink at all. Then we'll walk down to this funky little art gallery I visited last year. I bought this Chagall worth twice what I paid for it. And, of course, we'll have to get you some scrimshaw. You'll think you're in New England."

"I thought Simon wanted to set sail early," Michael said, wondering how he'd lost control of the day so quickly.

"He does, but it's barely noon. Simon will wait for me," she said with the confidence of a woman who had had many a man do just that. "And if he doesn't, I'll just stay with you two for a while."

Dear God, what a thought! Michael turned onto Front Street and prayed that Simon was a patient fellow.

"EVERY EVENING at sundown, they light the tiki torches," Charlotte was saying. "Then a young man climbs up to Black Rock, offers a lei to the waves and dives from the rocks into the sea."

"I've seen something similar in Mexico," Jo said.

Charlotte sipped the last of her mai-tai and signaled the waiter for another, then lighted a cigarette. "Ah yes, but that's to prove he's brave. At Kaanapali, it's a reenactment of King Kahekili's leap to defy the spirit world and conquer his demons, both personal and otherwise. It's marvelous."

Michael shook his head at the waiter, refusing another. The rum drinks were potent, and he was already feeling light-headed. He leaned back in his chair at their table under The Banyan Tree after a wonderful lunch and wondered if he was up to mind wrestling with Charlotte. "And just how does jumping off a rock and endangering your life conquer your demons?"

"Risk, Michael," Charlotte said emphatically. "You have to take risks to achieve anything worthwhile." She leaned closer to Jo Knight. "You believe that, don't you?"

"Yes, I do." She swirled the melting ice around in her half-finished drink. "Sometimes you have to risk everything, my father often says. But first you have to make sure the rewards are worth the gamble."

A lock of Charlotte's red hair came loose as she nodded her agreement. "Exactly. It's the same in relationships." She gave a dazzling smile to the waiter who set down her drink. "Nice buns, don't you think?" she asked Jo as the young man walked away.

As Jo angled in her chair to check out the waiter, Michael frowned. "Aunt Charlotte, really. He's younger than your son."

"I don't *want* him, dear boy. I'm just admiring. One's never too old to admire, you know." Except a few who were born too old. "As I was saying, relationships can be quite chancy. I remember this one relationship Michael had a few years ago."

Here we go, he thought. "Do we have to go into my checkered past?"

Hardly checkered enough, Charlotte thought. "I'm trying to make a point. I thought she was quite charming. Whatever happened to...Hyacinth, wasn't that her name?''

Michael shifted uneasily on his chair. He saw Jo raise an amused eyebrow at him and wondered why on earth he'd thought it a good idea to bring her. ''Her real name was Geraldine, but she liked Hyacinth better. And I haven't a clue as to what happened to her. That was years ago, when I was going through my insane stage.''

It was difficult to imagine Michael acting even mildly insane. Jo couldn't help but tease him a little. ''You two were a *thing?*''

Charlotte shook her head. ''Not for long. He decided she was too risky.''

He found he needed to explain. ''Risky? She was bizarre, bordering on crazy. She lived in this loft, wore lots of beads she strung herself, ate kelp washed down with carrot juice and played the banjo half the night on her fire escape.'' He turned to Jo, his eyes imploring her. ''What does that sound like to you?''

Jo shrugged. ''A little kooky, but she sounds like fun.''

''My thoughts exactly,'' Charlotte chimed in.

Michael almost groaned aloud. ''Well, fortunately I've outgrown all that nonsense.''

''I'm not convinced that's something to celebrate, dear boy. We should all retain a little of the Peter Pan in ourselves, that reluctance to completely grow up.'' Charlotte turned to Jo. ''Give me your hand, my dear.''

''My hand?''

Again, Michael thought he should explain. ''Charlotte reads palms,'' he said, as if it were a very ordinary thing.

Amused, Jo held out her hand.

Charlotte wrinkled her brow in thought. "Ah, it's as I thought. I see maturity here and intelligence. See this line? It indicates a long life. And this is your love line. See all those little tributaries? You should have an active and varied love life."

"Varied?" Jo shook her head. "I'm not really one to hop around much."

Charlotte sent her a knowing look. "Varied *can* mean with the same person, my dear."

Jo smiled. "Ah, yes, there is that."

Charlotte traced another zigzagging line on Jo's palm with a pink-tipped nail. "And that's your fun line. I would say you enjoy life."

"I try." As she took back her hand, she looked over at Michael. He was studying the huge branches of the banyan tree overhead as if he'd never seen a tree before, obviously trying to go unnoticed. "Are you going to read Mike's palm?" she asked.

"Michael doesn't believe in nonsense, Jo." Charlotte put out her cigarette and signaled the waiter.

He didn't, of course, Michael reminded himself as he stood. Then why was he annoyed when he heard it spoken aloud?

Charlotte signed the charge with a flourish and got to her feet in a swirl of purple and white. "Come. Let's stroll along the shops and then go find Simon. I have the slip number where his sailboat is docked."

IT WASN'T EXACTLY a sailboat. It was the largest yacht in sight, manned by a crew of three and with sleeping accommodations for eight. Jo stepped on board, her feet sinking into thick white carpeting and looked around at the blue and burgundy furnishings and the polished teakwood bar, awestruck.

"So glad you could come, Binky," Simon was saying to Charlotte as Michael set down her bags. Turning, he offered his hand to her nephew. "And you must the the Michael I've heard so much about."

Binky? "Good to know you, Mr. Wakefield." How did she find them? Michael wondered. Tall and lean, Simon Wakefield had a full head of white hair and a slim mustache. Though it was a warm afternoon, he wore white linen trousers, a navy blazer and a paisley scarf tied at his throat.

"Call me, Simon, please." Looking as if he'd just stepped out of an English tearoom, the yachtsman slipped his arm around Charlotte's waist and gave them all a small smile. "I've been so looking forward to this." He glanced down the corridor where a man wearing a blue cap sat on a high chair at the ship's wheel. "Shall we take her out for a spin?"

"I don't know, Simon," Charlotte said. "Michael's anxious to get back to work."

He was. Or rather, he had been. Except he was looking at Jo who'd already wandered outside to the railing. Her blond hair swept about her face in a playful breeze, and her eyes, when she swung around to hear his answer, were dark blue with excitement. The sensible thing would be to ignore how challenging she looked and how filled with sudden longing he felt. But he didn't feel very sensible. "I don't suppose another hour will matter."

"Quite right." Simon signaled the man up front to start the engine. "Why don't we go topside? The view is so much better from there."

Charlotte placed a hand on his sleeve. "Would you help me settle in first, Simon?"

"Of course, Binky."

She patted his cheek and turned to Michael. "You two go on up and we'll join you shortly."

Michael couldn't tell if she was flirting with Simon or making a clumsy attempt at matchmaking. But Jo was already climbing the short stairwell. He followed.

They were heading straight out to sea and it was magnificent. The day was perfect, only a few spotty clouds marring a flawless blue sky. Jo felt the wind grab her hair and fly with it, then leaned into the railing and felt the salt spray on her face. She laughed for no particular reason, then turned to see Michael standing several feet behind her, his gray eyes unreadable.

What was he thinking? she wondered. After that soul-shattering kissing session in the kitchen last night, then the abrupt ending to the evening, she'd been wary today. He'd been polite, vacillating between annoyance and delight over Charlotte's antics, alternating between stretches of silence and bursts of chatter, first joking with her, then frowning at her.

She would play her cards close to the chest, she decided as he started toward her. She swung around and he came up close behind her, running his hands down her bare arms, easing her back to lean against him.

She was wearing yellow today, the same pale color as her fantastic hair. She was messing up his work, his head, his life. And he couldn't seem to keep from touching her. "So you like boats, eh?"

"Mmm. My father used to have a sailboat. It was nice, but required a lot of work. This—now, this is living. I had no idea Charlotte's friend was so well-heeled."

"She does seem to gravitate to that species of the male animal. But then, they say most people are drawn to a certain type."

Jo saw an opportunity for a little probing and shifted within the circle of his arms so she could see his eyes. "Do you gravitate to a type?"

"Probably."

"Am I like Hyacinth?"

He moved his hands up her back, urging her fractionally closer. "There are similarities, but not really."

She cocked her head. "Am I like any of the women you date back home?"

He didn't have to think about that for long. "Not in the least."

She wondered if that was a compliment. Rising on tiptoe, she pressed her mouth to his, long and lingeringly. "Do I kiss like any of them?"

He was used to women who kissed well, practiced and smooth performances, satisfaction without the passion. Here was the passion. He could sense it humming just under the surface. But here also was turmoil, entanglement, madness. But he wouldn't think about that, not right this minute. Not when she was warm and willing in his arms where he finally admitted he'd been wanting her all day.

"You kiss like no one I've ever known." The yacht hit a big wave and bounced, causing them to sway. He tightened his hold on her. "Your kisses are better, more stirring, more exiting. Is that what you wanted to hear?"

Her eyes warmed at his words. "Yes," she told him with utter honesty. "But I'd rather do it than talk about it."

Dipping his head, Michael was glad to oblige as he took her mouth, his heart lurching as she wound her arms around him. Tomorrow. He would think tomorrow. Today was for feeling.

At the head of the stairs down the walkway, Charlotte paused on the teakwood deck as Simon came up behind her. "Shh," she whispered. Smiling her approval, she watched Michael and Jo a long moment, then turned around. "Why don't we go back down and you can fix me one of those exotic island drinks? I believe it's too breezy up here for me after all." Later, she decided, she would find her camera and take some pictures. She wanted to remember this day.

"I REALLY SHOULD get to work," Michael said as he stopped the car at the crossroads. To the right, the road led to Kaanapali and the tiki torch ceremony; to the left was the road to their cottage.

"That's fine," Jo said, checking the time on the dashboard clock. "I have a dinner date anyhow." She hadn't planned on having one, but she felt fairly certain she could coax Christy into meeting her somewhere. She hadn't spent much time with her friend. And besides, she wasn't about to sit in that little house like a pathetic wallflower while he returned to his precious sketches, which he obviously preferred over dining with her.

Surprised, Michael didn't move. "Who is he?" The words popped out before he could stop them. None of his business, really. But she was here in an unfamiliar place, and he felt oddly responsible for her.

"A friend," Jo answered casually.

The honking of a car horn behind them startled Michael into action and he quickly turned left. A friend, was it? No name, no explanation. She owed him none, he reminded himself. He wasn't jealous, either. Just concerned.

And more than a little disturbed. How could she kiss him so freely, even eagerly, just an hour ago out on the yacht's deck, then go out to dinner with another man? A man she'd had to have met since she'd arrived because she'd told him that first day that she knew no one on the island. Of course, she'd made friends with the gardener in three minutes. She could be going out with the grocer, for all he knew. She wasn't one to hop from man to man, she'd told Charlotte when his aunt had read her palm. Right!

He wouldn't ask any more questions. He wouldn't give her the satisfaction. His lips a thin line, Michael jerked the car around a bend in the road and glared ahead.

Testy again. Jo smothered a sigh. For a conservative workaholic, Michael Daye had more mercurial moods than anyone she knew. Last night he'd all but ravished her, then coolly dismissed her. On the yacht, he'd kissed her with a hunger that matched her own. Now he was pouting again.

This ambivalence was driving her bonkers.

Jo stretched out her long legs, leaned her head back and closed her eyes. She was too keyed up to nap, but she could pretend. It was infinitely preferable to watching him struggle with his emotions.

Charlotte had to be a throwback to a recessive gene in the Daye family, Jo decided. From what she'd heard, both Michael's parents and his sister were as restrained as he. But good old Charlotte was like a fresh breeze in a stagnant room.

She'd taken Jo on a private tour of the yacht while Simon had taken Michael up to examine the bridge. They'd wound up in her beautifully appointed stateroom across the hall from Simon's, and finally Charlotte had had her say.

"You're good for him, you know," Charlotte had begun, lighting up and blowing smoke ceilingward.

Jo was too honest to fence, most especially with a woman of Charlotte's experience. "I don't think he thinks so."

"It's going to be uphill all the way, you realize."

"Don't I know it." Jo ran her hand along the pink satin inset in the teakwood footboard of the bed. Obviously this cabin had been decorated with women in mind. "Are you trying to warn me off?"

Charlotte chuckled low in her throat. "On the contrary, my dear. I'm trying to encourage you to keep at it. I love my nephew a great deal, and I'm pleasantly surprised to see a different man after a mere week. Imagine what you could do in months, in years."

"It isn't that I want to change him..."

"I know that. You want to draw him out."

"Exactly. He represses so much, denies his feelings, fights his emotions. I'm not altogether sure why."

Charlotte adjusted a delicate mother-of-pearl comb more securely in her hair. The explanation wasn't difficult to give, for she'd detected the reason years ago. "Michael grew up in a very sumptuous house with everything a child could want, and was given the best education money could buy. My brother's a very good man, and Ilona is a strong, talented woman. But they're a couple of cold fish, and although, in their own way, I believe they care for Michael and Deborah, they seem unable to show love or affection. Probably because they have none for each other. A pity, but there it is."

Jo nodded. "I'd thought as much from the little he's told me. Yet you seem so different, and so is Noel."

Charlotte smiled, as if at a very flattering compliment, then inhaled deeply. "Our parents were divorced when Eugene and I were quite young. He was reared by our father, a stoic man. I was fortunate enough to be raised by our mother, a warm and generous woman. Perhaps Noel and I take after her. But getting back to Michael. The problem isn't that he's incapable of caring. It's that he's frightened to death of marriage because he views it as an irresistible force meeting an immovable object. Eugene and Ilona apparently didn't want to work on making something of their marriage, so they didn't. But two people who are different *can* make a go of it. If they love enough."

Jo sighed her agreement. "I've always thought so."

"Do you love him?"

The lady played hardball. Jo brushed back her hair, uncertain herself. "I could, I believe, if he'd let me. He's the first—the only—man I've ever felt so much for so quickly. It's frightening. I'm not sure I would call it love just yet. I mean, it's all happened so fast."

Charlotte smiled. "Love is like that, my dear. Like lightning. It just happens. No logical explanation as to where and when it'll hit. I should know. It struck me the first time I laid eyes on Henry Kramer."

Jo saw Charlotte's eyes soften. "Your first husband."

"Yes. Oh, I've married since, several times. I like a good time too much to be always alone. But I still love Henry and I always will. You're that way, I'd wager. You'll settle on one. And so did Jarrett. How that man adores your mother."

"I know. It's beautiful to see."

"And beautiful to share." Charlotte crushed out her cigarette. "Now, I have a piece of advice for you, my dear. A privilege of advancing age, you know, this need to share our wisdom with the young." She gave a self-deprecating laugh. "Push him a little. He has a ways to go, but Michael's always been a quick study. He wants you, I can see it. But he senses you won't settle for half a loaf, and he's never given anyone the whole Magilla. But he will, if you go about it right. Make him want you more, enough to want to change. I believe he already suspects he should. And when he comes around, you'll have quite a man."

Eyes still closed as the car hummed along, Jo smiled at Charlotte's advice, then let herself remember the moments in Michael's arms as the powerful boat had spun out to sea. Yes, quite a man, she thought drowsily. And definitely worth the effort.

"YOU'RE COMING IN a little late." Seated at the dining room table, Michael frowned through the archway as Jo shut the front door behind her.

She glanced at her watch. Eleven-fifteen. Hardly late. "I'm a big girl now, Mike, or haven't you noticed?" She bent to pet Heinz's head as the dog came up to greet her.

He'd noticed, all right. She'd left around seven wearing a turquoise dress that swirled around her shapely legs, leaving behind the lingering scent of honeysuckle that had intruded on his thoughts all evening. In slacks or shorts, she looked willowy. In a dress, her shape was more defined, more disturbing.

He'd drunk so much coffee that his hands weren't steady and his hair was tousled from his frustrated fingers combing through it. Papers were scattered all over the table, and the sketch he'd been working on wasn't going right. "Don't you know it's not safe for a woman alone to go roaming around in the middle of the night?"

With genuine effort, Jo kept her features even. The middle of the night, indeed. "Who appointed you my father? I've been going out alone for some time now. Even Dad's stopped hounding me."

"What kind of a man has you meet him rather than picking you up at the house as he should?"

She wasn't sure how long she could keep this up. "Let's see, a painfully shy man, an inconsiderate one, or an ax murderer. I would imagine that about covers it." She sauntered to the table to peer over his shoulder at his latest sketch.

"Right. Which one was he?"

Jo straightened to stare at him as he turned to look up. "I think you've had too much sun." She held up her hand to stop his next ridiculous statement. She would be angry if she wasn't just a little pleased at his silly jealousy. "Okay, okay. I was out with Christy. At her apartment, actually. We had dinner and conversation. Alone, just the two of us. I could probably get the names of a couple of her neighbors to verify this if you'd like." She watched him digest that and almost laughed out loud.

Michael felt the heat rise in his face and turned back to his sketch. "You could have said so."

"What, and spoil all this righteous indignation? Never." She leaned over again, studying the drawing. He really was a nice man, and she shouldn't have goaded him. But he'd been so ripe for it. Changing the subject so he could save face, she pointed to a stretch of buildings on his drawing. "What are these?"

Michael took a deep breath, letting go of his annoyance. He had acted like an overprotective parent. Pretty odd considering he didn't regard Jo in a fatherly way at all. "Storefronts and abandoned warehouses currently. They're going to be torn down and the whole area renovated into a shopping plaza."

"And you're designing the stores?"

"That's part of it." He reached for another preliminary drawing to explain the rest. This he was comfortable with, talking about his work. "There are rundown apartments around the corner from this area occupied by low-income families. They're the potential customers for the stores. But the housing is substandard, so we talked the government into subsidizing the buildings and putting up apartments over this whole stretch of stores, subject to approval of our designs, of course."

Jo found herself impressed. "It looks like a two-level shopping center when, in fact, there will be stores on the ground floor and living quarters above. That's neat."

He felt a flush of quick pride, then wondered why her opinion mattered to him. "Thanks."

She eased back to look at him. "Then it *was* your idea?"

"Well, yes."

But he hadn't boasted of that, just explained. And he cared about people less fortunate. Yes, Michael

Daye was definitely worth the effort. And quite won-derful when he forgot to be so intense. Absently she began to massage his tense neck muscles. "When will this project get under way?"

"After I return, we submit the plans for approval. When we have that, they start bulldozing." Michael felt his head grow heavy. Lord, but she had great hands.

"And occupancy when?"

"Under a year, if all goes well. It's tricky because we can't knock down those old tenements until we have a place for those people to live. And we can't complete the project until all the apartments are cleared away. Timing. It's all in the timing." He put down his pen-cil as his head dropped forward. On a sigh, he closed his eyes, feeling almost boneless.

"Yes," Jo murmured softly. "Timing is every-thing." Abruptly she straightened and stepped back. "It's been a long day. Good night, Mike. See you in the morning."

She wanted desperately to turn around at her bed-room door and catch his surprised expression. But it would spoil everything. Humming, she went inside.

Always leave them wanting just a little bit more, Jo thought as she flopped onto her bed with a very fem-inine smile.

Chapter Six

Michael stood at the kitchen window gazing out at the tropical scene of the ocean waves frothing the shoreline and palm trees dancing in a light breeze. And, for the first time in years, he wanted to set aside the work waiting for him in the next room and play hooky.

Not a good sign, he told himself.

His life had consisted of studying and learning in his youth, then of scheduled activities, meetings, timetables and deadlines. Yet he'd thrived on it, looking forward to the challenges of his work, the satisfaction of his designs taking shape, the pleasure of viewing the completed projects. Why, then suddenly, did he want to chuck it all and go out and frolic in the sea like some carefree kid?

Because Jo was out there.

He poured himself a glass of tea from the pitcher and added ice. Sipping, he strolled back to the window. She'd neatly one-upped him last night, letting him assume she was going out with another man, leaving him home with his fertile imagination. It wasn't that he was jealous necessarily. He was just the type of man who worried about his friends. Even his *new* friends.

Michael swallowed another gulp before he set the glass down and admitted the truth. Sure, he'd been worried. Worried she'd find some guy who was full of the fun she was always talking about. A man who would make her laugh. A man who would not turn from the kisses she offered with such open generosity.

He should feel relieved if she had, he'd told himself while he'd paced and watched the road for her return as the hour grew late. He should be glad she was out of the way so he could work uninterrupted. But he hadn't been. Whether with him or away, she was always on his mind.

How had that happened? Michael wondered, frowning. How had he let it? Ridiculous, a man his age standing around mooning over a woman. He would be thirty-four in a few days. He would do well to remember that. Women clouded a man's mind. It was a well-known fact. Case in point was his partner, Eric Stromberg.

Eric was a hell of a nice guy. But each time a woman came into his life and got her claws in him, Michael felt as though he might as well be dealing with Bozo the Clown for all the sense Eric made during their business discussions. Eric would get all dreamy-eyed, leaning back in his swivel chair, his feet propped on his desk while he babbled on the phone with his current lady, his mind turned to mush. If that was love, they could keep it.

Michael leaned closer to the window, trying to spot a blond head bobbing between the waves. She'd been out there an awfully long time. Why wasn't she sitting under her tree with her guitar where, as long as she was playing, he knew she was all right? Abruptly he straightened. He was doing it again, acting like a distressed father.

He ran a hand through his hair, disgusted with himself. She'd reduced him to this pitiful state. What right did she have to muddle his faculties when she knew he needed a clear mind to work? He wouldn't allow it to continue, he decided as he finished his iced tea. He would forget about her, get in there and complete his sketches. He didn't need this. He'd never in his life felt responsible for another human being other than himself. He'd never even owned a dog, a cat, a canary or a goldfish. Why was he taking on this added burden? No more, he vowed.

Turning away, his eyes drifted to the window for one last glance. He saw her then, swimming in, her strokes slow and somewhat sluggish. She'd probably worn herself out by going too far. She needed a damn keeper, that's what she needed. Didn't have the good sense God gave a newborn puppy. She...

Michael leaned closer. She was walking in through the shallow water now, but then she stumbled and went down on one knee. Could she be that tired? Narrowing his eyes, he saw her slowly get up, then stagger out. She was barely clear of the last swirling wave when she dropped to the sand like a collapsing rag doll.

Something was terribly wrong. Heinz, waiting for her at the water's edge, was dancing around, licking her face, yet she didn't move. Turning, he raced through the door and down to the beach.

Michael reached her side in moments. She was lying just as he'd seen her fall—absolutely still, her face as white as her suit, her hair shifting in a small pool of seawater. He crouched down and slipped a hand under her shoulders, lifting her from the water. "Jo, can you hear me?"

Pressing shaky fingers to her throat, he quickly found her pulse. Her heartbeat was steady if not terribly strong. Had she gotten a cramp, than worn herself out and fainted? About to slide his free hand under her knees to lift her, he saw the gash in her leg.

And he saw the sharp spine of a stingray sticking out of the angry cut.

Jo turned her head and moaned low in her throat. With the return of consciousness came the pain, blazing a trail from her leg to her brain, the ache so severe she stiffened in reaction, trying to return to the black oblivion. But the agony wouldn't let her be, clawing at her, so sharp she wanted to cry out.

"It's all right," Michael said, trying desperately to remain calm. He'd vacationed here often enough to know how wicked a stingray's saw-toothed tail could be. He had to get the sheath out if he could—and the sooner the better. Kneeling beside her, he pushed back her damp hair. "This is going to hurt, Jo, just for a minute."

Her eyes opened slowly, dazed with pain. She tried to focus on his face, to push back the panic. "A stingray," she said in a voice she didn't recognize. "I saw him. He brushed against me. I went out too far. I..."

He took her hands and squeezed them. "Don't talk. I'll take care of you."

"But...they're poison...I..."

"Shhh. Just hang on. The spine's not in very deep." He didn't want to do this. He was, in fact, not very good in medical emergencies, since he'd experienced very few. He could carry her to the house and call a doctor, but he was afraid to chance the wait. Even now the poison was seeping into her and spreading. "I'll do it as quickly as I can."

He watched her eyes, hoping she wasn't going into shock. He let go of her hands and took a deep breath, his heart pounding, then pushed a hovering Heinz out of his way.

Jo squeezed sand with her fingers and tried to concentrate on the red glow behind her closed eyelids, uncertain whether it was the sun or the blinding pain. She felt a rip, and her neck arched involuntarily as she let out a yell. Then she felt herself sink back into the welcome inky darkness.

Michael tossed the treacherous blade aside and saw the blood gush out of the open wound. Scooping salt water, he rinsed the wound repeatedly, letting the sea wash out as much of the poison as possible. She'd fainted again, and he was glad he wouldn't have to watch her struggle with the pain.

He ran to the lime tree at the sand's edge, pulled off a lime and split it open with his teeth as he ran back to her. He remembered reading that the acid in citrus fruits was also a good rinsing agent for poisonous wounds. He squeezed both halves over her leg wound, then splashed on more salt water. At last he picked her up and cradled her against his body.

He'd never carried a grown woman before, Michael realized as he rushed to the house. He wasn't the caveman type. He only wished it was under different circumstances.

Her head lolled against him as he hurried. She would be reviving soon and hurting again. He had to call a doctor and didn't know any. Praying he'd done the right thing for her wound so far and that he'd gotten most of the poison out, he took her inside, lay her on his bed and reached for the phone.

Heart thudding, he listened to the ringing. She had to be all right. She simply had to be.

THERE WERE LAYERS of fog drifting overhead. Jo fought through the gray swirls to consciousness, opening her eyes and blinking against the brightness. She closed them again, struggling with the mists. Memory slammed into her then, and with it a jolt of fear.

She'd been floating on a quiet sea, letting her mind drift. The stingray with its whipping tail had come out of nowhere. She'd tried to swim away, but he'd been too fast. Then there'd been the pain, sharper than she'd ever imagined. She made a protesting sound low in her throat.

"You're all right, Jo." Michael's voice seemed to be coming through a long tunnel as she forced herself not to give in to the blackness tugging at her. His hand took hold of hers and she felt the mattress dip as he sat next to her.

Again, she labored to open her eyes and found him watching her with a worried frown. She pulled in a shaky breath and was surprised that the pain was gone. She squeezed his fingers with ebbing strength and whispered his name in a weak voice.

"You're going to be fine. The doctor's been here and given you a shot. Short chubby man with a white beard. Do you remember Dr. Thaddeus?" He held her pale, fragile hand between both of his and stroked her soft skin. He'd never been so scared in his entire life. Until just now, when she'd finally opened her eyes, he hadn't believed the good doctor that she would come around. He saw she was trying to focus on the memory. "You're drowsy because of the medicine."

She blinked, trying to recall a doctor coming and going, but only hazy images surfaced. Her eyes scanned her surroundings. "Your room," she managed to get out, her voice sounding breathy.

He touched her warm cheek, brushed her hair back, needing the contact. For hours he'd sat here in the chair he'd pulled up alongside her bed. Watching her face bead with sweat, listening to her moan as he applied cold cloths to her head the way Dr. Thaddeus had instructed. "Yes, I brought you in here. It was closest and there's a phone in here. I didn't want to leave you while I called around for a doctor."

Her legs felt numb and tingly, her head spinning with the drug. "The poison..."

"Is no longer a threat. With a little rest, you'll be like new."

"You saved me," she said, finally realizing it was true. "Thank you."

"You scared the hell out of me." He brought her hand to his lips and kissed it gently. "Don't thank me, please."

He'd do the same for anyone, he'd told himself while he'd quickly located a doctor who would come out to the house. For reasons he didn't want to think about, he hadn't wanted to take her to a hospital, to let her out of his sight. He'd offered an outrageous amount of money and the second doctor he'd phoned had agreed to come right over.

Michael learned he'd done the right things, rinsed the wound well. Dr. Thaddeus had told him to apply hot compresses for an hour, then rebandage the wound. He'd left pills and left a very frightened man behind to deal with her raging fever. But he'd weathered it, Michael thought as he ran a hand over the stubble on his chin. And yes, he would have rescued a stranger if he'd have found them similarly injured.

But he wouldn't have spent twenty-four hours alongside a stranger, praying that she would be all right.

"Are you hungry?" he asked. "The doctor said soup would be good. There're some cans in the cupboard."

She shook her head, surprised again that she felt no pain. "Sleepy," she murmured.

He smiled down at her, his first in a long while. "Then rest. If you need anything, I'll be right here."

Jo raised an unsteady hand to touch his face. He hadn't shaved. He was always so neat. And his eyes were kind of hollow-looking. "Are you all right?"

"I am now." He leaned down and brushed his lips across hers. "Go to sleep."

She wanted to say more, to ask more, but she didn't have the strength. She closed her eyes and in moments was sound asleep.

Michael let out a shaky breath as he sat, still holding her hand. He needed a shower and shave, some clean clothes and something in his stomach besides black coffee. But he didn't want to leave her just yet.

She looked so small under the sheet, her pale hair fanned out on the pillow. The next time she'd awaken, she'd probably be stronger. And she'd probably be embarrassed and possibly angry when she realized she was wearing one of his long T-shirts, but he couldn't have let her lay in her wet bathing suit. He would gladly match tempers with her if only she would return to her old self.

Thank goodness, she was young, strong and healthy. The doctor had told him a weaker woman might have required hospitalization. All those years of swimming and running had paid off. And still, he worried.

Michael stroked her cheek again, but she didn't move. She was lovely, even after such an ordeal. Now that it was nearly over, he took a moment to examine his feelings about Jo Knight. It was more than desire that had him churning. A man doesn't struggle against desire so strongly. He usually acknowledges it, acts on it or takes a cold shower. But feelings of a deeper nature were not so easily handled.

She was tangling his emotions more each day, something he'd always fought against. They were all wrong for each other, yet he was inexplicably drawn to her. And he hadn't the foggiest notion how to handle that.

Rising and gently placing her hand on the sheet, he went in to clean up.

SHE AWOKE to a vaguely familiar scent. Jo opened her eyes and saw that she was lying in Michael's bed, her face buried in his pillow. It was his special fragrance she smelled, the one she'd inhaled each time he'd held her and kissed her. Rolling to her back, she groaned as the pain made itself known. It would seem the shot had finally worn off.

But the ache wasn't nearly as sharp. More like a dull throb in the general vicinity of her left leg. And her head hurt. But at least that terrible wooziness was gone. Her eyes drifted to the chair, and she noticed Michael wasn't with her. He was probably working or maybe taking a nap. She glanced up at the window and saw it was dusk. She'd gone swimming around ten and it had to be seven or eight. A long while to be out of commission.

Testing her strength, she moved her leg and felt a quick stab of pain, but manageable. Jo had enjoyed good health all her life and had been known to be impatient with even a head cold. She certainly wasn't about to let this keep her down too long. She still had several more songs to complete before next week's assembly program.

Feeling warm, she lifted back the sheet and light blanket. Gazing down, she saw she was wearing an unfamiliar long blue shirt that ended at mid-thigh. Quickly she felt around and realized her suit was gone. The blush spread slowly but surely.

She took a deep breath and frowned. Michael had undressed her, right down to the skin. Not much she could do after the fact, she supposed.

"You're hurting again," Michael said, entering the room and misinterpreting the look on her face.

"Not much." She pulled the sheet back over herself and tried to sit up, but a wave of pain had her eyes closing.

"Here, let me help you." Michael slipped his arm around her, quickly stacked the two pillows behind her head, then gently eased her back down. "It's probably time for a pain pill."

"No, they make me feel too floaty." She looked him over as he pulled the chair closer. He'd shaved and changed clothes, but there were smudges of fatigue under his eyes. What must she look like? she wondered as she ran a trembling hand through her tousled hair. "I must look a sight. Could you get my hairbrush, please?"

A good sign. She was worrying about her looks. "Sure. And there's soup heating. I'll be right back."

She insisted on fixing her hair first, and he insisted on feeding her the soup when he saw that she was weak as a kitten, worn out after a few brush strokes. "Chicken broth imported from France. Nothing but the best from Aunt Charlotte's private stock. It'll fix you right up."

Jo swallowed, the aroma alone arousing her hunger. "I can feed myself, you know."

"Humor me. Anyone who worries me for thirty-six hours owes me."

She choked down a swallow. "Thirty-six?" She glanced out the window again. "But I thought it was only early evening."

"It is. The day after. It was yesterday morning you tangled with the stingray." He continued spooning in the soup.

So that was why he'd looked so disheveled when she'd awakened earlier. And why he still looked tired. "You stayed up all night with me?" Other than her mother when she'd been about ten and had had a terrible case of the flu, she couldn't remember anyone ever doing that for her.

He shoved in another spoonful, then wiped her chin. "It was no big deal." He couldn't have slept anyhow, until her fever had broken. And afterward, she'd grabbed his hand and held on, like a young child needing the human contact. He hadn't had the heart to pull away that small measure of comfort.

"I'm sorry, Mike." She touched his hand before he could feed her more. "I know you weren't pleased that I was here in the first place. You certainly hadn't planned on nursing me."

He set down the bowl and met her eyes. "You'd have done it for me, right?" They both knew with utter certainty that she would have.

"That's not the point." She was grateful. She remembered clutching his hand, afraid he'd leave her, afraid she'd die.

"It's exactly the point. Besides, I *wanted* to, or I wouldn't have." He shook a pill out of the container the doctor had left, then poured cold water from the pitcher on the nightstand. "Take this."

"What is it?"

"It'll help you rest. Now, don't fight me on this."

She swallowed obediently, losing ground fast. How could she be so tired after eating half a bowl of soup? "Tomorrow," she said softly. "I'll find a way to thank you tomorrow."

"I don't want your gratitude." Why did that make him so angry? Because it reduced their relationship to favor for favor, tit for tat. That's how he'd wanted it to be, once. But things had shifted for Michael during his long night's vigil. He still didn't especially want to feel so much. Yet he had to admit that he cared about her far more than he'd planned to.

He saw her squirm a little, trying to get comfortable. "Want me to fix your pillows differently?" he asked.

She still had hold of his hand, but she wanted more. He'd already done so much that she wondered if she dare ask as she tried to read his eyes.

"What is it?" Michael asked as he leaned closer. "Tell me."

She would bury her pride, this one time. "Would you hold me, please, just for a little while?"

That he could do with the greatest pleasure. As gently as possible, he bunched the pillows against the headboard, eased behind her and cradled her to his chest. She settled, emitting soft sounds as she got comfortable. "Is this all right?"

"Perfect." The pill was dragging her under, the heaviness spreading. "Mike?"

He smoothed her hair back from her cheek, thinking he could use a little sleep himself. "Hmm?"

"I was so scared," she admitted on a shaky sigh.

He tightened his arms around her. "I know." Me, too, he thought.

She was silent for a long moment, and he thought she'd drifted off. But her hazy mind wouldn't let her until she asked him one more thing. "Have I told you yet that I'm nuts about you?"

Michael smiled as he heard her breathing deepen at last. It was the medicine talking, he told himself. She wouldn't remember what she'd said in the morning.

But he would. Feeling oddly content, he closed his eyes.

THERE WAS A KNOCKING sound, loud and insistent. Jo's eyes popped open. She was alone in Michael's bed, and the sun was streaming in the open window. Another knock and the door opened just as her head swiveled around.

"Are you decent? Dr. Thaddeus is here to check on you." Michael strolled into the room followed by a man resembling Santa Claus dressed in white slacks and a green-and-yellow aloha shirt.

"Well, young lady," Dr. Thaddeus said as he came alongside the bed. "You're certainly looking better than the last time I saw you."

Carefully Jo straightened, then flinched at the sudden throbbing in her left leg.

"Still painful, I see." The doctor pulled back the sheet. "Let's have a look."

Despite the discomfort the movement cost her, Jo reached down to straighten her tangled nightshirt. "I'm all right." She sent a look of dismay at Michael standing at the foot of the bed. "Did you call him again?"

"No, he did not," the doctor answered for him. "I always check back on my patients, especially one as pretty as you." With practiced hands, he removed the bandage. "Ah, yes, coming along nicely." From his bag, he removed antiseptic and a cotton pad, efficiently cleaning the wound. "You have your young man to thank for his quick thinking, you know."

With no small effort, she held still while he smeared antibiotic ointment on her leg. "Yes, I know."

"All but threatened me with dire calamities if I didn't drop everything and come attend to you." Dr. Thaddeus chuckled as he winked at her, then deftly rebandaged her cut.

Jo watched Michael walk to the window, looking disconcerted. Why did doing nice things for people embarrass the man? Odd.

The doctor checked the pill bottle on the nightstand. "You're not pain-free by a long shot, I'll wager. Don't be afraid to take these when you need them."

Michael turned back. "She has to stay in bed for a while yet, right?"

"No!" She didn't care if it hurt a little. She'd never been able to lie around for days on end. Seeing the stubborn look on Michael's face, she tried to reason with the doctor. "I'm not going hiking, but I want up. A shower and shampoo. I have some more work to do that I can't put off."

"What kind of work?" Dr. Thaddeus asked, zipping up his bag.

"Songwriting. I can sit under a tree. Or on the couch."

"All right, but keep off the leg for at least two more days unless it's absolutely necessary, okay?"

Finally she felt like smiling. "I will and thank you."

Michael sent her a glare, then escorted the doctor out.

She had to get up while he was out of the room and get into the bathroom quickly. If she didn't have a shower soon, she'd go crazy. And her hair must look like limp linguine. Carefully she swung her legs over the edge and sat upright.

The room swam for a moment, then righted. The lingering effects of the medication. No more damn pills, she thought as she eased up, letting her good leg take most of her weight. So far so good. Gingerly she tested the other leg, slowly pressing down. It hurt, but not unbearably.

She waited a moment, adjusting to the throbbing, then started toward his bathroom. She knew she couldn't chance making it to her own, all the way through the living room and around. Besides, he'd probably intercept her. She made it and closed the door. She nearly locked it, then thought better. After all, she could still pass out. No use being silly.

Moving to the mirror above the sink, she peered at her image. Lord, what a mess she was. Hair limp and hanging, her face white even under her ever-present tan, and eyes that looked a little bruised. Jo took a deep breath. She was young, she was strong. Another day or two and she'd be fine. She turned to pull back the shower curtain as a knock sounded at the door.

"Jo, are you all right?" Michael's voice sounded exasperated.

"Yes. I'll be out after I shower. Could you bring me my robe, please?" She'd put that on, then go to her own room and find some clothes. Invalids sat around in robes; she was *not* an invalid.

He muttered something, then walked away.

It seemed as if her male Florence Nightingale was growing fond of his role. Well, she wasn't used to being coddled. Shrugging out of his shirt, she turned on the water.

SHE WAS FALLING in love with him.

Sitting in the yard under her favorite palm tree, Jo gazed up at a brilliant blue sky. Odd how things happened. Since her mid-teens, she'd dreamed of falling in love with a man like her father. A big, solid man with gentle eyes and a hearty laugh, a man who unabashedly loved life and children and animals. And her. A reserved architect more comfortable with blueprints than people, who consistently denied his feelings even to himself, hadn't been considered as a candidate.

But when that architect kissed her, he didn't seem bookish or restrained.

Sighing, Jo looked over her notes. She had several new songs put together for the books she planned to use for the assembly program at Christy's school. And she'd rehearsed some of her old standards. It was all shaping up just fine.

Last week, the evening she'd visited her friend's apartment, they'd gone over the skits Jo wanted to do, and Christy had given her the names of the older students who'd volunteered to act out her songs. The principal, an avid amateur photographer, was planning to film her presentation. The program would be fun and a learning experience as well, and Jo was looking forward to it. Maybe she'd ask Michael to go along.

She stretched her left leg out. She was healing rapidly, a fact that pleased her no end. Four days after her accident, she had little pain and could walk without much discomfort. The bandage covering her cut was growing smaller each day.

She flopped back on the grass lazily. It had sprinkled this morning, but the clouds were gone and everything had dried up by now. The scent of rain coming in through her open window had awakened her and, restless from too much sitting around, she'd gotten up to make coffee. As she'd walked past Michael's door, she'd noticed that it was ajar. Cautiously she'd peeked in.

He'd been asleep in a tangle of sheets, one arm dangling over the edge of the bed. And curled up into his side was Floppy, who'd opened one yellow eye to check her out then promptly drifted off again. Smiling, she'd tiptoed on to the kitchen.

He'd looked so sweet, napping with Floppy, this man who'd said emphatically that he didn't like cats. She'd been wondering where Floppy had been spending his nights since he hadn't come in to her bedroom in some time, although Heinz played pillow tag with her regularly. And sweet wasn't the only impression she'd had of Michael as she'd caught him unaware.

Sexy. Turned on his side facing her, he'd had the sheet riding low on his hips and wrapped around his lower body. Jo was certain he slept in the raw. Interesting. The lingering memory gave way to daydreaming as she stuck a blade of grass between her teeth. A fine mind, a great body, a nice guy.

At first she'd thought him awfully grumpy. Even this morning he'd shuffled out before she'd plugged in the pot, wearing only shorts and a frown. Pouring a glass of juice, he'd silently sipped it. She'd come to the conclusion he wasn't a morning person. Not everyone was. He'd been so good to her, so considerate, that she couldn't really fault him.

Her accident had put him behind in his work, which she knew had to bother him. She'd suggested that perhaps he could stay another week if necessary, but his answer had been another frown. The past two days, he'd spent most hours hovered over his sketches, though he stopped often to check on her. Workaholic wasn't the word. Obsessed perhaps.

Jo rolled over on her stomach. Since Michael had cared for her through her recovery, since the night she'd slept in his arms, innocent as that had been, he was looking at her differently. Long, lingering, thoughtful looks. She'd give a lot to know what was going on in his mind.

Hearing a sound, she looked up and saw a vehicle pull into the drive leading to their cabin. A white van, she noticed as she carefully got to her feet. Heinz was already on his way to greet the driver.

"Morning, ma'am," the mustached driver said, climbing out. "Got a delivery for you."

"Really?" The name painted on the truck's door was Celebrations. Curiosity aroused, Jo trailed along to the rear double doors. The man leaned inside and reappeared with a cellophane-wrapped package sporting a huge silver balloon attached by a red ribbon.

"Special delivery gift for—" he squinted at the attached card "—a Mr. E. Michael Daye, Jr."

The balloon's message was Enjoy. Jo peeked through the clear, thin paper. Mounds of chocolates. "How nice. I wonder who sent them."

Obligingly the delivery man read the rest. "I wanted to be a part of your best birthday ever. Follow the directions on the numbered envelopes and enjoy. Love, Aunt Charlotte." He looked up. "Is Mr. Daye here?"

Michael's birthday and he hadn't even mentioned it. Why was she not surprised? "Yes, indeed. I'll take you to him." Humming, she led him inside.

Michael stared at the man, then at the package, feeling like a little boy again, receiving a gift from the only relative who'd ever bothered to pick out his presents herself. His father had always given him a check, and his mother had had her personal assistant who always traveled with her mail him a gift. Something expensive and usually from F. A. O. Schwartz when he was young, later from Neiman Marcus. June was a month his mother always spent on the road—a great concert month in Europe.

Michael swallowed and hoped his feelings weren't evident in his expression, especially to someone as astute as Jo. "Nice, nice," he said, for lack of a better reaction and gave the delivery man a tight smile and a tip.

"Thanks, but I'm supposed to wait until you take out the envelopes and read the first one." Seeing the puzzled look on Michael's face, the man held out the tag attached to the balloon.

Reading it, Michael frowned. There was no telling what Charlotte was up to this time. She was so unpredictable. Uneasily he pulled the envelopes out and opened the first one. As he read, a reluctant smile formed.

Remember the scavenger hunt I took you on when you were a little boy, Michael? This one's even better. Let the man bring in the next surprise, and when he leaves, read the second envelope.

Feeling a bit sheepish, Michael told the man to bring in whatever it was.

Jo watched him leave, then turned back to Michael, who was peeking inside the cellophane as she'd done. "You didn't tell me."

Deftly he extracted a large milk chocolate and took a bite. Grand Marnier burst from its juicy center. Savoring, he closed his eyes, chewed and swallowed. "Tell you what?" he managed.

"That it's your birthday. And neither did Charlotte."

Michael sat back down. "Have one. Charlotte knows I'm crazy about chocolates with liqueur fillings." He ate the other half.

"So what is he bringing in?"

"I don't know." He handed her the note from the first envelope and eyed a foil-wrapped candy while she read it. He knew he'd have to explain. "When I was around six, I got the chicken pox, a really bad case. My mother was out of town and I think the housekeeper of the moment was having trouble with me so she called Charlotte.''

Jo sat at the table, shaking her head at the chocolate he offered her. It was a little early in the day for liqueurs, with or without chocolate. "And she hurried right over with liquor and candy to distract you?''

"No. I developed a taste for these years later. Charlotte thought up something special, though." Michael sat back, smiling at the memory. "She told me if I promised not to scratch my terribly itchy sores and leave scars all over my face, she'd arrange a scavenger hunt for me. She made up these notes with elaborate clues and put each one in a separate envelope. When I figured out the clue, it led me to the location of a present. It really kept me occupied—and I got a present a day for a week. By the time I found the last present, my chicken pox were gone.''

"What a clever woman Charlotte is.''

Michael saw the delivery man returning, carrying a large zippered bag with a hanger in each hand. "Looks like Charlotte's done it again.''

The man from Celebrations laid each bag over a chair and got Michael's signature on his form, then left. Dangling from one was a name tag reading Michael and from the other, Jo. "Looks like she's dragging you into this one.''

Jo stood. "I love surprises." Slowly she unzippered the bag with her name on it and pulled out the hanger. A halter-style dress, long and white, with yards of chiffon in the skirt. "Will you look at this?''

Michael was beginning to figure it out. He unzipped his own bag and found a tuxedo with a white dinner jacket. He should have explained to Charlotte that he and Jo were just friends—before she got the matchmaking gleam in her eye. Maybe it wasn't too late to put a halt to all this. Then, he looked into Jo's eyes and saw they were dancing with excitement.

"Let's open the next envelope and see what she has in mind." Jo was beginning to appreciate Charlotte more every minute.

Michael took his time rezipping the bag, needing a moment. He was handling this well, he knew, but birthday celebrations—the few he'd had—unnerved him. He remembered one when he'd turned eight. The housekeeper had arranged it since both his parents had been away. She'd invited several boys and girls from his class at school and, of course, Deborah. Seated around the long formal dining room table, the kids had hurriedly eaten and found reasons to leave. They hadn't even waited for him to open the presents they'd brought, obviously picked out by their parents.

Michael couldn't blame them. He'd been such a loner that he didn't know any of them well. They'd been forced to attend his party by parents who hadn't wanted to offend his father. He'd pretended their indifference hadn't hurt. But it had. He hadn't made a real friend until he'd met Eric Stromberg in high school.

"I've never been one to fuss over birthdays." He opened the envelope as Jo leaned in to read the note with him. Charlotte's handwriting was large and bold.

And so we begin. First, a champagne dinner for two. Be dressed and ready at 7 p.m. You will be taken to a secluded location. Tonight, dear boy, is for romance—the greatest gift I could give you.

"I like your aunt," Jo said with a dreamy sigh. A

mysterious evening. Just what they'd been needing. She, too, would have to think of something special to give him.

But Michael was hesitant, looking for a way out. "I'm not sure you should go out just yet. Your leg…"

"Is fine. And I'm going." Gathering up her gorgeous dress, she headed for her room. "I certainly hope you can join me."

Michael selected another chocolate and chewed resignedly. He hadn't planned on even mentioning his birthday, and now the decision had been taken out of his hands. In spades.

Despite his desire to pull back from this relationship, he was being suckered in. Jo was probably already trying on the dress. He couldn't be a heel and disappoint her. What was one evening anyhow?

He would watch himself, Michael decided. He would keep his distance and not allow himself to be snared by Charlotte's scheme. He would resist romance and the places it led, as he had in the past. Charlotte and Jo were a formidable pair. But he could outwit them.

That decided, he set the candy aside and went back to work.

Chapter Seven

Romance. An elusive thing, Michael thought as he showered. Women longed for romance, or so he'd read often enough. But men viewed such things differently.

Differently and nervously. He had no idea what this mysterious evening that Charlotte had obviously painstakingly planned for them was all about. But it worried him. While he admitted to himself that he'd come to care about Jo, romancing her had not been in his thoughts. Women equated romance with love, and he didn't even want to think along those lines.

Shampooing his hair, he acknowledged that a part of him was looking forward to the evening, knowing that Charlotte's surprises were usually terrific. And he might even have fun, if only Jo wasn't expecting more than he was willing to give.

It would probably be good for him to get out, Michael decided as he rinsed off. About six months ago, he'd been having intermittent stomach pains and had finally gone to see his doctor. Tests had been taken and the doctor had informed him that he had all the signs of an ulcer beginning. Michael's father had had an ulcer for years. Right then, Michael had decided that he was turning into a chip off the old block, and the image hadn't pleased him.

So he'd altered his ways. He'd quit smoking. Well, almost. He'd limited his intake of junk food and he'd tried to eliminate major stress from his life. The work load at the office was heavy and hectic, so he'd decided to take his latest project and complete it in the quiet atmosphere of Aunt Charlotte's isolated house in Maui.

But he hadn't planned to do something out of character just for the hell of it. And then he'd met Jo.

Michael smiled, remembering that first afternoon when she'd trouped in with her entourage of animals. Oddly, he who'd never been allowed to have a pet as a kid—a fact Jo couldn't get over—had grown fond of Heinz with his frantic energy and his need to please. He was also surprised that when Floppy curled up next to him occasionally and began purring, he felt a reluctant contentment that he would have once laughed at. Perhaps it was the trust that animals gave so completely that had gotten to him.

Michael shut off the water and reached for a towel. But it was the woman herself who'd managed to change him somewhat without his realizing it. She'd slowed him down and warmed him up. She'd made him stop to smell the flowers, so to speak, figuratively and literally. She'd aroused protective instincts inside him that he hadn't even suspected he had. She'd dared him to do things, and his male pride had forced him to accept the challenge. He hadn't guessed he'd wind up relishing things he'd once labeled nonsensical.

Of course, most of this was temporary, Michael reminded himself as he wrapped the towel around his waist. He'd return to San Francisco and gradually resume his old ways. But he'd return a better man for having had the diversion of new activities. He remembered when he'd studied languages in college he'd learned that the word *vacation* was derived from the Latin word for change. Yes, he was having a change—of scenery, of plans—which would refresh and renew him.

Stepping into his room, he decided he would enjoy his birthday tonight, perhaps for the first time ever, as Charlotte wanted him to. And he would enjoy Jo. Carefully, because he didn't want her to get the impression that his intentions had changed. He'd begun to think of her as a fairly sensible woman after all, stemming mostly from the way she'd handled that accident and her recovery with bravery and a minimum of fuss. She would undoubtedly come to the same conclusion, that their stay on Maui was a moment out of time when they could have fun together, then go back to their separate lives.

Pleased with his conclusions, he began to dress.

Jo STOOD in front of the cheval mirror by her bedroom window. How Charlotte had done it, she didn't know, but the dress seemed made for her.

Picking up her evening bag, she smiled dreamily. She was going out with a man she was crazy about, and they were going to have fun. She felt only an occasional twinge of pain in her left leg, and she was determined to ignore that. Life somehow seemed more precious to her these days. The accident, which could have turned out so much worse, had pointed out something that she'd always known but had some-

how forgotten. That each day was to be savored and
enjoyed for no one knew if it might be their last.

Humming, Jo left the room.

Walking from the kitchen, Michael stopped to stare.
She was stunning. The dress clung to her upper body,
then drifted down to yards of white chiffon swirling
around her slim ankles. It fastened behind her neck,
leaving a delicious expanse of bare back. She wore
strappy white shoes, showing off toenails painted
bright pink. Wide gold hoop earrings caught the rays
of evening sun as she moved her head, causing her hair
to shift sexily. He swallowed around a dry throat.
"You're beautiful," he whispered.

Jo closed the distance between them. "Thank you."
He was a man born to wear formal attire, she thought.
The contrast of his new tan against the white dinner
jacket was striking. Running her hands slowly along
the lapels, she smiled up at him. "Nice threads."

"I'm having trouble with this cuff link." He held up
his right arm. "Can't seem to get it with my left
hand."

She took the cuff link from him and bent to fix it,
her hair falling forward.

Honeysuckle. Years from now, he would associate
the scent of honeysuckle with Jo. When she finished,
she looked up at him. Distance, Michael reminded
himself. Then he saw her eyes darken and shatter his
resolve. "I hate to ruin your makeup, but I have to kiss
you."

She raised her hands to his shoulders. "I'd rather
have a kiss than a perfect face."

It should be familiar by now, Michael thought as his
mouth touched hers. Old hat, ordinary, casual. But
kissing her was somehow new each time. As he drew

her closer and deepened the kiss, he wondered how long that would keep happening. Surely tomorrow, holding her would lose its powerful grip on him. Certainly soon, touching her would no longer quicken his heartbeat. Undeniably the day would come when wanting her would diminish.

But not yet, he thought. No, definitely not yet.

Layers of sensation piled up as Jo leaned into the kiss. Her mouth answered his suddenly demanding lips as her hands slipped up into his hair. During her more lucid moments, lying around recovering the past few days, she'd tried to convince herself she didn't want this, didn't need this. This race into madness, this dive into delirium. She could live without it, she'd told herself, desperately afraid she would have to.

Like she could live without air. She needed him. The thought both terrified and delighted her. Hadn't she waited a lifetime to need like this, to feel like this, to love like this? Hadn't she daydreamed and night-dreamed of a man who could awaken her woman's heart and make it his? The fear came when she let herself realize what Michael had made perfectly clear from the beginning. He wasn't a forever man.

Jo stepped back, trembling. This was to be a celebration, a birthday dinner, a happy occasion. She wouldn't let herself think disturbing thoughts tonight. She tried a smile. "I've mussed your hair," she said in a voice still thick with passion.

Michael wasn't ready to let her go, not nearly ready. "Muss it some more." He pulled her back, his lips trailing down her throat then returning to plunder her mouth. The kiss was deep and intimate, leaving both of them shaken when at last he drew back.

Breathing hard, Jo shook back her hair, feeling unsteady on her feet in a way that had nothing to do with the cut on her leg.

"You make me crazy, you know that?"

She was calmer now and enormously pleased at his reaction. "Good. I'm glad." He needed to be a little crazier.

Michael heard footsteps on the porch. Turning, he looked through the screen and saw a short man with skin tanned to nut-brown, wearing a waiter's jacket and a beaming smile.

"Good evening. My name is Cado from Celebrations. Ms. Kramer has put me in charge of your birthday evening."

Michael opened the door. "Good evening, Cado. We're at your disposal."

"Very good, sir. My first instruction is to ask you to open envelope number three and to bring the others along."

Michael ripped open the envelope and held the note so Jo could read it with him. "Go with Cado and *enjoy!*" He sent Jo a skeptical look. "I hope you're up to this. When Charlotte's at the helm, you never know what's in store."

"I'm game for anything."

Slipping the other envelopes in his pocket, Michael led the way out to the porch.

"Oh, just a minute," Jo said. "I want to put Heinz in my room. He chewed one of your socks yesterday."

Michael raised a brow, but didn't comment. He could see no limousine as he'd been expecting, since that definitely was Charlotte's style. Only the Celebrations van stood in the drive behind his own rental car. His curiosity high, he turned to Cado who was smiling with patient politeness. "Have you done business with Ms. Kramer before, Cado?"

"No, sir. She telephoned from Mr. Wakefield's yacht. We've done many celebrations for him."

So that was how the sly fox had come up with the idea. "Where to?" he asked Cado when Jo rejoined them.

"Follow me, please." Cado started across the grass in the direction of the beach.

Eyebrows raised, Jo grinned. "A picnic in the sand, do you think?" she whispered to Michael. "Formal, of course."

"It doesn't seem like something Charlotte would dream up, but you can never tell."

When they reached the sandy area, Cado kept on walking, turning left down the beach as they followed.

The sun was inching lower, causing the sky to look like God's palette streaked with reds and golds, a delicate mauve and a deeper purple. Mesmerized, they trod along the sand, captivated by the view, scarcely aware they'd reached their destination until Cado spoke.

"Your champagne dinner, sir," he said, bowing as he swept one hand to the left.

Michael's mouth nearly dropped open as Jo, beside him, gave a delighted squeal. Set on the sand, poised between two swaying palm trees, was a wooden platform holding a table with two chairs. A pale blue cloth hung almost to the ground. The white china plates were trimmed in dark blue, the smoky champagne glasses were tulip-shaped and a hurricane lamp sat in the center. Cado stepped forward to light it. Only Charlotte, he thought.

Jo was struggling with incredulity. "I don't believe it."

"This is as close as Charlotte gets to picnicking," Michael said with a chuckle as he held out her chair.

Cado brought over the ice bucket containing the chilled champagne, popped the cork and poured, leaving the bucket next to Michael. "Happy birthday, sir." With another small bow, he retreated behind the palm trees.

"Yes, happy birthday," Jo echoed. His eyes were smiling as if he were genuinely happy, something she felt didn't happen often. Michael Daye was a success in many ways, yet he'd had too little spoiling, and far too little fun in his life. With the help of his caring aunt, she meant to see that tonight he would have generous portions of both.

Michael tapped his glass to hers and sipped. Her mouth, damp from the wine, was so inviting. He wanted to kiss her again, but instead searched his mind for something to say. Something appropriate. "If someone had told me when I arrived in Maui that I'd be sitting here like this tonight, I'd have probably laughed."

Remembering how disconcerted they'd both been that first afternoon, Jo smiled. "Me, too, probably."

"And yet I find that this is exactly where I want to be, here with you." He laced his fingers with hers, realizing he meant every word.

Jo felt her eyes fill, and blinked back the moisture. "That's the second time you've said something truly lovely. Be careful, I might begin to think you've set aside your cynicism."

"I have, at least for tonight."

"It's a start." A pale gold light fell softly onto the platform area just then, and she turned to look behind where Cado had set up his work table. Malibu lights had winked on, one under each palm tree, followed by music, soft and low, with Hawaiian strings. She recognized "Tiny Bubbles" and smiled at Michael. "It would seem that Charlotte's thought of everything."

"She's terrific at arranging parties. I used to love to go to them when I was a teenager, especially since the dinner gatherings my folks put together were so boring. Charlotte used to have a theme for each festivity. Like Aloha Night, or a Caribbean dinner or a Fourth of July supper with everyone wearing red, white and blue."

Jo let the champagne tease her tongue, then slide down her throat. "I'll bet she really went all out at Halloween."

"Did she ever. She even got me in costume, which wasn't easy, because I thought it was most undignified to dress up in silly clothes in my teens."

Jo would wager he still thought so, but didn't comment. She wanted to draw him out while he was in a talkative mood. The key to understanding Michael, she'd decided, was probably intertwined with understanding his background. "Did she bring you here to this beach house often?"

He shook his head. "The first time I came here was with my father."

Cado appeared then and served their Caesar salads, placing a basket of hot rolls on the table as well.

"I can tell that the menu's one of my favorites, but I'm not sure you're going to be pleased."

Jo pictured a half-raw steak and hoped it wasn't so. "I'll manage." She tasted the salad and decided it was excellent, but she wanted to get back to their conversation. "You said you came here with your father. Just the two of you?"

"No. He'd brought me along with one of his banker friends and that man's son. Dad had arranged to have us all go deep-sea fishing, mountain climbing, golfing. Two fathers teaching two sons all the manly things men do together."

She caught the bitter note. "How old were you?"

"Sixteen."

"And did you learn them all?"

Michael sighed. "I suppose I did, though perhaps not well enough, since Dad never asked me to go away with him again. I think it was too little too late, and we both realized it. A man can't get to know his son over a long weekend."

Jo reached for his hand, feeling a flush of anger for the man who'd fathered a son then left him to flounder. "His loss, Mike."

He glanced up and saw not pity but honesty in her eyes. "Thanks. I guess it was your turn to say something nice."

She wanted to say a great deal more, but instead went back to eating her salad.

Why had he told her about that trip? Michael wondered as he sipped his champagne. He watched the way the gentle lamplight flickered over her lovely features. Because she was easy to talk to, a good listener. And because she seemed to care, genuinely. On the one hand, he was drawn to that the way a wilting flower is drawn to water. On the other hand, it scared the hell out of him. He sat back as Cado stepped up to clear their plates.

The dinner was going to be scrumptious. Beef Wellington just as he liked it, the crust crispy, the meat fork-tender, with a pepper sauce that teased the taste buds. Baby asparagus and tiny new potatoes. More champagne. Cado served, then quietly withdrew behind the palms to pack up his hot pads and warming plates. Michael was going to enjoy every mouthful.

But he was going to enjoy looking at Jo even more.

She was breathtaking with the scarlet sun setting behind her, sinking into an azure sea. She was slender and graceful, every man's dream, and her eyes were on him. Only him. He wanted to reach out and touch the satiny skin of her bare back, to run his fingers through the silken strands of her hair. He wanted to be alone with her, completely alone in some quiet place meant for lovers. He wanted badly to tell her so, but he hesitated.

Looking into his eyes, Jo felt emotion tighten her throat. She was good at reading expressions, and she doubted if she was mistaken this time. He wanted her, but he was afraid. Afraid that she would want more than he was willing to give.

Perhaps she did. And perhaps he was the wrong man, after all. Oh, she cared, more each day. But would she be happy with a man who had to be persuaded, coaxed, cajoled into a serious relationship?

She had accused him of overthinking things. Maybe she should take her own advice and just go with the flow. Turning to him, Jo smiled. "Do you think he'll ever finish puttering back there and leave us alone?"

"My thoughts exactly." He shoved aside his plate and cleared his throat noisily. Perhaps he could hurry Cado along.

The waiter appeared immediately and offered coffee. They both refused. He hurried to clear the table.

Jo strolled out toward the rolling waves and minutes later turned back to see that Cado had removed everything from the platform.

"Tomorrow, my staff will come pick up everything. I will leave the lights and radio for you. When you're ready, please read the next envelope, which will explain dessert." He gave a short bow. "It's been a pleasure serving you both."

Michael slipped him a folded bill and waited until he left. Stepping onto the platform, he held out his hand. "Dessert can wait. I believe this is our dance."

She moved into his arms, wanting his touch. Of course, he would know how to dance, she thought. He would likely have been given lessons, probably under duress. They'd paid off though, as he carefully stepped her around the small floor.

The soft lighting played on them as they swayed to the strains of a melancholy tune. The scent of flowers was heavy in the sultry air. Jo felt a shiver take her as Michael pressed a light kiss to her bare shoulder.

"The first time I saw you, I thought you were a crazy lady," he told her, shifting so he could see her eyes.

"The first time I saw you, I thought you were an uptight snob," she confessed as well. "I've changed my mind."

She waited until he whirled her out of the turn. "And what is it you think now?"

"What would you say if I said I think you're the loveliest woman I've ever known?"

Her mouth twitched into a smile. "I'd say you're reaching, but I'll accept the compliment graciously."

"There's more." He rubbed his lips over hers lingeringly. In this he could speak from the heart. "I want you more than I've ever wanted anyone." He trailed his fingertips over her cheek, cupping her chin, then skimming down the long line of her throat. "I can't look at you without wanting to kiss you. I can't touch your hand without wanting to touch more."

"Oh, Mike." She went on tiptoe, seeking his mouth. The kiss went on and on, yet was too short. When she eased back, she saw that he was trembling. Her own hands were none too steady. "I suppose we owe it to Charlotte to open the next envelope."

Reluctantly Michael stepped back and took it from her. "She says dessert is waiting thirty yards past the second palm tree." Though he'd all but lost interest, he walked over to the darkening area.

A fire had been laid, and beside it sat a package of marshmallows and two long sticks. Michael found a smile. "Good old Charlotte." He crouched down to light the fire. "I told her once when I was a kid that I'd wanted to roast marshmallows and I'd tried to in our fireplace. But our housekeeper had stopped me. So Charlotte bundled me into her car, drove me to the beach and we roasted marshmallows, just the two of us. I remember she was wearing this colorful caftan with big billowy sleeves, and I was worried she'd set herself on fire. I think that's the closest she's ever been to a picnic."

Coming alongside, Jo slipped off her shoes and settled on the sand, arranging her skirt around her.

She took the stick Michael offered and stuck a fat marshmallow on the end. "We used to do this a lot when I was younger. I couldn't eat very many—too sweet—but my brothers would go through a couple of packages."

Michael's cooked the fastest. "The way to do this is you feed each other." Needing to make up for his odd mood, he moved beside her and held up the browned confection.

She stuck her tongue out, testing. She bit in cautiously, then took the rest into her mouth.

"Didn't your mother ever teach you to share?" He rolled her over onto the dry sand and touched his mouth to hers. She laughed from deep in her throat as he ran his tongue over her lips, removing the last of the sticky stuff. But his mouth didn't leave hers, and suddenly they forgot the humor of the situation as the kiss took over.

It was long minutes later when Michael finally pulled back and helped Jo sit up. Never in his life had he grappled on the ground with a woman, most especially not in the sand wearing evening clothes. "You're still doing it, making me crazy."

She laughed, delighted. "I'm *so* glad." She found her stick and tossed the ruined marshmallow aside, then got another.

They ate several, more to please the absent Charlotte than out of hunger. Finally Michael doused the fire and reached for envelope number five. "My next surprise is behind the first palm tree," he told her as they walked over.

"How many more envelopes do you have after that?"

"Only one." He bent to pick up the long, thin package. "I'll bet I know what this is." Pulling off the tissue, he nodded. "A kite, complete with tail." At the platform, he removed his jacket and sat to assemble the kite.

Jo finger-combed her hair as the evening breeze blew it about. "Is that something you've always wanted, a kite?"

"I used to collect them when I was a kid. My mother brought all kinds of unusual ones home from her travels. Kites are real big in the Orient, you know."

She sat beside him as he carefully inserted the sticks, looking as happy as a little boy. Tonight he was having his childhood back, courtesy of Charlotte, and enjoying it more this time around, Jo decided. A lock of hair had fallen onto his forehead. She started to reach to brush it back, then thought better of it. She would curb her urge to touch and let him play. She would leave the next move to him.

Finished, Michael slipped off his shoes and socks, then started down the beach, letting the string out gradually. Then he was running and the kite caught the breeze. Soon it was sailing high and he was laughing as he raced with it.

Unbelievable, she thought, watching him. It was as if Michael Daye were several people. The cautious, bookish architect often obsessed about his work. The boy inside the man who'd missed out on a childhood. The lover inside the man who touched her with a reverence she'd seldom known.

And she was charmed by all three.

Tiring finally of his solitary play, Michael returned, reeling in his kite. Out of breath, he dropped down beside her. "You must think me silly," he said as he anchored his kite.

She reached to touch his face. "I think you're wonderful." She brushed back his hair then. "And a little warm."

He took her hand, placing a gentle kiss in her palm. "Time to cool off a little, don't you think?"

She raised a questioning brow.

Rising, he untied his tie and whipped it off, then hooked his thumbs into his suspenders and eased them down. "Last one in is a wet hen."

"Swimming? What about..." Caring as much as she did, wanting him, was she suddenly shy?

"Suits?" he asked, shoving off his pants and tossing them aside. "We don't need suits."

Tentatively her hand went to the ties of her dress at her nape. This wasn't exactly as she'd pictured the scene unfolding.

"I don't suppose you're aware of it," Michael went on, unbuttoning his shirt, "but I undressed you after your accident."

The blush came, though she'd always considered herself a liberated woman. "That was different. I was out cold."

"But I wasn't." Grinning, he leaned down to kiss her lightly. In moments, he was down to just his briefs. "I'll take pity on you and go in ahead so you can undress." With that, he turned and ran into the sea.

Sighing, Jo stood. She'd been after him to loosen up, so it would be contradictory to stop him now. It was just that she had so little on under the dress, and it was such a gradual slope out to deeper water.

He was already out quite a ways, she could see in the moonlight. Quickly she stepped out of the dress and carefully lay it on top of his clothes. Wearing only a swatch of pale silk low on her hips, she ran to join him.

Michael had reason to be glad that he had excellent distance vision. Standing in shoulder-high water, he watched her walk toward him in the shifting sand. Her long hair brushed the top of her breasts, and her skin shimmered in the silvery light. He felt his breath catch at the sight. Then, she dived under.

He rolled with a high wave just as she came up beside him. He wondered how much longer he could keep from touching her. "Want to race?" he challenged.

So he wanted to play games still. "Certainly. Where to?"

"First we swim out a ways, then race back to where we can stand."

Jo dipped her head back, rearranging her wet hair. "And the prize?"

He gave a low chuckle. "We'll think of something. Ready?"

She was, and they swam out lazily, then stopped, treading water. Fingertips touching, they floated a moment, catching their breath. Playfully he reached out and ducked her under.

Sputtering, she rose and tangled with him, laughing as she shoved him under. A large wave roared past, and they bounced with it. Kicking hard, she swiveled, heading for shore.

Reaching sandy bottom, she lowered her feet as he came alongside. "I won," she said, tossing her hair back.

But Michael's mood had shifted again. He drew her back to where he stood. Shorter than him, she was on tiptoe here. "You're like a mermaid with the moonlight in your hair."

The water was cool, yet she felt warm. "But I'm not. I'm very much flesh and blood." With a quick tug of her hand, he had her close up against him. When her breasts touched the solid width of his chest and settled there, Jo released a soft sigh. She closed her eyes as his hands moved over her back.

"You certainly are." His voice was husky, his breathing unsteady. He kissed her then, deeply, slowly.

Jo was far from passive when it came to this man. She wound her legs around his waist, and her arms around his neck, letting him take her weight and giving herself over to the kiss. It started immediately, the fire inside, as it always did when he held her.

His mouth still on hers, he walked toward shore. When the water was only waist-high, he stopped, setting her on her feet. Her breasts were sleek and wet, the peaks hard from the chill of the water. He closed his hands over them and heard a sound from deep in her throat.

His pulse racing, Michael met her eyes. "I can't wait. I want to make love with you. Right here. Right now."

Jo could hardly speak. "I want that, too."

Chapter Eight

He was carrying her out of the sea, much as he'd done last week. Only this time, she hadn't passed out from pain but rather was wide awake and aware.

At the water's edge, Michael set her on her feet. In the spotty moonlight, he met her gaze. The scent of the sea drifted from her, tangling his senses. Her eyes were luminous and a little wary as she studied him almost shyly. He dropped to the sand and tugged her down with him.

She was on top of him, damp flesh touching damp flesh. Jo felt a shiver of anticipation as his long fingers thrust into her wet hair, making her scalp tingle. "Kiss me, Mike. Kiss me the way you did that first time up on Mount Haleakala. Let me see the fireworks."

He reached to take her mouth. Tonight he would feel and not think, he told himself. He fought to keep the kiss gentle, to hold back and not rush. They had hours ahead of them, he knew, yet he struggled with the repressed passion that had been an almost constant companion since meeting her.

She recognized the passion in his kiss. And something more, something she'd been searching for. Ten-

derness. Most men were capable of passion, but
tenderness was foreign to many. Michael understood
it and, unlike his day-to-day encounters, was unafraid to show it when he kissed her. She wondered if
he knew how sweet that was.

How had he thought he could casually walk away
from this woman? Michael wondered. His heartbeat
thundered in his ears as she wound her long limbs
around him. She was strong, yet seemingly fragile, her
skin silvery in the moonlight.

He became fascinated with trailing his hands down
the smooth column of her throat, across the slope of
her shoulders and skimming along her slender arms.
No matter how often a man and a woman made love,
there was only one first time, and he wanted to make
it perfect for her, to have her feel cherished. With
trembling fingertips, he traced the translucent skin of
her breasts. When he put his mouth to her, he heard
her answering gasp.

Needing to touch as well as be touched, she lifted
her suddenly heavy arms, her hands moving to inves-
tigate him as she'd been longing to do. The nape of his
neck was sweet and vulnerable. The hair on his chest
was soft, yet crisp. The muscles rippling along his back
as he moved were firm and exciting. Growing impatient, her fingers raced over him, then settled at the
waistband of his wet briefs.

Too soon, he thought and shifted their positions,
pinning her beneath him on the cool sand. He heard
the roar of the ocean, or was that his hot blood rushing through his veins? A wave washed onto their intertwined legs, the sensual feel of the sea adding to his
excitement. "Can you feel how much I want you?" he
asked huskily.

"Yes, as much as I want you." No man had ever touched her with such infinite care, such gentle adoration. Then he eased sideways and pulled off her panties, tossing them away. Jo lay in a hazé of feeling as his seeking fingers touched her more boldly, more intimately. In moments he had her arching, her head thrashing restlessly as the mists closed in. She felt drugged, floating, yet wonderfully alive. Closing her eyes, she shuddered as he continued his journey over her sensitized skin.

The sand was cool beneath her hands; his mouth as it shimmered along her inner thigh was warm. A light breeze had her shivering, or was it Michael's touch, his lips, his loving? Senses heightened, Jo moaned softly as his mouth found her.

The ocean, the moonlit sky and all night sounds disappeared for Jo. Her hands clenched on his shoulders and she jolted as hot waves of pleasure slammed into her. Careening out of control, she cried out his name.

Michael paused to catch his breath, watching her lovely face flush. For the first time in recent memory, he had no desire to think, to plan the next move, to race to the finish line. He wanted to savor and linger, to make it the very best for her. Stunned by the depth of his feelings, he held back his own needs as he moved up her and gazed into her eyes dark with passion.

This time he wanted more than quick release, the frantic completion his body craved. This time he wanted intimacy of mind and soul, not just a physical union. This time, with this woman, he honestly felt he could achieve that.

It took Jo long moments to recover. When she could speak again, she touched his face, wondering if he would be able to lose himself in her as she had in him. "You're so strong, Mike, always so in command of your emotions. Do you lose control when you make love? Do you really let go then?"

He accepted the challenge with a smile. "Why don't we find out?" Another wave crashed over them as his mouth crushed hers, while his busy hands drove her back up.

Then she was lost again, shifting beneath the onslaught of his mouth searing her everywhere. With the patience she knew him capable of, he tasted, tortured, devoured. They rolled together on the sand and the restless waves chased them. Nerves again screaming for release, Jo closed her eyes and let him take her where he would.

Her avid response had him near the breaking point. He tugged off his briefs and touched his hands to hers, stretching her arms up over her head. He felt her pulse thunder against his fingertips and gloried in the knowledge that it pounded there for him. Only for him.

He had no intention of letting her rest. He pressed his mouth to hers, quieting the soft sounds she made. He'd never known how much pleasure could be had in just watching her reaction to the passion he'd brought out in her. He'd never known how much joy he would feel in seeing her eyes darken as he filled her completely.

Trembling with the effort to make it last, Michael moved, setting the pace and watching her find the rhythm and follow. Her eyes were locked with his, and he saw her struggle to remain focused as they moved as one.

And then they were soaring, past the mountain they'd been standing on, the ethereal sunlight bathing them in its fiery glow. Para-sailing in an endless blue sky, locked together. And suddenly Michael saw the fireworks, just as she'd predicted, bursting into a million technicolor pieces.

Jo felt the shattering explosion, holding on to it as long as possible, feeling the waves take her. And when at last she was able to open her eyes, she saw she was safe in the arms of her lover.

LOVE. Mom hadn't misled her. If she'd seen fireworks when Michael kissed her, she'd seen a centennial celebration light up the sky when he'd made love with her. Jo took in a shaky breath, still staggering from the impact.

After the wonder of their first coupling on the beach, Michael had carried her to the house where they'd rinsed away the clinging sand, dried each other off, then fallen on his bed and made love a second time. More slowly, drawing out the pleasure. And it had been as glorious as the first time.

She wasn't naive enough to believe that lovemaking alone guaranteed that love was present. But for her, it was. Everything added up just right. Michael Daye fit perfectly—in her bed, in her plans, in her life.

What a pity she couldn't tell him.

Michael found his face cradled in the crook of her neck as his breathing slowed. She smelled of seawater and honeysuckle and their combined scent, a heady combination. He took a moment to think about how he felt, and decided it was a little as if he'd taken a lightning bolt to the solar plexus.

Lying there with her arms still wrapped around him, he knew he ought to say something. Something meaningful and momentous. His mind felt incapable of the ordinary right now, much less the remarkable. He was a man shaken to his very soul.

Because what had taken place between them—not once but twice—hadn't been in the least ordinary. He was a man who prided himself on knowing what he was, what he wanted—from life, from women. But something had happened that had blown the lid off his lifelong preconceptions.

He'd enjoyed sex before, but not with such heedless passion. He'd made a woman cry out before in pleasure, but never had her enjoyment thrilled him to such extent. He'd lost control before, something that happened when people made love. But not with such abandon, such a feeling of complete unity, such intensity of need.

It had probably been a fluke, something that wouldn't happen again even if he made love with Jo again and again. The very thought of another repeat caused an instant response in his body that stunned him.

He would have to think about that, long and hard, he decided. But not now. He lifted his head and met her eyes.

There was wariness there, he saw, an uncertainty. Even when she'd been recovering in his bed from her accident, she hadn't looked as vulnerable as tonight. He felt an unexpected wave of tenderness as he brushed back her hair. "That was very special. *You're* very special, Jo."

She smiled hesitantly. She didn't want to talk, afraid that words would spoil the wonderful afterglow she was feeling.

"I should move from you..."

Her hands at his back tightened. "Not yet, please." She touched his hair, easing his head onto her breast. "Just a little longer." He settled against her and she sighed.

It had begun to rain, a soft summer shower, the drops sliding off the palm tree outside the window and bouncing into the pool. The sound was soothing, calming.

She was all right now. She would go on playing the game, attraction without commitment, lovemaking without the loving. Until he was ready to accept her love, to listen to her words of love.

She ran her fingers slowly through his hair. "What are you thinking?" she asked.

"That I'm crushing you."

"Besides that. And you aren't."

He eased back, supporting his weight on his elbows, and frowned. "That I forgot about protection."

His practicality pleased her this time. "Not to worry. I may be impetuous at times, but I'm not careless about important things."

He let out a long, relieved breath. "Neither am I, usually. I don't know what happened."

She smiled. "You lost control, my friend. You *really* lost control."

"Yeah, well, I..."

"Hey! It doesn't require an apology." She wiggled around beneath him, snuggling into him. "It's one of the times you can give yourself permission to let go."

She trailed her fingers down his back, her nails lightly raking his skin, and felt him shiver. "And I won't tell if you won't."

"You're so different than anyone I've known, Jo."

He was looking at her as if trying to understand a difficult puzzle. "Am I?" She stretched her neck to kiss him. "How am I different?"

Her movements beneath him had his body tightening again with renewed desire. Amazing. He didn't know how to tell her, or even if he should. "Nice different," he answered vaguely.

She squirmed again and her eyes grew cloudy as she felt his response. "I'm not, you know. Maybe it's just that you're different when you're with me."

"Maybe." He didn't want to think about that, or anything else right now. "Want to see if we can lose control again?" He heard her murmured assent and pressed his lips to hers, effectively ending their conversation.

There would be time enough later to think, to contemplate the wisdom of his actions, Michael decided as he began to move.

HE AWOKE to a tantalizing smell. Still in the snares of a lovely dream, he was reluctant to open his eyes. The smell grew stronger. Chocolate. Yes, definitely chocolate. In his bed? Impossible. Michael lifted his heavy lids.

The first thing he saw was a cup of steaming hot chocolate almost under his nose. His eyes drifted to the woman holding the cup. She was seated on the edge of his bed wearing his formal white shirt haphazardly buttoned. A long length of thigh teased him as she crossed her legs and wiggled her painted toes.

Traveling back up, he saw tousled blond hair in careless disarray trailing down into the open V of his shirt. He swallowed hard.

"Is it morning?" he asked as she moved back enough to allow him to sit up.

Jo glanced toward the window. "Barely. It's six and raining."

Michael ran a hand across his face. "Then why are we up?"

"Because you like to drink hot chocolate on rainy days, remember?"

He had told her that once. Was she keeping track of his every word? Still, she was being sweet and he was being grumpy. "Thanks." He reached for the cup and sipped cautiously.

Heinz chose that moment to come racing in and almost made it onto the bed before Jo stopped him in mid-jump. "Hey, you're all wet, pal." She grabbed a discarded towel to rub him dry, then set him down. "He's not speaking to me, still mad because I locked him up all night." She remembered the envelope she'd taken from his pocket earlier and held it out. "Don't you want to know what Charlotte's last note says?"

Michael bunched the pillows behind his back and grunted.

"You surely aren't a morning person, are you?"

He sent her an exaggerated leer. "Depends on what you have in mind to do first thing in the morning."

She flopped onto his chest, crossing her arms and gazing into his eyes, nearly upsetting the remaining hot chocolate. "Insatiable, are you?"

He considered that. "I don't think so. At least, I haven't been, up to now."

She grinned happily. "Must be me, then."

He was feeding her ego inadvertently, Michael realized, which was fine. What he didn't want to feed was her hopes. When a person began to hope for something another person wasn't willing to give, things inevitably ended between them. He didn't want things to end between Jo and him. But he also didn't want to get her hopes up that, just because they'd made love, because he did care for her, she should start picking orange blossoms and hunting down houses with picket fences.

He gulped his drink. Their relationship had shifted unquestionably. Unalterably, even. But Jo had this fairy-tale vision of love, marriage and happiness coming as a prescribed package. She had witnessed one such marriage and decided that hers could be like that because she so badly wanted it to be. He, on the other hand, had seen several marriages up close, each in their own way knocking the pins out of her conclusions.

He doubted if his parents had ever loved to begin with, and though they had a marriage, happiness had eluded both. One out of three. Deborah and Kerry had fallen in love, moved into a marriage, and happiness still hadn't entered the picture. Two out of three. Then there was Charlotte, who'd had one successful marriage and three failures. Michael didn't like the odds.

As he set the cup on the nightstand, Jo lay her cheek on his chest and sighed contentedly. He found himself giving in to that always unexpected wave of tenderness she seemed to evoke in him so easily. Lazily he stroked her silken hair, marveling at how good it felt to have her here with him, to awaken and be able to look at her.

And looking at her was something he enjoyed almost as much as touching her. She'd come into his life, brash and confident and independent as hell. But immediately he'd noticed a softness to her that drew him inexplicably. A gentleness with her animals, a poignancy with her music, a sensitivity with him.

Other women he'd known had returned to being themselves very quickly after the loving, back to being separate and self-reliant. Jo retained an openness, an innocence, her huge eyes revealing her every emotion. He prayed he wouldn't hurt her even as he feared he would have to.

"So let's see what's in the envelope," he said because it would divert him from his thoughts. He read the note. Charlotte knew him perhaps better than he knew himself, he thought wryly.

"What does it say?" Jo asked impatiently.

"The night is for lovers. Enjoy!" he quoted.

She slithered back onto him. "And we did, didn't we?" Just as quickly, she got up again. "But it's time to get moving."

He frowned. "Moving where?"

Jo tossed a pair of white shorts at him. "First, a walk on the beach."

"It's raining and scarcely light out."

"That's when it's most fun." Slowly she began unbuttoning his shirt that she still wore.

Michael screwed up his nose, then lost his train of thought as his eyes fastened on the bare skin revealed between the folds of his shirt.

"Are you going to turn stodgy on me again?" she asked, hands on her hips.

Stodgy was far from what he felt. "Come here," he ordered.

Jo smiled. "I love it when you're masterful." She went to him. "Yes?"

He kissed her soundly. "Now, why should we go out there and get all wet when we have this warm and cozy bed right here?" He tossed the sheet aside and drew her up close.

"Mmm, point well made." Wrapping herself around him, she pressed her mouth to his. She was just really getting into the kiss when the phone rang.

Michael jerked back. "Who'd be calling at this hour?"

"No sane person," Jo grumbled. "Let it ring."

But he simply couldn't. Disentangling himself, he answered on the third ring.

"Michael, is that you?" said a voice laced with static.

He sat up straighter. "Deborah?"

"Yes. I tried calling last night, but there was no answer."

No, he'd been preoccupied on the beach last night. "Where are you?"

"We just landed on Honolulu, Shawn and I." She sounded weary and hesitant. "Our flight to Maui gets in in two hours. I know it's a terrible imposition, but could you come get us?"

"Is anything wrong? Where's Kerry?"

He heard a sound that resembled a sob. "I've left him."

"THIS DOESN'T SURPRISE ME a bit," Michael said as he maneuvered the car out of the airport parking lot. It had stopped raining by midmorning and already the sun had chased away all traces. "You never should have married him in the first place."

Beside him, her face pale and strained, Deborah nodded. "So you've said many times."

In the back seat with Shawn, Jo grimaced. None of her business, she knew, yet Michael's strong censure and Deborah's defeated tone bothered her. And it bothered her that the five-year-old might understand their words. "Shawn, look over there," she said in an effort to distract him. They were on the coastal road on the way back to Charlotte's house. "See that red-and-white striped parachute up in the sky in the distance? Your uncle and I went para-sailing in one of those last week."

"Honest?" Shawn asked, his voice sounding amazed. "Can I go while we're here, Uncle Michael?"

"We'll see, Shawn," Michael answered.

"You went para-sailing?" Deborah asked Michael incredulously.

"Yes," he admitted somewhat proudly. "Terrific experience."

Deborah glanced at her brother, the first chance she'd had after their hectic arrival to really look him over. She was tired from the harrowing day she'd spent yesterday after her impulsive decision to leave and from the long flight. Michael looked good, tanned and fit, relaxed despite his present annoyance with her sudden announcement. And he looked somehow different. His hair, usually combed to perfection, was actually windblown. And he was wearing shorts and a knit shirt, an outfit she'd not seen on him since he was a boy.

"Michael, you look so...so casual," she told him.

"Are you going to tell me you didn't recognize me without a tie, like Charlotte did?"

"Well, she's right. You're seldom without one."

Jo wanted to jump in and say he hadn't had one on, except for the one he'd worn last night with his tux, since arriving in Maui, but decided to keep still. He was touchy about his family and she thought it best to let him set the pace.

"Did you tell Kerry you were coming here?" Michael asked.

"I left him a note. I know it was cowardly of me, but I just couldn't face another scene." Deborah shook back her short dark hair. "He's leaving tomorrow on his Canadian tour anyway. Eight shows a week. He'll be too busy to miss us." She heard the self-pity in her voice and hated it.

Michael reached out and squeezed her hands tightly curled in her lap. "Don't worry. You and Shawn can relax here awhile, then when we go back, I'll help you find a place. Unless you want to move back with Mother and Dad."

"Oh, no. I... I'd rather not." They would never understand, Deborah thought. Nor did Kerry. She fought back the panic and the hurt, remembering their last quarrel. It's time to grow up, Deborah, Kerry had said. Time to be a real wife. Turning from the memory, she glanced back at the woman who was quietly pointing out things of interest to Shawn.

"I'm sorry to intrude on your stay, Jo," she said by way of apology. "I didn't realize anyone else was at the house." Michael's hasty explanation of the mix-up over Charlotte's cottage had scarcely registered. Yet now she found herself curious about Jo Knight.

"It's no intrusion, really." Jo turned back to Shawn who was studying her with eyes such a dark brown they were almost black. With his blond curly hair, he was truly a picture-poster child. "Do you like animals, Shawn?"

"Yeah. We can't have any 'cause we're always moving."

"I know what that's like. When I was your age, I used to move around a lot, too."

"Is your daddy an ice skater, too?"

"No, he sold insurance. I couldn't have pets then, but I've got all kinds now. I brought along my dog and one of my cats."

The boy's eyes widened. "Right here, you mean? At the house we're going to?"

She nodded, smiling at his delight. "You bet. The cat's name is Floppy and the dog is Heinz."

"Wow! Did you hear that, Mom?"

Deborah all but turned around in her seat. "You brought two animals with you across the ocean?"

"Oh, sure. They love to travel."

"I see." Deborah cast a hesitant glance at her brother. As she recalled, Michael didn't much care for animals. How had he managed to put up with this stranger and her pets for over a week? Only years of politeness, instilled by several stern housekeepers, kept her from commenting further.

Jo hid a smile. Deborah Daye English was a pretty woman, about her own age, and as uptight as Michael. Correction. As Michael *had been,* she thought, remembering last evening. And the wonderful night that followed.

Michael had hung up after Deborah's call, looking not terribly surprised by her announcement of the end of her marriage. He was, however, surprised she had hopped on a plane to visit him without ever reaching him first by phone. She was not in the least impulsive, he'd explained to Jo. Jo had no trouble believing that.

She'd suggested that he go alone to the airport to pick up his sister and nephew. But he had asked her to come along, looking as if he would appreciate a feminine shoulder in case his sister had turned weepy. Jo had agreed and gone in to shower.

She'd scarcely turned on the water when he'd joined her. The shower had lasted until the water had almost cooled. She'd warned him they'd be late, but still he'd lingered for another kiss. And another, until finally they'd had to hurry into their clothes and dash out the door.

No, Michael wasn't nearly as tense as he'd been a mere ten days ago, Jo thought with a smile. She hoped his sister wouldn't be shocked at the changes.

"Here we are, Shawn," Michael said as he turned into the drive leading to the oceanside house. "Have you kept up your swimming lessons? We have a big pool in the backyard."

"Sort of," Shawn answered, anxiously peering out the window.

"I used to teach swimming," Jo said. "Maybe we can pick up where you left off."

"Okay. Where's your dog?"

"In the house," Jo answered, opening the door as Michael turned off the engine. "Come on and I'll introduce you." Thinking Michael and Deborah might want a private moment, she led Shawn inside.

"She seems very nice," Deborah said somewhat carefully as Michael took their luggage out of the trunk. She hadn't seen the two of them so much as touch, yet there seemed to be something between her brother and Jo Knight. Or was her fatigue causing her to see things that weren't there?

"She is nice." Michael grabbed the two bags.

"What does she do? I mean, most of Noel's friends are sort of drifters."

"Not Jo. She's involved with the government literacy program. She writes music, songs she plays on her guitar and acts out to get kids interested in reading. At schools, libraries, parties." He recognized a note of pride in his voice and realized that getting to know Jo had made him rearrange his first impression. He hadn't seen her in action, but he felt strongly that Jo would attack her work with the same intensity she brought to everything she did.

"Children's songs. I see."

Michael frowned as he closed the trunk, annoyed that Deborah seemed to trivialize Jo's talent without knowing much about her. As he had done. "It's important that children learn to read, Deborah. Do you know how many illiterate adults there are in the world today, people who find it difficult to make a living, people who have low self-esteem?"

Deborah arranged the strap of her leather bag on her shoulder. "I had no idea you'd turned into a crusader for literacy."

"It's not that. Jo's putting on a program next week at the local school. Maybe you should go and see for yourself. Maybe we all should. Shawn would probably enjoy it." He started for the house.

Defensive, Deborah thought and wondered why. "Undoubtedly."

"Are you hungry? Jo's a fantastic cook."

"My, my. A musician, a teacher *and* a fantastic cook. There doesn't seem to be much your new and unexpected roommate can't do." Catching up with him at the door, she put her hand on the knob and gave him a teasing sisterly smile. "I don't suppose the fact that she has gorgeous hair, lovely eyes and a smashing figure has anything to do with the way you feel, now does it, Michael?"

Michael went in, feeling the heat rising in his face. Were his feelings for Jo that evident that even his sister with her many personal problems could see through him? He saw that Jo and Shawn were sitting on the floor with both animals sniffing around the boy, and wondered if she'd overheard. "You two take my room," he called over his shoulder. "I'll bunk on the couch."

Deborah sagged wearily into the rocking chair. "We can sleep out here," she said. "I don't want to put you out."

"You're not." Michael returned and caught Jo's eye. She winked at him. Yes, she'd overheard. And seemed oddly pleased. She would be.

He cleared his throat and rubbed his hands together, considering his options. He rarely played host, and never unexpectedly. He still had work to complete and wondered when he'd find the time. He loved his sister and Shawn, but their timing couldn't have been worse. And, he acknowledged with disappointment, he'd just discovered the wonder of Jo and would have preferred to be alone with her during this last week together. Ah, well.

"So, what would you like to do?" he asked Deborah. "It's about noon. Want some lunch, or a nap, or a swim?"

"I'm too big to nap," Shawn protested.

"Usually," his mother answered, "but today might be an exception. Neither of us slept much last night."

She hadn't slept much, either, Jo thought as she rose to her feet. But she didn't regret a moment. "Why don't I put together a quick lunch while you unpack, Deborah? Then you can take it from there."

Deborah dragged herself up. "Sounds good."

Michael walked over and ruffled his nephew's hair. "And Shawn, you look after Floppy and Heinz while I help Jo in the kitchen, all right?"

The boy jumped to his feet. "Can we go outside?"

"Yes, but stay on the patio." With a sigh, Deborah walked into the room she'd been given.

"Most kids don't like salads," Jo said, bending to peer into the refrigerator. "How about cold chicken for us and grilled cheese for Shawn?"

"Fine," Michael answered distractedly. Alone again. Touching her shoulders, he brought her to him and bumped the door shut with his hip. As a desert walker is drawn to water, his mouth lowered eagerly to cover hers. His arms wound around her as he lost himself in the kiss. After a satisfying minute, he pulled back. "Thanks, I needed that."

"Me, too." She smiled up at him. "Cute kid. Nice sister."

"Yeah, but bad timing. I hope you understand. I couldn't turn them away." He nuzzled her neck, inhaling her special scent.

"Of course not. I feel bad for Deborah. She looks so deep-down sad. Maybe, after some time apart, they'll think things over and be able to work out their problems."

"Their problems won't change or go away. They are two very different people." He shifted her hair and nibbled her ear. How could he want her so much after he'd had her all night?

Jo shivered, trying to keep her mind on their conversation, because they weren't alone and because she had a point to make. "People *can* change, Mike. They do it all the time."

He let out a ragged breath. "In books, in movies. But in real life? Seldom." He didn't want to discuss Deborah's problems at the moment. "Are you really going to let me sleep all scrunched up out there alone on that couch tonight?"

He was evading. She would let him because this wasn't the right time for this debate. "Mmm, what else did you have in mind?" She moved her hands up his back and curled them around his shoulders.

"An invitation, perhaps, to join you in your room."

"Why, Mr. Daye," she whispered, as if shocked, "I'm stunned at such a bawdy suggestion."

"I don't believe you are in the least, Miss Knight."

"You found me out. It's a date." On tiptoe, she reached for his kiss.

The same quick tug of reaction, the same thrill of delight. Every time his mouth touched hers, Jo thought, the fireworks followed. Even more so now, now that she knew what a wondrous place he could take her to. Pressing closer, she let his lips and tongue seduce her.

Footsteps and a startled gasp. "Oh, I'm terribly sorry."

They jumped apart guiltily.

Standing in the doorway, Deborah looked embarrassed. "I came out to see if I could borrow the iron."

Michael drew back, not meeting her eyes. "It's in the linen closet of your bathroom," he told her.

"Thanks." Deborah left them alone.

He turned to look at Jo and saw that she was having trouble containing a laugh.

"I feel like a teenager caught necking in the back seat," she confessed.

"Me, too." Grinning, he pulled her back into his arms. "Since we have the name, we might as well have the game." And he bent his head to kiss her again most thoroughly.

Chapter Nine

"The shark was wonderful," Deborah told Jo as she finished wiping the kitchen table. "Where did you learn to cook like that?"

Exactly the same question Michael had asked her last week, Jo thought as she stacked dishes in the dishwasher. Had they both always had live-in cooks? "When you live alone, you learn to cook or you go hungry."

Deborah walked to the sink and gazed out at the evening sky. Michael had taken Shawn for a walk on the beach after dinner. She felt rested from her nap, yet unaccountably restless. "I've never lived alone. I went from my parents' home to college, then quit school to marry."

Jo had listened to them talking about Kerry English at dinner, Shawn chattering away about watching his daddy skate. Her heart went out to the little boy who would no longer be having daily contact with his father. She closed the dishwasher and turned to Deborah. "It's none of my business, I know, and I don't know either one of you. But I just have to tell you how sorry I am that you and your husband have split."

Deborah's soft gray eyes, so like Michael's, filled with tears and she blinked rapidly. "Me, too."

"Do you love him, Deborah?" Jo asked. She had no business being so personal with a veritable stranger, yet this sad-eyed woman seemed to want to talk.

"Yes, but that's not enough."

Jo didn't believe that, not for a minute. "Are you so sure?"

"We're too different, in too many ways. Not just our personalities, bad as that is." Deborah swiped at a lone tear that trailed down her cheek. "Kerry's so...so outgoing. He loves people around all the time. He *needs* people. And I'm more a homebody. I'm content to be with just him and Shawn most of the time."

Pretty much as Michael had said. "But surely, there are compromises you can both make."

Deborah sighed. "We've tried. Almost from day one, I've traveled with Kerry. It was fun at first. Then Shawn arrived, and it became more cumbersome. So many baby things to drag around, his clothes, toys. Sometimes we stay in one city only a week, then we're off again. The places we visited became a blur. Kerry was hardly ever with us, either rehearsing or performing. He tries to understand how I feel, but he loves that life and can't see why I don't."

Jo searched for an answer. "Couldn't you set up a home somewhere as a base, and Kerry could travel to his performances from there?"

"We tried that once, but I got sick and Kerry got worried and came back. He missed a whole season and almost lost his position with the show. We were nearly broke and he wouldn't let me accept a dime from my folks." She shook her head. "So I went back to traveling with him. But now it's time for Shawn to start school in the fall. I can't deprive my son. I want him to have a secure home and a good education. A child growing up on the road misses out on both."

Jo shrugged as she hung up the dish towel. "Oh, I don't know. I traveled with my folks until I was about ten. My brothers started coming along then and my father had a good foothold in the insurance business and a solid book of clients. He bought a house in California and finally we planted roots. Maybe you could look at Kerry's need to travel as temporary. I mean, how long do professional skaters keep performing?"

Deborah slid her hands into the pockets of her linen slacks. "As long as people will pay to watch them and they can still skate, I suppose."

"If he did it for another five or ten years, perhaps you'd have enough to settle down. Maybe then he could teach skating locally. You know, Kerry might even tire of the circuit himself."

"He thrives on it."

"Now. People change."

Deborah looked doubtful. "All those years on the road, you had to be dragged from school to school. You probably had trouble making friends since you never stayed in one place long enough. Michael and I had a home, a proper school from start to finish. That's important."

And where did all that proper upbringing get either of them? Jo was tempted to ask. Uptight, filled with tension, unhappy. Great beginning. Instead she said, "I think I learned to relate to people quickly and to make friends easily because of all that early moving around. But the other thing, the best thing that happened, was that it made the three of us very close."

Looking out the window, Deborah saw Michael walking back with Shawn, her son jumping about as he always did. "Shawn's very close to both of us now. But I have to think of his education. What kind of man will he turn out to be, growing up with only performers as role models?"

Jo was certain that Deborah didn't regard her as a performer and therefore hadn't intended her remarks as an insult. It was more a snobbish commentary than anything. Again, she found herself feeling sorry for Michael's sister, and not just about her separation. "There are worse ways to grow up, Deborah." She stood for a moment, studying the woman who stood gazing unhappily out the window. Then Jo turned and walked outside, feeling the sudden need for some fresh air.

Michael came up to her as she joined him and Shawn on the front lawn. "Did I time it right? Are the dishes done?" he joked as he slid his arm around her waist and drew her close for a quick hug.

"Yes, you owe me."

He moved his mouth close to her ear. "And I always pay my debts."

"I'll hold you to that." She turned away to watch Shawn leaping up and trying to capture a firefly. "You want to get a jar, poke some holes in the lid and catch fireflies?" she asked the little towhead.

"Yeah, can we?"

"Sure. I think I saw a jar in the shed out back. Come help me find it." She held out her hand.

"Play nice, children," Michael commented. "I'm going to go in and talk with Deborah."

Jo paused. "She's going through a difficult time." And she hoped he wouldn't make it worse by rushing her into a divorce. Time might well be all Deborah and Kerry needed, time to realize that being apart hurt more than living together and compromising.

"I know." Michael went in through the open patio doors and found his sister huddled in a corner of the couch, looking thoughtful. "Are you all right?" he asked, dropping into the chair opposite her.

Deborah shrugged. "As all right as I can be under the circumstances."

"You should have been prepared for this eventuality. You should have married someone like Kent." Kent Baxter was a neighbor who'd grown up with Deborah, gone to the same school and eventually to work in their father's bank. Shy and a little bookish, he was a solid young man whose career was on the rise.

Annoyed at the introduction of an old discussion, Deborah frowned at her brother. "Let's not bring up good old Kent. I didn't love him then nor could I ever."

Michael stretched out his long legs. "Love. More mistakes are made in the rosy glow of love than in anything else I can think of."

She heard Jo pass by the open doors with an excited Shawn trailing after her. "You're a fine one to talk. That kiss I witnessed between you and Jo looked like your relationship with her has progressed a step or two beyond casual. Are you in love with her?"

It was Michael's turn at annoyance. On his own for years now, he was unused to people questioning his relationships. "You should know by now, I don't fall in love. Love is for romantics." The words hung between them as Deborah's steady gaze stayed on his face while the memory of a recent very romantic night had him shifting uncomfortably.

"Is that a fact? Immune to love, are you, big brother?"

"Love is a word that florists and the writers of greeting cards invented to pep up their business, and it works. People fall for all that nonsense and make stupid decisions. Like marrying someone wrong for them. They don't stop to think that they don't like the same things or want the same out of life." Growing irritated, he got up to move around. "Growing up in our parents' home, you had a prime example right in front of you of marrying for the wrong reasons."

Interesting, Deborah thought, crossing her arms over her chest. She so seldom witnessed Michael, a man always in control of his emotions, pacing in agitation. "Are you saying you feel nothing for Jo Knight?"

Michael ran his fingers through his hair, wondering why he felt so defensive. "Of course, I feel something. I like her and I'm obviously attracted to her. She's charming and considerate and . ... fun."

Deborah's brows shot upward. "Fun?" Odd, but that was a word she'd never associated with her brother. Kerry was fun, but Michael thought fun was going over blueprints.

"Yes, fun. It's not a four-letter word." Echoing Jo's words bothered him, yet it was the only answer that came to mind.

"Oh, but love is, right?"

"Yes. *If* I ever decide to fall in love . . ."

"Decide to?" Despite the seriousness of the subject, she almost laughed. "Michael, people don't *decide* to fall in love. They just do."

Michael's strides increased in length. "That's where they make their mistake. People pick out cars with more care than marriage partners. They should select with their heads, not some foolish romantic notion. They should make a list of compatible traits, of requirements—some negotiable, some not—and of future goals. Then they should choose someone who fits at least ninety-five percent of their requisites. That way, the chances of coexisting harmoniously would be greatly increased while the failure rate would be minimal."

Pleased with that analysis, he marched back, his hands in his pants pockets. "As I started to say, *if* I ever decide to fall in love, that's how I'd go about it. The intelligent way."

She couldn't help herself. Deborah's mouth had dropped open halfway through his speech. "You're not serious. Michael, I know you intellectualize everything, but this is one thing that can't be approached rationally. Tell me, seriously, have you ever loved anyone?"

"Of course," he almost spit out. "I love our parents, you and Shawn, Charlotte—"

She waved a dismissing hand. "I don't mean family. A woman. I know you've had relationships. I remember someone named after a flower. Carnation or—"

"Hyacinth, and that was years ago. And no, I didn't love her. Lord, we were nothing alike."

"You're right. You were drawn to her possibly because opposites attract. And that's why you're attracted to Jo." She turned to glance out the open patio doors and saw Jo crouched in the grass with Shawn, studying something in a jar. "And probably why she's in love with you."

"She most certainly is not."

Deborah smiled tolerantly at her brother. "Look, I know you're very smart and highly successful. But this is one area where I'm definitely more experienced than you. I've been in love since the day I met Kerry. I know what it feels like and what a woman in love looks like. And Jo's got the look, whether you like it or not."

He badly needed a cigarette. But he refused to give in to his craving. "That's ridiculous. She's attracted, as I am. We're having an interlude here, enjoying each other, then moving on and returning to our lives, which are vastly different."

An interlude. She'd never met a woman who thought of love as an interlude. "Have you discussed this with Jo in just those words?"

"More or less. I told her right from the start my views on marriage and my ideas on compatibility."

"And she still fell for you?" Deborah shook her head in wonder. "She must be a masochist."

Michael stopped his pacing and paused at the doors. Barefoot, Jo ran in wide circles on the green grass, her golden hair flying out behind her. Fast on her heels was a giggling Shawn, with Heinz joining in the fracas, his long ears flopping. Suddenly she stopped and let Shawn catch her, then stooped to pick him up and twirl him around. He saw the boy hug her hard as he laughed. And he'd only met her a few hours ago.

Children and animals, he'd once read, have good instincts about people. Jo enjoyed life, embraced it with open arms, drawing people to her like a magnet.

With all his heart, Michael wished he could be more like that, able to let go and show his feelings unafraid. But he also knew he wasn't and could never be. He turned away from the scene and saw his sister studying him again.

"I rest my case, Michael," she said softly. "You may not want to, you may deny it, but you're in love with her. You've got the look."

"And where has love gotten you, little sister?" he asked sadly. "You've loved Kerry for years, you just admitted, yet you left him because you want different things. If I give in to my feelings for Jo—even if I go so far as to admit I care more than I ever have before—it might be wonderful. For a short time. But eventually we'd wind up like you and Kerry, unable to live together. And by then, there might be a child. I grew up, as you did, in a house with two incompatible parents. I won't do that to a child of mine."

His words depressed her more than she could say. Silently Deborah got up and went into her bedroom.

Hands in his pockets, Michael stood gazing after his sister, on his face a troubled frown. Despite his adamant statements to the contrary, the truth was that he had his doubts.

Could Deborah be right?

HE WANTED HER desperately.

That was the one thought that consumed him as he turned over restlessly on the living room couch that evening. He wasn't a man who'd ever let his cravings rule him. But he'd never known hunger this strong before, either. It was even more than a craving. It was the fact that he was beginning to *need* her. Michael swung his feet to the floor and leaned forward, holding his head in his hands.

Deborah's earlier observations had scared the hell out of him. That was why he hadn't given in to his screaming need to go to Jo's bed. He was well aware he was fighting himself more than her. Each time he touched her, he was being snared further. Each time her velvet arms opened and he melted into her, he wanted her more than the last time. And he knew it was wrong because he knew he had no intention of giving her that which he'd come to realize she was after: a future with him.

He didn't want to hurt her. He cared about her too much to deliberately hurt her. Yet he had no intention of repeating his family's inherent weakness, that of marrying a person wrong for them.

Life had been so simple just a short time ago. Before Jo had careened into his life and turned it upside down. And the really frightening thing was that he was beginning to enjoy the unconventional chaos she'd introduced him to. He knew he had a tendency to overthink things, and this was certainly one of those times.

Perhaps he was making another mountain out of a molehill. Perhaps he should just go in to her, enjoy her physically while being careful to avoid saying words that would come back to haunt him. Yes, that was the right approach. Michael stood.

He paused outside Deborah's closed door. Shawn had been asleep for hours. His sister likely was also, her body still adjusting to the time change. He'd creep back onto the couch before daylight and they'd never be the wiser. It wasn't that he felt guilty. He just didn't want to put up with Deborah's knowing looks after their last discussion.

On bare feet, he tiptoed to Jo's room and quietly opened the door.

A candle was burning on the nightstand, but the bed was empty. She was standing at the window, looking out. When she heard the door close, she turned. She wore white, a floor-length gown, sheer and feminine, her hair a pale yellow frame around her shadowed face. She wasn't smiling.

Michael hitched up his gray jogging pants and took a hesitant step toward her. "Is it all right if I come in?"

She'd about given up on him. He'd been quiet all evening, obviously troubled by Deborah's marital problems. Jo knew she couldn't change his thinking. But she could make sure that if he walked away from her, he'd lie awake nights with memories that would haunt him.

She crossed the room wordlessly, opened her arms and met his kiss.

Slow loving and soft sighs. Tender touches and racing hearts. The lemon scent of candles and sweet fragrance of honeysuckle. She gave him all that and more.

The flame didn't burn in an incandescent rush, but rather glowed gently on his skin as her cool hands roamed over him. His hands reached to slip off her gown. Her fingers inched down to push aside his pants. Her lips caressed, her teeth nipped, her slender body eased onto his.

A gentle coupling, as gentle as the summer breeze that blew in and had the candlelight dancing. Slow withdrawal and a welcome return. Movements synchronized as if by a lifetime of practice. Only then did heartbeats increase and breathing quicken. Urgent hands closed over damp flesh and feelings surged and merged. Eyes on each other, two lovers spun out of control together.

And when it was over, Michael shifted to his side, curling into her back. He rearranged her hair, placing a soft kiss on the nape of her neck before gathering her closer, his arms encircling her. Still in the afterglow, he closed his eyes.

She didn't reach up to brush aside the tears that fell silently onto the pillow beneath her head. Beautiful loving, yet something was wrong. It had felt like the prelude to a goodbye. In moments, she felt his breathing even out.

"I love you," she whispered into the silent night, knowing he couldn't hear, wouldn't want to hear.

Behind her, his eyes flying open, Michael's heart skipped a beat. Deborah had been right.

What the hell was he going to do now?

IT WAS THE LAST full day of school, and a holiday atmosphere prevailed. Peeking out from the side of the stage curtain, Christy smiled. "A full house," she told Jo as she pulled her head back. "Half the school is out there, from kindergarten through fourth grade."

Seated on a high stool on stage left, Jo was tuning her guitar. "Great. Did you find seats for Mike, Deborah and Shawn?"

"Sure did. Right in the front row." Behind them, some of the staff were moving backdrops into place. Christy walked closer. "That hunk out there, he's the one you've been rooming with all this time?"

"Yes."

"No wonder you look so terrific." Noticing that her friend didn't meet her eyes or even smile, Christy touched Jo's chin, causing her to look up. "You haven't gone and fallen for him, have you?" She gave a disgusted shake of her brown curls. "You have. And judging by those sad blue eyes, I'd say the guy's not interested in marriage and kiddies."

Jo lay her guitar across her lap with trembling hands. "No, he's not."

"Damn, Jo, why don't you listen to me? Men like him are for fun and games until Mr. Moneybags comes along, didn't I tell you?"

She could almost smile. "Yes, you did, many times. I guess I'm a slow study."

"I'm sorry, Jo."

"Me, too." Time for a change of subject. "How are things between you and Pete?"

"Wonderful. He's close to popping the question, I can feel it."

A loveless marriage with all the amenities. Jo felt like crying, for both of them. "I hope you get what you want, Christy."

"Want me to snare one of Pete's friends and introduce you? Someone single and loaded?"

"No, thanks." She saw Naomi Werner, the music teacher who'd helped her put together the program, walking toward them. "Are we all set, Naomi?"

"Not quite." Naomi's chubby face moved into a frown. "I've got my two volunteers all in costume. Andrew's our American Indian and Terrence is our coyote."

"But we're supposed to have three," Jo reminded her.

Naomi's frown deepened. "Yes, I know, but I just learned that William Boyd, our vice principal, went home ill at lunchtime and the older students have all been dismissed after their own earlier assembly program. We don't have a young man available for the part of the buffalo."

Maybe she *would* cry, Jo thought. The buffalo was an important part of her show. Maybe she could get one of the taller teachers to help out.

"I suppose I could do it," Christy suggested reluctantly.

"The costume's designed for someone six feet tall and you're barely five." Naomi looked down at her own short, rotund figure. "And I wouldn't do. I don't think we can find a six-foot man at the last minute like this."

Jo's lips twitched as a thought hit her, and she gave in to a smile. "I just thought of one." She thrust her guitar at Christy. "Here, hold this. I'll be right back."

Christy giggled. "You wouldn't!"

"Watch me." Hair flying out behind her, Jo left the stage.

"You're crazy," Michael told her. "I can't do that." A look of panic on his face, he glanced around at the rows of rolled-up backdrops behind the scenes. He'd been sitting out front waiting for the show to begin when she'd motioned to him. He'd followed her backstage, never dreaming she wanted him to make a fool of himself. "Absolutely not."

"Sure you can." She held up the buffalo costume. "Look, no one will even know it's you. You'll be covered from head to toe."

"*I'll* know it's me. I'm not a performer."

She lay a hand on his arm, trying her most persuasive tone. "You just have to follow my directions. I sit on a stool, play the guitar and read the book. You and the others act out the story as I tell it. Sometimes I sing the instructions. It's that easy."

She'd gone mad. "I'm not good at this sort of thing."

"A child of eight could follow simple commands like ... and so the buffalo walked over to the campfire to guard the Indian. Things like that. Only we don't have a six-foot-tall child of eight handy."

Stubbornly Michael shook his head. "I don't want to do this, Jo. It's undignified for a grown man to dress up in costume just to entertain children. Get someone else."

"I don't *have* anyone else." Suddenly she lost it. How could she have thought he'd actually begun to enjoy doing something crazy occasionally? Michael Daye was positively the most repressed man she'd ever met. "Oh, never mind. Just go back and sit down. Don't do anything spontaneous or silly or impulsive. Someone might laugh at you and that someone may be a child who will undoubtedly tarnish your precious image."

He was getting angry. "Now wait a minute..."

"Forget it. I'll manage somehow. Forgive me for asking."

His anger deflated and turned into hurt. "That's not fair."

"At least we agree on that." She started walking away, then whirled back. "Why can't you loosen up, Mike? It only hurts for a little while."

IT WAS DIFFICULT to smile when she was fuming. But she would manage, by God, Jo thought as she settled herself on her stool. The natives were getting restless out there. She'd delayed the start of the show too long as it was. Taking a deep breath, she signaled Naomi to get her helpers in place and take the curtain up.

Once she was into the program, Jo forgot her anger. Her joy at looking into the enthralled faces of the children cheered her as always. She finished the first book she'd sung, a first-grade volume filled with silly rhymes. The kids had giggled and squirmed in their seats. Deborah in the front row had even smiled, and Shawn was watching her intently.

Quickly she set the second book on her stand and played the guitar as soft background to the reading. The first two pages were serious. Then the American Indian came whooping onto the stage and the kids perked up. A bit later, as the story progressed, a howling started backstage and in came the coyote. The audience clapped loudly at his arrival.

She was about to set aside book three, which was about the buffalo, when Naomi caught her eye from the sidelines. Grinning, she pointed to someone next to her wearing the buffalo costume. Who had she scrounged up on such short notice? Jo wondered. Surely reticent E. Michael Daye, Jr. hadn't changed his mind.

She began the story. The children were quiet, listening. As Jo introduced the buffalo, the big lumbering figure wandered onto stage center. The costume was quite realistic, and the audience oohed and ahhed. She drifted into the song section, drawing out the lyrics filled with instructions.

The buffalo waddled around the stage, lay down by the campfire and chased the coyote away from the Indian's tepee. As they all three exited, the children applauded.

But the best was yet to come, Jo knew as she hurried into the next book. The music picked up in tempo, a song she'd written. The first part featured an Indian war dance that had the kids fascinated. Then the coyote came dancing out to a snappy tune, choreographed to include a rubber chicken. In the end, the chicken manages to elude the forlorn coyote.

Wondering if the buffalo had hung around, she came to his part. A fast-tempo song with a rock-and-roll beat, she played the tune with enthusiasm. To her delight, the hairy buffalo came charging out, shaking his ample hips in time to the music. The laughter of the children almost drowned out her words.

Because everyone was having such a good time, including the buffalo, Jo repeated the chorus. The animal really was getting into it now. Grabbing hold of his long tail, he draped it over one beefy front paw as he wiggled and sashayed, bumped and twirled around the floor, clowning with the best of them.

The children, many on their feet, were clapping along in time to the music as the song ended. The buffalo did a final jig on his way off stage, then coyly kicked back one foot as he exited at the curtain and waved his tail at the kids. They burst into wild applause.

As pleased as the audience, Jo smiled as they sat back down noisily, still discussing the buffalo dance. She ended the program as always with a tune familiar to most children. The young voices rang out with a rousing rendition of "I'm a little teapot, short and stout..." Many rose to their feet again, going through the motions called for in the song. Without her having to call them back, her three helpers came on stage and sang along, pantomiming the movements. The applause was generous, then it was time to thank her costumed performers.

To the strum of the strings, she introduced the American Indian by name. He whipped off his feathery headband and bowed to their applause. Next came the coyote who skipped onto the stage, evidently caught up in the merriment. As she spoke his name, he yanked off his coyote headgear and bowed low. Finally the buffalo ambled out.

The kids cheered and applauded before she had a chance to tell them who it was. Since she wasn't certain anyway, she just played a few chords. To her amazement, he tugged off his head mask and grinned at the kids.

In the front row, Deborah gasped audibly.

Beside her, Shawn leaped to his feet. "Uncle Michael," he shouted.

Chapter Ten

Michael stood with his feet in the frothy water, watching the waves lazily roll in while the morning sun inched upward in a clear blue sky. Jo had jumped out of their bed a little later than usual to do her pool laps and had tried to coax him to join her. But he'd opted instead for a walk on the beach. He needed a little time alone.

Hands thrust into the pockets of his shorts, he began walking slowly down the beach. The uncomplicated life-style he'd carefully cultivated gave him the freedom to work when he wanted to and to play only when he truly felt the need. Yet lately he couldn't seem to work up the necessary concentration to finish the last couple of sketches.

He'd talked with Eric by phone yesterday, half-heartedly checking on things at the office and been told that everything was fine. Leaning down to pick up a piece of driftwood, Michael wondered at the change in himself. He knew that he'd shocked Deborah yesterday with his buffalo performance. He'd managed to shock himself as well.

He'd done it because Jo had challenged him, made him feel small for stubbornly hanging on to what she referred to as his stuffed-shirt image. So he'd had to prove to her that he could loosen up with the best of them. But somewhere along the line, out there on the stage, a peculiar thing had happened to him. Watching the rapt attention of those kids, seeing their smiling faces, hearing their laughter, he'd begun to enjoy himself.

Privately he'd belittled his brother-in-law Kerry's profession as an entertainer, labeling it childish and unimportant. Donning that silly costume and dancing around for a short time had been infinitely less important. Yet it had been fun. And oddly fulfilling to give pleasure to those kids. He'd certainly thrilled Shawn.

And the look on Jo's face, the warm hug she'd given him when the curtain went down, had been worth every second.

But he'd confused Deborah. They'd all but quarreled the day she'd arrived, and last evening she'd looked at him strangely and accused him of changing into someone she no longer recognized. When he'd denied that, explaining that he thought it was time he loosened up a little, she'd walked away, her brow furrowed. Michael sighed. This business of trying to please people wasn't easy.

He kicked his bare foot at a small sinkhole in the sand. What was he going to do about Jo? Deborah wasn't the only one wallowing in confusion. She loved her husband, she claimed, yet their differences made it difficult if not impossible to live together happily. He...cared for Jo. And she'd said she loved him. Sooner or later he would have to deal with that.

Tossing the driftwood inland, he began the stroll back toward the house. They could never make it together, he decided again as he put one heavy foot in front of the other. Yet the thought of separating from her made his stomach queasy.

The physical aspect of their relationship was wonderful. Superb even. But what about the daily stuff? He'd never lived with a woman before sharing the cabin with Jo, even for a short time. Once he'd gotten used to her ways, he had to admit he enjoyed it. The shared meals, the conversations, the pleasure of having her in his bed. But this wasn't reality; it was a vacation paradise.

Back in California, he had a high-rise apartment, an orderly life, and work that occupied him nearly eighteen hours a day. She lived near the sea in an isolated hilltop house miles from the civilization he required. She spent her days playing the guitar, dreaming up songs, entertaining children. He spent his time catching cabs, attending meetings, traveling to explain his projects. She was crazy about kids and would undoubtedly want several. He'd rarely spent more than an afternoon in the company of a child. Incompatible life-styles, goals, needs.

No, it would never work. Why was he even thinking about it?

Leaving the sandy area, Michael stepped onto the grass and stared across the yard at Jo stretching on tiptoes to toss a wet towel on the clothesline. Her impossibly long legs ended in some kind of a terry shorts outfit in bright yellow. She looked up, smiled and waved. His heart flipped right over.

He knew exactly why he'd been considering a future with Jo. He cared, he wanted, he needed. If only caring alone could dissolve their difference, he would—

Michael stopped in mid-thought and turned to watch a big station wagon coming up their drive. Hearing the vehicle approach, Jo left the side yard and came forward. Heinz came tearing after her, barking a welcome. A large man got out from behind the wheel and stood shading his eyes as he gazed in their direction.

"Dad!" Jo yelped and ran toward the station wagon as a blond woman emerged on the other side.

Flabbergasted, Michael stood watching as three boys of varying ages and heights piled out of the back. She hadn't been kidding, she really did have three brothers. But what was the entire Knight clan doing here? Trying to suppress a groan, he walked to meet them.

"What a surprise," Jo was saying, turning from her father's embrace to hug her mother, then her brothers.

Jarrett Knight hitched up his pants and smiled at his only daughter. "I told you we might surprise you."

Her arm still around her mother's waist, Jo tugged eight-year-old Jon closer on her other side. "I thought you were kidding. It's great to see all of you. Where are you staying?"

"The Wailea Beach Resort."

Twelve-year-old Jason stepped in. "You should see the place, Jo. This big old suite. We had room service last night."

"Burgers, I'll bet," she teased him.

"What else?" Annie Knight interjected.

An impatient sixteen, Jerry was anxious to get going. "We're going snorkeling. Want to come?"

"Just hold on a minute," Jo said. She motioned Michael over. "I want you to meet Mike Daye. He's an architect from San Francisco.'' She saw the hesitancy, but he came closer, offering his hand to her father.

As she introduced her family to Michael, Jo studied his face. He was polite as always, but not particularly warm. No one would ever guess he was the same man who'd done a buffalo jig just yesterday. She wondered if he thought she'd called and asked her family to join them. Already she could tell he was feeling hemmed in by having Deborah and Shawn around.

Just then, Shawn came running out through the patio doors followed by his mother. Michael stood back and let Jo take over, introducing everyone.

Quite a family, he thought. Her three brothers all had hair the color of Jo's and the same blue eyes. He turned to look at her mother and saw how Jo would look twenty years from now. Slender, smiling, hair just a shade lighter and cut considerably shorter. The softness, the gentleness, were there in her face and in the laugh lines etched into the corners of her eyes.

Jarrett Knight was the surprise. Tall, tanned and generously built, he wasn't at all as Michael had pictured him. Jo's father had a rumpled look about him, from his dark windblown hair to his expanding waistline. But his handshake had been firm and friendly, and his eyes were dark brown and intelligent. Michael had the impression the man was comfortable within his own skin, a goal he knew he hadn't quite reached.

As Heinz raced around the boys and the three women stood chatting, Jarrett came over to Michael. ''Hope you don't mind the interruption. We didn't know Jo was sharing the house.''

"No problem," Michael said. So she hadn't called them since arriving. "There was a little mix-up on dates, but we've worked it out. My sister and her son surprised us a couple of days ago, too."

Jarrett's eyes narrowed thoughtfully as he realized that his daughter and this man had been staying here alone for over a week. Of course, Jo was a big girl. Still...

Michael couldn't help but comment on something puzzling. "I thought that blond hair and blue eyes were recessive genes. Your family seems to be the exception."

Fondly patting two cigars in his shirt pocket, Jarrett chuckled. "My wife's an O'Leary, all blue-eyed blondes dating back to the old sod. The O'Leary clan runs to a strong strain, especially the women."

"So I'm finding out." He watched Jo persuade her youngest brother into showing Shawn his water pistol. "Your daughter's pretty terrific with kids. Shawn's nuts about her already."

Jarrett followed his gaze and nodded. "Yes, she always has been, just like her mother. She's a talented musician, too."

"I know. We saw her perform yesterday at her friend's school."

"Did you like the show?"

I *was* the show, Michael thought, as he cleared his throat and hoped his first and last theatrical appearance wouldn't come up. "Everyone seemed to enjoy it," he answered carefully. "Why don't we go in out of the sun and get something cold to drink?"

"Good idea." Jarrett followed, planning to slip in some subtle questions. "So you're an architect," he began.

Noticing the men going inside, Jo thought it wouldn't hurt to join them. Her relationship with Michael currently was iffy at best, and her father, though a kind man, was often blunt. She didn't need anyone upsetting the applecart further right now.

She'd been so pleased with Michael yesterday after he'd come through for her so beautifully at the school. They'd shared a tension-free dinner last night, the four of them, with Shawn suddenly enthralled with his uncle. Deborah had looked a little drawn and uneasy, as she did this morning, but that was to be expected, Jo supposed, since she was wrestling with some important decisions.

When the house had quieted, Michael had come to her bed again. This time he'd been the one who hadn't been in the mood for conversation. Their lovemaking had had an unmistakable poignancy that had frightened her more than the previous night. Afterward, lying in the circle of his arms, she hadn't cried. She'd forced herself to accept the inevitable. Michael, she was certain, was trying to think of an easy way to say goodbye.

She would not make it difficult for him, she'd decided. There would be no point. She loved him more each day. But she wanted a lifetime of love, and that took two willing people. She would not try to hold him or make him feel guilty. She would walk away with her dignity intact, despite a broken heart. Now if only she could carry that off, she thought.

"Hey, boys," she called to Shawn and her brothers, "how about a game of horseshoes while the rest of us go inside and talk?"

"Mom," Jerry protested, "I thought we were going snorkeling."

"We will, Jerry," Annie answered. "We're here for an entire week. Please help the younger boys set up."

"The horseshoes are in the shed around the side," Jo told them as she led her mother inside, followed by a nervous Deborah.

"Horseshoes," Deborah said. "I don't know. Shawn's awfully young and he's never played."

Annie slipped her arm around the sad-eyed woman. "Please don't worry. Jerry's sixteen and very good with youngsters, despite his anxiety to leave. And we'll be right inside the door."

Reassured, Deborah went along.

Jo saw that Michael was pouring iced tea for two. "I'll make some lemonade," she offered, going into the kitchen. "Please, sit down and I'll be right back."

Jarrett joined his wife and Deborah as Jo opened the refrigerator to get the lemons. She glanced up at Michael's unsmiling face as he got down more glasses. She moved closer to him. "I didn't know they were coming. That is, Dad had teased me before I left that they might surprise me, but he so seldom goes on a trip this far from his office that I really didn't take him seriously."

"I know." He really didn't mind, except that he wondered how he'd complete his work. Perhaps he'd have to get an extension on the deadline, something he rarely needed. But this wasn't Jo's fault. He slipped his arm around her waist as she cut the lemons. "Your mother's almost as beautiful as you are."

That made her smile warmly. She turned her face up to his. "Thank you. That was lovely."

Michael glanced over his shoulder. They were all three seated and talking in the living room. He lowered his head and kissed her. "You taste like lemons," he said, smiling.

"You taste like the sea," she whispered back, inordinately pleased that he wasn't upset by her family's arrival.

"Can't be. I didn't drink any salt water." His arm at her waist turned her to him. "Want to check that out again?"

"Maybe I'd better." Jo put down the knife and slid her arms up over his shoulders, offering her mouth.

The kiss was long and thorough, warming her everywhere. A few days ago, this man never would have kissed her while others were in the same house, much less only about twenty feet away through the dining room arch. Somehow that made the kiss all the sweeter, knowing he wanted her enough to disregard them.

Annie Knight sat back in the rocking chair across from the couch and looked into the mirror above the fireplace. Perfectly reflected there was an image of her daughter kissing Michael Daye, a man she'd met a very short time ago. Kissing him passionately, if Annie was any judge, and she was.

At forty-eight, Annie enjoyed an active love life with a man she loved with all her heart, which made it relatively easy for her to spot the real thing when she saw it. She also knew her daughter, knew that Jo wouldn't be kissing a man so thoroughly in a house filled with relatives unless she simply couldn't help herself. Annie also recognized that feeling.

So that's how it is, Annie thought, rocking gently. Maybe she'd find a quiet moment later to talk with Jo. Not to question, but to be available if she needed to talk. She'd only spent minutes with Jo since arriving, yet something bothered Annie. Her daughter's eyes looked sad. If Jo was in love, why didn't she look happier? Annie had lived too long not to know that the course of love rarely ran smoothly, especially in the beginning. With effort, she returned her gaze and her attention to Michael's sister.

MICHAEL TOSSED THE BALL into the air with his left hand, then hit it with his right fist. Up and over the net it flew. Jason, guarding close to the net on the opposite side, leaped up and returned the ball with a sharp punch. It sailed to the far side, but Jo scrambled over and hit it back. Hard and high. So high it flew past Jerry's head in the back and hit the sand rolling.

"Out of bounds," Jerry called. "We won."

"It was not," Jo shouted, mostly just to be argumentative. The boundary lines they'd drawn in the sand weren't really clear.

"Come on, it was out by a mile," Jason joined in.

"You erased the back boundary line," Jo said with a grin.

"Not this time, Jo," her father said as he walked back from retrieving the ball. "Concede gracefully."

Annie, who'd been sitting on the sidelines on a towel, rose laughing as she walked over to Deborah. "This family *never* concedes gracefully," she explained with an odd note of pride.

Deborah, who'd been trying valiantly to catch on to volleyball and to get into a lighthearted mood, smiled back at her. She knew she looked out of place out here. And she felt out of place as the Knight family converged at the net and continued to hash out the results of their second game. Wiping her brow, she wondered how she'd allowed herself to be talked into participating. She'd never cared for sports and it showed.

Turning, she saw Jo's mother looking at her sympathetically. She didn't want the woman's pity, but she had to admit that here was someone who epitomized the word *mother,* someone who looked as if she cared for everyone in need. Unused to confiding in anyone, Deborah suddenly felt as if Annie Knight would understand if she dared be so bold as to discuss anything with her. She could readily see why Jo was such an open and caring person, raised by such a mother.

The discussion at the net was settled with Jo finally giving in. She jogged over to the dry sand to where the two women stood on the sidelines. "Those men sure won't give an inch," she complained good-naturedly.

"Nor do you," her mother commented.

Jo hugged her mom. "Right again." She glanced up at the sun drifting lower in the sky. "Should we go back and get things started for dinner?" When they'd been in the kitchen, she'd asked Michael if he'd mind if the Knight clan hung around for a while. To her surprise, he'd readily agreed and invited them to stay for dinner.

After that, she'd cooked breakfast for those who hadn't eaten and they'd sat around talking for a while. Soon most everyone decided a swim would be fun. While they'd played in the ocean, she and Michael had driven to the store, as much to be alone for a few minutes as to get groceries for the evening meal. He'd further shocked her by pulling over to the side of the road in a wooded section and necking with her like a teenager.

"I'm ready to go back," Deborah said with a grateful sigh. "Shawn, come along."

"Aw, Mom," the boy protested.

Michael walked over. "Don't tell me you're not going to make it best two out of three?" he asked Jo. He hadn't played sports much growing up, and he realized now it had been because no one had offered to play with him. He'd been a swimmer, though, and ran frequently, so he was in good shape. He'd caught on quickly to volleyball and had enjoyed the exercise.

"Not if you want to eat tonight," Jo answered, looking up at him. This is how she liked to see him, relaxed, smiling. He'd removed his shirt and wore only shorts. It was all she could do not to reach out and touch him in front of all these people. But her mother was already giving her speculative glances, so she decided to behave.

"Do I have to go back, Mom?" Shawn asked. "I want to stay with the guys."

Michael put his hands on his nephew's shoulders. "I'll watch him, Deborah."

Deborah sent him an odd look. Michael had never offered to look after a child. "Are you sure?"

"We'll all keep an eye on him," Jarrett said reassuringly. "Come on, team. Let's line up."

Annie shook her head affectionately. "That man is always organizing." She started back toward the house with Deborah.

Jo turned to follow, but Michael took hold of her fingertips and coaxed her back for a private word. Looking down into her flushed face, he smelled the sunshine in her hair. "You need any help?" he asked, wondering why suddenly working in the kitchen alongside Jo held more appeal than playing volleyball.

"Thanks, but I think we can manage."

"Then how about a kiss?" An impulse, more to see her reaction to his question than because he really thought she'd kiss him in front of her whole family.

Her eyes softened. "Okay, sweet talker. But my father's watching and he's—"

"Liable to break both my kneecaps if I compromise his daughter?"

"Is that a fancy word for seduce?"

"I thought I'd already done that."

"Mmm. Hard to tell who was the seducer and who was the seducee."

His fingers stroked hers. "Later, then?"

"Yes, later."

Michael squeezed her hand and let her go. But he stood watching her long-legged strides for some moments. When he turned back, he found the boys engaged in finding seashells and throwing them back into the sea.

But Jarrett Knight was standing quietly studying him. Michael put on a smile. "Ready to start?" he asked.

Jo STOOD at the kitchen counter chopping celery for potato salad while her mother sliced the cooked potatoes at the sink. Deborah had excused herself to take a quick shower, complaining that she felt uncomfortable with salt spray and sand on her skin.

"Michael's sister seems unhappy," Annie said to her daughter. "Is anything wrong?"

Jo sighed. Yes, a lot was wrong. "She left her husband. He's a skater who travels much of the year with the ice show. Deborah hates that life and feels Shawn needs to be enrolled in a proper school."

"I see." Annie rinsed her hands. "Did you tell her that you attended five schools before your tenth birthday?"

"Yes, but she didn't want to hear it." Jo reached for the onion and shook her head. "I believe she loves him. I wish she'd try to work things out. I hate to think how a divorce will affect that darling little boy."

"What does Michael think?"

Jo frowned. "That Deborah and Kerry never should have married in the first place because they're too different."

Annie peeled hard-cooked eggs. "So who wants to marry someone who's just like themselves? What a bore that would be."

"I think so, too, Mom. But Mike and Deb's parents aren't a bit alike, and I guess they don't have much of a marriage. He believes things would have been better if they'd been more alike."

"Where's he going to find a woman who likes everything he does, and vice versa?"

Jo scooped the chopped vegetables into a big bowl. "Beats me."

Annie stepped back, drying her hands, her eyes on her daughter's profile. "And you're attracted to him." It wasn't a question. She'd been watching the two of them most of the day, seen Michael reach for her hand, trying to look nonchalant, and the way Jo wrapped her fingers with his so willingly. Such a casual gesture, yet it spoke of intimacy understood. Yet there was that worrisome underlying sadness.

"Much more than that." Jo reached into the refrigerator for the mayonnaise. "I love him, Mom. And it took me less than a week to realize it. Do you think I'm crazy?"

Her mother laughed. "Me? I met your father at seven in the evening and went home at midnight to announce to my mother that I'd just left the man I was going to marry."

She'd heard the story before and smiled. But her eyes remained serious. "But there's one difference between the two stories. Dad loved you instantly, too. Mike doesn't love me."

Annie handed her the salt and pepper. "I wouldn't be too sure about that, dear. I've seen how he looks at you, the way his eyes follow you."

"Oh, I think that's just a little healthy lust."

"I believe I'm old enough to recognize the difference in a man's eyes."

"Perhaps a little, then, but not enough to take a risk like marriage. In his own words, he's not the risk-taking type. He doesn't believe in love, and the very word *marriage* scares him." Finishing, she spooned a taste and offered it to her mother.

"Delicious," Annie said. "So what do you plan to do?"

Jo arranged plastic wrap to cover the bowl. "Nothing. He's a smart man. He knows I care. The next step's up to him. I don't want him unless he wants me enough to take that risk." She placed the salad in the refrigerator, hoping she had the courage of her convictions.

Annie's heart was already hurting for her daughter. "Are you sure there's not a better way?"

Jo closed the refrigerator door slightly harder than she'd intended. "What other way? Throw myself at him, beg him to love me? I've still got a little pride left. Not much, but a little." She felt the tears building and prayed she wouldn't cry.

"No, that's not what I had in mind," her mother said quietly.

Jo shoved her hair back from her face. "Then what?"

"Keep your head high and walk away with a smile. If it's real, Jo, he'll come after you. When he wakes up."

Jo swallowed around a lump in her throat. "What if he doesn't, Mom?"

Annie reached to hold her close. "He will, sweetheart. He will."

Men and boys came noisily trooping in with Heinz at their heels. Annie went to greet them, letting Jo finish up alone so she could gather her composure. "Jarrett, isn't it time you started the fire? The chickens are ready to be grilled."

After the boys grabbed something cold to drink and the adults trooped back out to watch the chef cook, Michael found Jo at the sink husking the corn. "Are you all right?" he asked, noticing that she was unusually quiet.

She'd buried the urge to weep and let him turn her to face him. "Certainly. Are you thirsty?"

Her eyes were overly bright and he wondered at the cause. Later he would ask her. "Yes, thirsty." He pulled her close up against his body. "For this." Tenderly he touched his mouth to hers.

It was almost her undoing. She couldn't prevent the tiny, muffled sob as she dropped the corn and reached for him. She would take what she could, for now, because it might very well be all she would ever have. She badly wanted to believe her mother, but she doubted that Michael would admit he was wrong and go after any woman. Jo put her heart into the kiss, telling him in that way what her lips couldn't say.

Shaken and breathless, Michael pulled back. "Did anyone ever tell you you're some kisser, lady?"

She smiled up at him. "You ain't seen nothing yet, buddy."

"How about tonight about midnight, we take up where we left off?" he suggested.

"You're on."

THE BACKYARD was bathed in moonlight at midnight. Michael stepped out the kitchen door into the soft night sounds. Palm trees rustling in the breeze. In the distance, the ocean sweeping the sandy beach. And the cooing sound of a bird somewhere overhead.

The pool looked inviting, shadowed, very still. He dropped his towel on a chair and wondered where Jo was. He hadn't checked the bedroom, had instead slipped outside to grab his suit from the clothesline, changed and come out. Then a ripple of water in the far corner caught his eye.

She was floating on her back, arms outstretched, her suit very white in the dark water. Automatically his eyes went to the window of Deborah's bedroom. But the blinds were drawn and he hadn't heard a sound from in there in hours. Jo's family had left about nine, and an exhausted Shawn had all but fallen asleep during his bath. But not before he'd told Jo repeatedly how "really neat" her brothers were.

Michael walked to the pool's edge and sat, dangling his feet in the water. The Knight family was not only neat, they were exceptional, he thought. Jarrett and Annie smiled at each other and touched often, holding hands after dinner like young lovers. There was respect and admiration and genuine caring between the two of them, and reflected in their children. Michael felt at a loss to explain how they'd managed that.

No wonder Shawn had been drawn to them. Even Deborah had loosened, going for a walk on the beach with Annie, returning with a smile, but looking as if she'd shed a tear or two. His sister needed a woman to talk to and had never really had one. If she'd met someone like Annie years ago, perhaps her life wouldn't be such a mess.

"Hey, fella," Jo whispered into the still night air as she moved her hands, floating closer to him. "Aren't you coming in?"

She'd drifted into a patch of moonlight and, gazing at her, Michael lost his train of thought. Her skin was like marble, smooth and perfect. Only it wasn't cold like marble, he was well aware. His own blood began to heat just watching her, remembering how his hands had skimmed over her, touching everywhere. And his mouth had leisurely brushed over her, tasting.

Her eyes were dark and intensely aware of the effect she had on him. Suddenly she jackknifed and dived under, then shimmered along just beneath the surface. Michael let out a shaky breath and eased into the pool.

In moments she rose up near him, her head tilted back so the water dripped off. "So, have you gotten over my family's sudden arrival, chaotic stay and mass exodus?"

On top of the water, his fingertips toyed with hers. "They're nice, Jo. Very nice."

Genuinely pleased, she smiled. "I think so, too. But a little overwhelming sometimes."

"Yes." He moved closer. "Collectively and individually."

"My father mentioned that your company has its liability insurance through him."

"I guess so. My partner handles that end of things."

"Small world." She was near enough to slide one foot up his calf slowly. "Ever make love in a pool, Mike?"

His eyes drifted again to Deborah's window. "Think she's asleep?"

"Yup." She rubbed against his chest and heard his sharp intake of breath. Laughing, she turned and kicked off. "But that doesn't mean I'm going to make it easy for you."

Blood churning, he started after her. "We have to keep quiet."

At the far end, she let him catch her. "I'll try not to scream and thrash about as you ravish me." She kissed him lightly.

But Michael wasn't in the mood for games. He felt tense and anxious, like a man on the verge of making a big decision, with neither choice satisfactory. He couldn't stay with Jo, yet he couldn't bear the thought of letting her go.

As he drew her close, he saw her read the raw need in his eyes. Taking her mouth, he kissed her hungrily, overcome with feelings he couldn't explain. His tongue invaded, plunged, plundered. He could taste the surprise as Jo struggled to keep up.

Wrapping his arms around her, he deepened the kiss and took them both under. Fighting the water, fighting the urgency, he kept them moving. His air was running out so he finally gave a push against the pool bottom and they rose together in a gush of spraying water.

Eyes wide open and dark with desire, Jo came back for more. He was fighting his own demons, she knew. She couldn't offer her love when he didn't want it, but she would give him this. Desperate now and as eager as he, she clung to him as his hands slipped her suit from her, then moved over her wet flesh. When his mouth settled on her breast, she closed her eyes and fought not to moan out loud.

This was how he wanted her, limp and in his arms yet not submissive, pliant yet not quite surrendering. Her hands skimming over him, leaving a trail of fire. Her breath hot in his ear, her mouth searching for his. This was what he'd wanted with the woman he wanted more than his next breath.

He moved them to where the water was only chest-high and stepped out of his suit. Gently he backed her against the pool wall, then lifted her. Breathing hard, he waited until her eyes locked with his. Then he filled her as she wrapped her legs around him.

Michael watched her face as he moved with her, moved within her. Her heavy eyelids wanted to close, but she wouldn't allow it as her hands gripped his shoulders. Moonlight danced around them as he increased the rhythm, wanting this feeling to go on forever. Wanting her with him forever.

When the tidal wave hit, Jo's head fell backward. Michael buried his face in the slim line of her throat and wished that this moment would never end.

Chapter Eleven

They were shivering from the coolish night air when they came in the kitchen door, both wrapped in towels, trying to keep quiet. Heinz came rushing over to greet Jo, giving her a short bark of welcome.

"Shh, we don't want to wake Deborah and Shawn," Jo told him, then rubbed his chin to show him she hadn't meant to scold.

Michael took a can of cola from the refrigerator and snapped the top with a loud fizz. He tilted his head back and drank thirstily, then offered the can to Jo and watched her take a sip. "You don't think Deborah would approve of skinny-dipping?" he asked as he grabbed a hold of the end of her towel and pulled her close.

In the moonlight coming in through the window, Jo's eyes were thoughtful. "Maybe. You said Kerry's outgoing and gregarious. Perhaps he's introduced her to some of the more bold pastimes." She angled her head to look up at him. "Have you ever been swimming sans suit before tonight?"

"No." His arms slid around her. "If you want credit for changing a conservative architect into a liberated man, you've got it."

It wasn't credit she wanted, but the man himself. She was still a little shaken from his edgy desperation during their lovemaking in the pool. Although he'd alternated between lovingly playful and thoughtfully silent the past few days, she knew something was bothering him.

And that something had to do with a decision about her.

Maybe it was time to bring the subject they'd both been avoiding out in the open. Taking a step back, she shook out her wet hair. "I suppose you've enjoyed your fling at liberation, but when you return, you'll go back to living the same as before, won't you?"

Somehow he'd known he'd be having this conversation. He'd hoped they could postpone it until they were truly alone. He kept his voice low. "Yes, I probably will. People don't really change their basic makeup, Jo. Certainly not during the course of a two-week vacation."

A two-week vacation. Is that how he thought of the time they'd spent together? A little sun, a little unconventional recreation, an unorthodox woman in his bed. But soon it would be time to return to reality. And in the future, occasionally he would take out the memory of his Hawaiian trip and smile at how foolishly romantic he'd allowed himself to be for a couple of short weeks.

"That's where we differ. I believe people do change. If they want to. If what they want is greater than the pain change brings about.'' She looked at him point-edly.

Michael let out a quiet breath. She was pushing. He'd never reacted well to being pushed. ''If you painted over the spots on a leopard and added stripes, you could call him a zebra, but it wouldn't change what he really was. And if you put that made-over leopard in a cage to live with a zebra, you would have an incompatible pair.''

Jo turned to gaze unseeingly out the window. He still didn't get it. It wasn't his conservative ways she thought needed changing as much as his unbending viewpoint. He cared for her; she was certain of it. Yet he wouldn't bend enough to give their love a chance, wouldn't learn to compromise. He'd rather spend a lifetime alone than risk getting hurt.

She'd asked for this, Jo reminded herself, had walked into this with eyes wide open, leading with her heart. She had no one to blame but herself.

Watching her profile, Michael felt terrible, and wondered why. He hadn't done anything to deliberately hurt her. He hadn't misled her. He'd been straight with her from the beginning. ''I never lied to you, Jo.''

His quiet statement settled in her chest like a chunk of heavy metal. Slowly she turned back to him. ''No, you didn't.'' She'd lied to herself, made herself believe that because she loved, he would love.

Her eyes were dark and solemn, when just minutes ago, it seemed, they'd been soft and inviting. He hated the fact that he'd taken that zest for life and replaced it with that lost look. She didn't realize that he was doing her a favor. It was far better to hurt her now than to hurt her daily for the rest of their lives, the way his parents went on hurting each other. Separate lives filled with quiet frustration and growing indifference. That's what they'd have to settle for. Or a painful divorce like Kerry and Deborah were now facing.

How could he convince Jo without twisting the knife further? "I don't believe in marriage and happily ever after, Jo. I wish I did, for both our sakes."

She prayed she wouldn't cry. "It's more than that, Mike. You've decided that loving someone has to be painful. And you've arranged your life so you'll never have to feel that possible pain."

He took another swallow from the can, then tried to keep his voice calm so Deborah wouldn't come out to check on them. He'd always hated quarrels, especially in front of others. "I don't want to fight with you."

"I'm sure you don't." Giving in to her anger, she tossed back her hair and paced the length of the small kitchen. Anger was so much easier to deal with than the hurt she'd been dreading. "Well, I happen to think a good fight now and then clears the air. But it's risky, and you run from risk."

She stopped in front of him, knowing if she didn't end this soon, she'd say too much. Perhaps she already had. "Go ahead and run, Mike. Go back to your solid, comfortable life. You've been right about me from the beginning. I'm wrong for you. I'm a little crazy, unpredictable, spontaneous. Those words put fear in your heart."

Her quiet delivery made her words all the more effective. Michael rubbed a hand along the back of his tense neck. "I never said you were those things."

"You didn't have to. Did you think I was blind? I saw all the differences between us long before you pointed them out. But I also see all the similarities you won't." She wet her dry lips. "I wish you well, truly I do. Yet I can't help but wonder about your life. Whose heart skips a beat when you walk in the door? Who gives you pleasure, makes you laugh, warms you? Who holds your hand when you're sick or hurting? In years to come, how will you spend your Christmases, Mike? Who will you buy for, decorate a tree with, drink eggnog in front of the fire with? Who will you call to share your celebrations?"

He didn't answer because there were no answers.

She felt the pressure building behind her eyes. She had to leave and started to. At the doorway she swung around. "You can find a lot of women far more experienced to replace me in your bed. I should have guessed you'd prefer competence over love."

She saw his face turn white. Finally she'd gotten a reaction from him. Barefoot, she stomped through the living room. Floppy and Heinz were curled up at opposite ends of the couch he'd made up into his bed, still keeping up the pretense. Well tonight, he could damn well stay right there. She fervently hoped they'd keep him awake all night.

Blinking back tears, she went into the bedroom and quietly closed the door.

In the kitchen, Michael rummaged around in a drawer and found the rumpled pack of cigarettes he'd left there last week. Quickly, he lighted one and inhaled deeply. He almost staggered back from the nicotine head rush. Staring out the window, he braced one hand on the sink's edge and took another punishing drag.

It was going to be a long night.

JO WAS STANDING at her bedroom window when the first rays of the morning sun began to lighten the sky. She seriously doubted if she'd slept more than minutes snatched between bouts of restless tossing and turning. Finally she'd risen and showered, then pulled on a roomy pink T-shirt that came down nearly to the cuffs of her white shorts. She didn't feel better, just fresher.

It was time to leave, she thought, watching the sky turn pink and gold. She'd wanted to visit Hawaii for years, and now she had. Perhaps in time she'd stop thinking of this lovely place with sadness. She wanted to go home to the safety of her house and the familiarity of her things. Her work here was finished. She'd accomplished what she'd set out to do. And much more.

There was no phone in her room or she'd have called the airline already. She would as soon as she found the opportunity, change her reservation and pack up. She'd already overstayed her welcome.

She badly wanted some coffee, but she wasn't anxious to encounter Michael so early. She had little energy left for Round Two. But, of course, he wouldn't begin it. His way was to retreat, not fight. She opened her bedroom door a crack.

Seated in the corner of the couch, wearing a blue silk nightshirt, her feet curled up under her, was Deborah. The bedding was neatly folded and stacked on a chair. Michael was nowhere to be seen. Jo stepped out. "You're up early," she said.

"I couldn't sleep." Deborah ran a hand through her dark curls, already disheveled from earlier such gestures. "There's coffee, if you'd like some."

Jo glanced toward the dining room and on into the kitchen.

"Michael's gone for a walk on the beach, if you're looking for him, and Shawn's still asleep. The animals seemed anxious to go out so I let them. I hope that was all right." Deborah sipped coffee from a mug.

"Yes, fine." Jo went to the kitchen and came back to sit in the opposite corner of the couch. She sipped her coffee, finding it hot, strong and very welcome. She raised her eyes to Deborah and thought she looked as bad as Jo felt. "Did you, uh, talk with Mike this morning?"

Deborah shook her head. "When I came out, he was walking toward the beach."

"I guess it's uncomfortable sleeping on this couch."

Deborah smiled then, a woman-to-woman smile. "We both know he hasn't been sleeping here, Jo. You don't have to pretend with me. I'm not a prude, and I'm not one to sit in judgment."

Jo relaxed, finding she liked Deborah after all. "Well, he slept here last night."

"I don't think he slept much. I heard him moving around quite a bit."

She had, too, but she'd thought it was because the animals had kept him awake. But she was hesitant to discuss all this with Michael's sister, a woman she didn't know very well. "I suppose he's concerned about not completing his project. I've learned that Mike hates anything to interfere with his work schedule.''

Deborah set down her mug and stretched an arm along the couch back. "I thought we were going to stop pretending."

Perhaps they'd been louder than she'd thought. "You heard us last night?"

"I heard you talking, then heard you go into your room while Michael stayed out here pacing and grumbling. After the episode in the pool, I thought—"

"Oh, Lord!" Jo groaned.

"I wasn't watching, but I heard you laughing." She leaned to touch Jo's shoulder. She hadn't been a toucher, not growing up in the Daye household. Kerry had taught her the value of a touch. "You sounded like you were having such fun. I lay there envying you both."

Jo shook her head sadly. "There's nothing to envy, Deb."

"You're good for him, you know."

Jo gave a short laugh. "Funny, that's what Charlotte said. Everyone seems to think I'm good for Mike. Except the man himself."

Deborah considered that. "We're a difficult twosome, the grown Daye children. We grew up without love, and it's foreign to us. We don't know how to act when it's offered. We're very good at heading it off at the pass or killing it even when it's freely given."

Frowning, Jo tried to understand. "But you met Kerry when you were young, fell in love and ran off with him against everyone's advice. You followed your heart, not your head. I'd say that's the right way to act."

Deborah shrugged. "But I can't seem to hang in there for the long haul. I'm afraid to trust, afraid to believe that love will be enough. I have a son to protect, to guide. I feel torn between my concern for Shawn and my need for Kerry. I've never had a role model to show me how to handle these things. Sometimes the heart misleads us, too."

Jo shook her head. "No, it doesn't. All right, so you had lousy role models. Probably half of the people in the world, maybe more, have no better. I believe you have to go with your instincts. If you love Kerry, you need to work out this family problem together, with him. Surely he wants what's best for your son, too. Perhaps he can arrange to travel less. And when it's necessary for you two to go with him, maybe you could take along a tutor for Shawn. There must be a compromise here somewhere. A family that cares needs to be together."

"I don't know, Jo. Michael and I were raised together under the same roof with both our parents, and we didn't turn out so hot."

"Because an important ingredient was missing. Love. Mike tells me he doesn't think your parents ever really loved each other."

"I agree. They probably didn't. In those days..."

"Oh, brother!" Jo got up, unable to sit still. Evidently she was still too agitated to discuss anything calmly. "Love has been around for centuries. Some people marry for love, others for whatever reasons. Your folks picked door number two. Your bad luck." She stepped closer, desperate to make her point. "You can overcome this, and so could Mike, if he'd just quit being so bullheaded. You're not your parents. You married for love. You're not going to repeat their pattern. *That's* the difference."

Running out of steam, Jo went to the kitchen and brought back the coffeepot, refilling each of their cups, then sat back down. She took a calming sip.

"You really think so?" Deborah asked after a pensive moment.

There was hope here, at least for one of them. Jo swung one knee up and angled her body toward Michael's sister. "Yes, I do. I think you two have been hiding behind this business of your indifferent parents long enough. I was fortunate enough to be raised by wonderful parents in a very loving atmosphere. That was great, but then I had the misfortune to fall in love with a pigheaded man who doesn't believe in love or marriage or happiness. With vastly different backgrounds, we're at the same crossroads, Deb. Only *you* can do something about your situation."

"Then you do love Michael?"

Jo sagged wearily. "Yes, I love him, for all the good that'll do me. But we're talking about you here, and you told me you love Kerry, right?"

"Yes, I always have. But—"

"But, nothing! Go to him, swallow your pride. Work things out. That little boy needs *both* of you."

"That's quite enough." Michael's quietly controlled voice echoed in the suddenly silent room, followed by his footsteps as he walked in through the patio doors.

Startled, Jo swung about, wondering how long he'd been there and just how much he'd heard.

His windblown hair was hanging forward onto his forehead, and on his tanned face was a scowl. He had on only his gray jogging pants, wet around the ankles. His stance was angry as he placed clenched fists on his slim hips and sent Jo an icy glare. "What right do you have to give advice to my family?"

Deborah rose to Jo's defense. "I asked her, Michael."

His eyes stayed on Jo as he answered his sister. "She has a big family. She should tell them how to live their lives and leave us alone." He saw the color drain from her face and wanted to pull back his cruel words. But he knew it was too late.

He was miserable, down to his soul. He hadn't slept, hadn't been able to think of anything except the argument they'd had last night, the hurtful words she'd hurled at him. He'd gone walking at daybreak, trying to come to grips with the dichotomy of his emotions. It hadn't helped. He felt like a man torn in two.

He could have ended it, had her back in his arms in minutes, just by whispering those three little words he knew she wanted to hear. He also knew he felt what was probably love for her, not that his experience in that department was vast. But admitting it to himself was as far as he was prepared to go. Because the next logical step—marriage—was the really frightening move.

Everything was against them. Life-styles, vocations, future plans. To say nothing of statistics. The latest he'd read had confirmed what he already knew, that over fifty percent of all marriages ended in failure. With her eternal optimism, he knew that Jo would probably tell him that a fifty-percent victory rate was pretty high. Was the glass half full or half empty? It all depended on viewpoint.

Walking back, he realized he was no closer to viable answers than he'd been last night.

As he'd reached the patio, he'd heard voices and stopped. When he realized Jo was advising Deborah to return to Kerry and more misery, he'd all but lost it. How dare she!

Now he watched her pull herself together and square her shoulders.

"You're right, for once," Jo said quietly. "I need to leave you alone." Moving slowly, as if her body were that of an old woman, she got her ticket and went into Deborah's room to phone the airline.

"Weren't you a little hard on her?" Deborah asked. Not since they were children had she heard Michael raise his voice or seen him lose his temper. Perhaps it was because not since then had he cared about anyone or anything enough to get emotionally involved.

"Has she brainwashed you in just a couple of days?" Feeling defeated, Michael poured coffee from the pot on the table into Jo's discarded cup and took a hefty swallow.

"Hardly." Deborah didn't want to argue with Michael. Not just because she rarely won against him, but because she was bone-tired of discussing this matter. With Kerry, with Jo and now with Michael. Yet she couldn't sit by and let him think he was right when she was no longer certain. "But she made some good points."

Reaching for patience, Michael turned to his sister. "Let us be reasonable about this and consider it like civilized adults. Marriages between opposites are doomed almost from the moment the man and woman say 'I do.' Have you forgotten what it was like to grow up in the Daye household? Did Mother and Dad ever agree on anything that you can recall? Do you remember the quarrels late at night in their bedroom, and even at those stilted dinners in the dining room? No shouting, of course. Just cold, cutting conversation. Then the silences, the strained looks. Then Mother would leave on tour and Dad would be at his club, night after night, while assorted housekeepers tried to pretend with us that we were a normal family."

Deborah did remember, and hated the memories. "But Michael, it doesn't have to be that way."

He was past listening, his eyes seeing myriad hurtful scenes. "Remember how you used to hide out in your room on your birthday so you wouldn't have to deal with no one home to celebrate with? Remember how it felt to open Christmas presents with only Aunt Charlotte and Noel there, all falsely gay, presents chosen by secretaries?" Perhaps Jo's comments on Christmas last night had stung the most. Because they'd been so accurate. To this day, he hated the holidays, often going in to the office even on Christmas Day.

Deborah touched his arm, as she had Jo's earlier, in a plea for understanding this time. Michael intimidated her often and made her feel inadequate. But of one thing she felt confident. "If there's love, Michael, the kind of love you couldn't help but notice between Annie and Jarrett Daye, it isn't like that, even if two people are very different. I took a walk with

Annie yesterday and she told me some interesting stories about..."

He got to his feet abruptly. "I don't want to hear any more. You do what you want." He walked into the kitchen, disgusted with himself. He never lost his temper. Wondering when he'd even developed one, he stood staring out the kitchen window.

Jo came out of the bedroom. The house was old and the walls thinner than she'd realized. She'd heard most of the exchange between Michael and his sister. Her heart went out to the youngsters they'd been, neglected and abandoned. Deborah had a chance with Kerry to overcome her hurtful history, if only she would see it, grab it. But Michael had buried so much and refused to forgive his parents, to let go of his past. She hadn't understood until just now how closed his mind had become.

Deborah stood. "I hate to see you rush off like this, Jo. Maybe if you stayed..."

Jo shook her head. "It's best that I leave."

Deborah sighed unhappily. "What time does your flight take off?"

Not soon enough. "Four. I think I'll go pack."

Michael came to the doorway. He'd calmed down and cooled off somewhat. There was no point in ending things on a nasty note. "I'll drive you to the airport."

No, she wasn't going to put herself through that. No goodbye scenes, no silent ride, no public tears. "Thanks, but I'll call a cab."

His temper flared anew. "I *said* I'd drive you."

Two could play this game and she was in no mood for compromises. "I'd sooner walk." Turning on her heel, she marched into her bedroom and shut the door.

Standing in the other bedroom doorway wearing bright green Ninja Turtle pajamas, Shawn rubbed his eyes sleepily. "I'm hungry, Mom."

"Good morning, sweetheart." Exasperated at the way Michael was treating Jo, Deborah frowned at him as she went to her son. "Well, that was certainly the civilized, adult way to handle the situation. Got any more good advice, big brother?"

Chapter Twelve

The view from Michael's seventh-floor office was of San Francisco Bay. It was one of the reasons he and Eric had taken the lease on this particular building. Whenever he felt tired or uninspired, the water and sky, the boats coming and going, the magnificent bridge to the north, would inevitably cheer him. He stood there now staring out and felt nothing but annoyance.

Turning away from the wall of windows, he walked back to his desk and sat in his leather chair. He should be feeling on top of the world. He'd finished the work on the urban renewal project before returning two weeks ago, and he should be hearing from the committee regarding the approval of his designs any day now. The grant for the inclusion of the low-income housing would follow and then he'd get the go-ahead to begin clearing the area. Everything was about to fall into place neatly.

Why then didn't he feel terrific? Where was the elation, the sense of satisfaction he always felt at times like this? Irritated with himself, he loosened his tie and undid his top button. The laundry had evidently ignored his long-standing instructions and put starch in his shirt. Why else would he suddenly feel that his collar was too tight?

Michael leaned back in his chair and gazed at the ceiling. He longed to whip off his tie and exchange his starched white shirt for a soft knit shirt, open at the throat. He longed to take off somewhere, on a boat or a plane, where no one knew him. Where he could start over. Now, where had that thought come from? he asked himself. He'd never been a daydreamer.

Correction. He had dreamed a lot, as a child. Left alone too much, he'd withdrawn into a better world he'd created in his mind. An escape. There, he'd designed wondrous buildings, been acclaimed by thousands as imaginative and far ahead of his time. He'd built castles with turrets and secret passages and towers where lovely ladies waited to be rescued. By him.

He'd had an opportunity to rescue a lovely lady recently, and hadn't taken the bait. Not that Jo Knight needed rescuing, really. Only by the broadest stretch of the imagination could he believe that she needed anything. Or anyone. She was self-sufficient, independent, unconstrained.

Except the day she'd tangled with the stingray. Michael closed his eyes, remembering the way hers had looked as she'd lain on the beach bleeding, filled with pain and fear. He'd done something he'd never done before that day. He'd acted like a hero in some romance novel. He'd certainly never seen himself in that role before. But that night, as he'd watched over her, and the next when she was finally out of danger and asked him to hold her—just hold her—he'd felt like a hero.

But other than that incident, Jo didn't need anyone. She had her own house, a loving supportive family, work she enjoyed. She didn't need him; she just thought she did. In the long run, he'd done her a tremendous favor by getting out of her life before they did something foolish, like get further involved.

Someone as beautiful, as warm and giving as Jo, would have no trouble finding a man. Some nine-to-five guy, a big blustery man like her father, who'd want to settle down and raise flowers and children with her. Someone who'd hurry home to find her waiting for him after a long day, to see that slow smile that made a man's heart lurch. She'd fill his house with kids and animals and confusion, his days with spontaneous laughter and his nights with those soft sounds she made as she opened her arms to hold him.

Lord, how he missed her. He should have adjusted to being without her by now. Michael became aware that his hands were clutching the arms of his chair in a death grip. With effort, he forced his fingers to relax.

"You look mighty grim this morning, partner." Eric breezed into Michael's office and folded his long frame into the chair opposite the desk. A big man, several inches over six feet with a head of thick blond hair and dark brown eyes, Eric wore his expensive clothes with a flair that was the envy of many of his friends. Most of them knew that behind his congenial good humor was a sharp intellect and a dogged persistence. Today his usual smile was missing. "And what I've got to tell you isn't going to improve your mood."

Great. Just what he needed. Bad news on a bad day. "Lay it on me," Michael said with a resigned look.

"The committee's approved your sketches and the rest of the plan for the urban renewal project for the shopping plaza. That's the good news. But the government subsidy for the second-phase housing development won't be forthcoming."

Michael bounced forward in his chair. "Why the hell not? I thought we had that wrapped."

Eric considered his partner. He'd never been as intense as Michael, even when they'd been teenagers growing up together. Sure, he hated these frustrating delays, but he was a man who'd long ago learned to roll with the punches. Michael resisted change with an iron fist. "They ran out of money, plain and simple." He tossed a sheet of paper onto Michael's desk. "Here's the report. Told us we could reapply next year, and that's only a maybe."

"Damn. We don't have a year to waste waiting around." He turned to glower out his window. "All that work, down the drain."

"Not necessarily." Eric had given this some thought since receiving the notice. "There are other ways."

"Right. You know some other way to get two million dollars pronto?"

"I have some ideas, and I think you might, too, as soon as you adjust to losing the government subsidy. Come on, Michael. Are we going to let one no stop us cold?"

"It's a damn big no."

"Then let's look for a yes." Eric enjoyed working with Michael and cared for him like a brother. But this was where they always locked horns. Michael wasn't good at compromising.

Michael swung back dejectedly. Why was his life, personally and now in his work, suddenly in shambles? he wondered. "Where do you propose looking?"

Eric shrugged. "How about private funding? Or approaching city government. That substandard housing is creating problems for the city, and they might welcome a solution. Then there's the people at the state level that we haven't tried. It's a bit of a risk, but I think we can manage it."

There was that damn word *risk* again. "Any of that could take weeks, months."

"Of course, but delays are part of this business. You know that. No one could accuse you of being adaptable, Michael, but I never thought you were stubbornly pigheaded and only able to see one answer to a problem."

Pigheaded. That was what he'd overheard Jo labeling him the morning she'd been talking to Deborah. The last morning he'd seen her. He struggled with a sense of anger—at Jo, at Eric. Yet, if he were to be brutally honest, perhaps it should be directed at himself. "Maybe I am stubborn. That's just the way I am."

Eric studied his oldest and best friend. Since returning from his trip to Hawaii, Michael had been moody and distracted. Eric had attributed it to the fact that his partner had been working too hard. But during this discussion, Eric had begun to lean in another direction. When a serious guy like Michael grew distracted, forgetful and uncharacteristically argumentative, it usually meant only one thing: a woman. Eric decided he'd better yank Michael's chain and get him back on track.

"People aren't born stubborn, Michael. I'd say you choose to be. I've known you a long time, and I've always admired your tenacity. But there are times when it takes on the form of bullheadedness."

It was only because they did go back a lot of years that Michael didn't lose his temper at Eric's comment. "I'm getting a little tired of everyone analyzing me."

"Who besides me?"

"My sister and...and someone else." Feeling defiant, Michael picked up his cigarettes and stared at the pack. It was crazy, but he didn't even want one. He tossed them aside.

Getting closer. Eric placed his left ankle on his right knee and kept his expression bland. "Want to tell me about her?"

Michael let out a ragged sigh. "No." Yes, he did, badly. But he didn't know how to begin. He'd never discussed women problems with Eric, mainly because he'd never really had a problem with a woman that he didn't know how to solve himself. And he still didn't. Jo wasn't a problem, because she was out of his life. "There's nothing to discuss."

"I see," Eric said, seeing far more than Michael might have guessed. "She must really be something to have you in such knots two weeks after your return."

"I'm not in knots. I'm perfectly fine." To prove he was indeed in charge of his own life, Michael lighted a cigarette, ignoring the stale taste in his mouth.

"Good, good. Women, they're not worth the aggravation. Always wanting elaborate gifts and expensive dinners."

Michael coughed into his fist. "She isn't like that." The most he'd ever given her was a rose, and she'd made certain they split all the expenses right down the middle.

"Well then, she was probably one of those talkers. Blabbering all the time about her life, her career."

Actually, Jo was a wonderful listener, seemingly more interested in opening him up than going on about herself. "Not exactly." Michael snuffed out the unsmoked cigarette with a look of distaste.

"Uh-huh. Most likely she was beautiful—I've seen the type. Gorgeous but a little hung up on herself, fussing with her hair, her nails, perfect makeup, fantastic clothes. Don't touch her 'cause you might wrinkle her."

Fair was fair. "No, not at all. She's naturally beautiful." And never objected when he touched her. Remembering how it felt to touch her, Michael shifted his gaze out the window again.

Eric fooled with the tassle on his loafer, wondering if Michael had any idea how transparent he was. He'd seen his friend date a lot of women over the years and never once get really hung up on one. Eric had privately predicted that when that happened to a man as intense as Michael, he would fall like a ton of bricks, but fighting it all the way. "I suppose then that she's too much like you. Likes everything you do and you'd be bored to tears with her in no time.''

Bored? With Jo? A contradiction, Michael thought. "One thing for certain, Jo's not in the least boring." He swung troubled eyes back to Eric. All right, so he'd tell him a little. How could he feel any worse than he already did? "The problem is that we're nothing alike. She wants all the things I want to avoid: home, hearth and kiddies. She needs a solid family man like her father."

"Who's her father?"

"Jarrett Knight from—"

"Southwest Insurance. Hell, I know Jarrett and he's only got one daughter." It was beginning to make sense. "You met Jo Knight in Hawaii, didn't you?"

Michael frowned. "How do you know her?"

"I used to date her friend, Christy Hanes, three or four years ago. The three of us stood up in the wedding of mutual friends." Eric laughed. "Christy's good for a couple of laughs, but Jo wouldn't give me a tumble."

That perked Michael up. "She wouldn't?"

"Not on your life. A group of us went out for breakfast after the wedding reception. We were all sitting around in this big booth in this late-night diner, and Jo was next to me. So I started moving in on her. She was easily the best-looking woman there."

Why did hearing that bother him? Michael asked himself. It had happened years ago. Because he knew exactly how Eric operated. Smoothly, swiftly. "Go on."

He certainly had his friend's attention now. "So after we ate, I walked Jo to her car and asked her for a date. She kind of studied me for a minute, then shook her head. She said she'd rather be my friend than take her place in a long line of women she was sure I had. The lady's hard on the ego."

"Yeah, that sounds like Jo."

Eric shook his head good-naturedly. "I tried to get her to change her mind, but she wouldn't budge. So I switched to Christy." Eric shifted in his chair, studying his friend. "You're better off without Jo Knight, buddy. That woman's got marriage on her mind and she's not apt to settle for less."

"You've got that right."

"And who needs it, right?"

"Right." Why wasn't this conversation making him feel better? Michael wondered.

"So she gave you the cold shoulder, too, eh? Well, consider yourself lucky."

It wasn't exactly a cold shoulder, not till that last day, but Michael didn't want to go into all that. "Yeah, lucky."

"Right. Like you said, you're too different, you and Jo. Hell, you don't want to settle down with *one* woman. You don't want some little house in the suburbs, kids and dogs. A mortgage and braces."

"Yes."

"Yes?"

"I mean, no. No, I don't want that." Michael ran a hand through his hair. It was longer than he usually wore it. Jo had remarked once when they'd been lying in bed that she liked his hair a little on the shaggy side, so she could run her fingers through it and . . .

"Glad you came to your senses before she got her hooks in you. I have to admit that Jo Knight is gorgeous." Eric straightened his already-perfect tie and shook his head. "But guys like us, we're too smart to get taken in. There're tons of women out there. Footloose and fancy free, that's what we are. Go where we want, when we want, right?"

Why was it, Michael wondered, that the only place he wanted to go was wherever Jo was? This was crazy. This wasn't *him*. Glumly he nodded, because Eric seemed to be waiting for some response.

"Yes, sir. You and I figured things out early the hard way. I grew up in a dysfunctional family much like yours. Watching my father have his little affairs while my mother looked the other way and pretended we were some TV sitcom perfection like Ozzie and Harriet. After living like that, we'd be crazy to get serious about any woman. Smart men don't take stupid risks. Not in business and not in their personal lives."

Eric was beginning to sound like dialogue from a bad book, Michael thought with annoyance. "Look, I don't want to dwell on this anymore."

"Good idea." Eric rose. "Listen, I know this flight attendant. Bambi really knows how to have a good time. She'll be in town tonight. What do you say I have her ask a friend along and the four of us go out? Nothing like a little wine, women and song to bring you out of your doldrums."

Michael thought that suggestion held about as much appeal as a dip in the Arctic Ocean in January. He ran a hand over his chin, his fingers finding the spot he'd nicked shaving that morning. Because he'd been distracted. Because instead of his own image in the mirror, he'd seen a sweet oval face, pale yellow hair and huge blue eyes. Not just in the mirror, but everywhere he looked. He cleared his throat. "Thanks. Maybe another time."

Eric took the refusal good-naturedly. "Suit yourself. I'll be around if you change your mind."

Feeling drained, Michael watched Eric turn to leave. "Eric, what's Bambi's last name?"

Eric paused, then grinned. "Hell, I don't know. Who cares? They come and they go, good buddy."

When he heard his door close, Michael swiveled in his chair to again gaze out the window. Is that what his life had become, nameless people coming and going?

Outside Michael's office, Eric was enveloped in a big hug.

"Eric, dear boy, you're as handsome as ever," Charlotte Kramer said, offering her cheek for his kiss.

He smiled, pleased to see Michael's aunt, as always. "You're a sight for sore eyes, Charlotte. Tell me the truth, did you just have a face-lift or are you getting younger-looking every day?"

Beaming, Charlotte stepped back. "You must practice a lot to know the exact thing to say to a woman so readily."

"Not at all," Eric protested. "That was very sincere. You look wonderful." In fact, she did. She was wearing a hot-pink blousy jumpsuit belted at the waist with a bright purple sash, purple high heels and dangle earrings that just brushed her shoulders. Her hair this week was black as coal and piled high on her head. "I like your hair."

Charlotte patted her heavy curls. One of the things she was most vain about was her hair, still thick and curly. "Did you know that eight out of ten women surveyed confessed that they had more fun as brunettes than as blondes?" She winked at the blond secretary seated at the reception desk who was gazing at her with something bordering on awe to show she was only kidding.

"I don't doubt it." Eric waved toward Michael's open door. "Your nephew's in if you're looking for him." He stepped closer with the ease of an old family friend, which he was. "But he's not in the best of moods, I can tell you."

"Is that right?" She'd spoken to Michael on the phone twice since they'd both returned, and each time he'd been vague and distracted. Not that he ever had been the bubbly sort. Except the afternoon she'd spent with him and Jo Knight. She held up a packet of snapshots. "Perhaps these will cheer him. Pictures I took when we were both in Hawaii, some quite interesting."

Eric bent to look at the top one. Michael and Jo were standing at the railing of a cruiser, each with an arm around the other's waist. They were looking at each other, their hair windblown, their smiles soft. "She's a beautiful woman."

"Has Michael told you about her?" There was hope if he had.

"Very little." Eric gave Charlotte's hand a squeeze. "Listen, see what you can do. I told him no woman was worth all that, but I'm not sure I got through."

Charlotte's eyes narrowed. "Did you, now?" With a little wave of her fingers, she sailed into Michael's office, closing the door. She found him staring moodily out the window. Charlotte took a bracing breath and put on a big smile. "Michael, it's good to see you."

Of course, he'd heard her arrive. Charlotte never did anything quietly. He'd talked with her briefly last week, thanking her somewhat curtly for his birthday surprises. If she'd wondered at his abrupt manner, she hadn't let on. He swung his chair around slowly. "Sorry, I'm a bit preoccupied. Got a lot on my mind." He stood and walked around to hug her warmly.

"Of course you do. And I won't stay but a minute. I have some wonderful news to share with you." With a flourish, she settled in the chair Eric had just vacated.

Michael leaned against his desk and crossed his arms over his chest. He made a bet with himself on what her news was. She had that giddy look about her and was undoubtedly going to get married again. To the yachtsman, Simon whatever. "I could use some good news."

She thought he could, at that. She'd never seen Michael with his shirt collar open and his tie crooked during business hours. His hair was disheveled as if he'd been thrusting his fingers through it repeatedly, and he had a small cut on his chin. Yes, he certainly had all the signs, Charlotte decided with satisfaction. "It's about your sister."

Michael frowned, totally thrown off track. "Deborah? What's happening with her?" She and Shawn had flown back with him, but he hadn't seen her since.

"She's gone back to Kerry. Isn't that wonderful?"

"I don't know that it is." Michael rubbed the back of his neck and wondered if his secretary had a bottle of aspirin in her desk.

"It most certainly is." Charlotte crossed her still-trim legs. "We had dinner together last evening, the four of us. Kerry flew in and they talked all one night. They both have come to the realization that it isn't where they live that matters but that they'll be together." She sighed audibly. "Isn't that romantic?"

Michael's frown deepened. "What about Shawn's schooling and the fact that Deborah hates to travel?"

"Well, they're working all that out, dear boy. In the fall, before Shawn starts school, they're going to buy a house in California. That'll be their home base. Kerry's making decent money now and he won't be doing as much with the road shows as before. But when he has to be away for more than a week, Deborah and Shawn will go with them and they'll take along a tutor so the boy won't get behind. A good solution, don't you think?"

Walking around to sit back down, Michael shrugged. "Maybe." He picked up his pen and toyed with it. Of course, he wanted Deborah to be happy. But compromising was so damn difficult.

"*I* certainly think so. And they have Jo to thank for the suggestion."

His head shot up. "Jo? Is she here in San Francisco?"

She'd been right, Charlotte thought and nearly smiled smugly. Michael was in love with Jo just as Deborah had told her. But he was too stubborn to bend a little. "No, I believe they had several talks when you were all in the Maui house. Don't you remember?"

He remembered, all right. Remembered the days, the nights, everything that had happened at the Maui house. He wished to hell he could forget. Without answering, he swung his gaze out the window, wishing Charlotte would leave.

"Wonderful girl, that Jo Knight," Charlotte went on as if he hadn't ignored her last remark. "Comes from a beautiful family. Don't you see her anymore?"

"No. She's out of my life."

"Pity. She changed you, Michael, and all for the better."

He turned back then, his eyes narrowing. "She changed me, all right. She's damn neared ruined me." Rising, he began to pace on the thick gray carpeting. "I have responsibilities, obligations, commitments. And look at me. I can't sleep, I can't work, I can't concentrate. And why? Because of this dreamy-eyed singer of children's songs. I have goals for myself, a picture of where I want to be next year, five years from now. She lives moment to moment." He stopped at the bank of windows, feeling as if he were losing his grip.

Charlotte almost felt sorry for him, but this was no time to let up. "And where do you see yourself five years from now, dear boy?"

"Where?" Turning, he marched back. "Here, doing work I enjoy, being successful, answering to no one. Happy, fulfilled, content."

Charlotte nodded agreeably. "And Jo would keep you from achieving all that?"

"Yes. No. I mean, she doesn't want the same things I do."

Charlotte raised a penciled brow. "She doesn't want to be happy, fulfilled, content? Oh, I believe she does. I think we all do. Some of us just go about it differently."

Michael came closer, easing a hip onto the edge of his desk, letting her see his red-rimmed eyes. "Do you know that I haven't had a decent night's sleep since meeting Jo? She makes me crazy. She has me sitting here daydreaming, for God's sake. She makes me wish I had a suit of armor and a white horse standing by." He ran a shaky hand through his hair. "I think I've gone around the bend this time."

Charlotte smiled broadly. "Yes, dear boy, I think you have. Finally, you have. And about time, too."

Aunt or no aunt, he had to get this wacky woman out of his office. "What are you talking about?"

"You've fallen in love and you're fighting it. Because this is one thing you can't logically explain away in that maddening manner you men have. You can't make it go away, and it frustrates you. You can't even orchestrate it or control it." She laughed, delighted. "Why not just say 'uncle'? Did you know that statistics prove that ninety-eight percent of the world's population fall in love at sometime in their lives? And I feel truly sorry for that other two percent. Their lives must be grim indeed."

He was angry, perhaps because he was deathly afraid she was probably right. He walked back to sit down, searching for a way to end this. "You're wrong. It's not love. It was merely passion and I'll get over it."

He was disappointing her, and she let her expression show him. "Don't be crass, Michael. What you feel for Jo is far more than passion, and you know it, deep inside. If you're fool enough to walk away from this...this gift you've been given, then you're not the man I thought you were. Because when it's right between two people, when passion moves on—as it will, my dear—we are left with the tenderness." Her eyes grew cloudy. "Oh, Michael, I could wish for you nothing better than to spend your life with a mate who understands tenderness."

Shaking off the mood, Charlotte stood and removed the packet of pictures from her roomy canvas bag. She laid them on his desktop right in front of him. "Take a look at the faces of those two people. That's not lust I see. It's that other four-letter word, the one you're running so hard from."

She adjusted her bag's strap on her shoulder. "Be careful what you give up, Michael. Most of the time, we don't get a second chance." Quietly she turned and left the room.

Michael swallowed hard and picked up the pictures.

JO GRABBED A TOWEL and hurried inside, wrapping it around her as she walked. She'd been doing some afternoon laps in her backyard pool when she heard the phone ring. Heinz, scooting between her legs, zoomed past her as she answered somewhat breathlessly.

"Is that you, Jo?" Christy's voice was clear enough, but with a definite note of strain.

"Hi. I just ran in from outside. How are you?" She'd left Maui so hurriedly that she hadn't thought to call her friend, but she'd written her a short note with a vague explanation about needing to get home because of other commitments. That was probably why Christy was calling now.

"Oh, I've been better."

Jo thought she heard something that sounded like a sob at the end of Christy's comment. "Is anything wrong?"

Christy sniffed. "You could say that. Pete eloped last night and it wasn't with me."

"Oh, no." Jo eased onto a stool at her breakfast bar. "Can you tell me what happened?"

"His note—the coward couldn't face me in person—says that it was love at first sight. He only met her two weeks ago, Jo. She's his new secretary, a mousy little thing with stringy hair. That is, she *was* his new secretary. Now, she's Mrs. Peter White. Oh, damn, I told myself I wouldn't cry anymore."

"Listen, it's okay to cry." Goodness knows she'd spilled her fair share of tears lately.

"No one can fall in love in two short weeks, Jo. I can't believe this." The tears were heavy in her voice now.

Oh yes they can. One week even. She brushed back her wet hair. "But I thought you didn't love Pete, Christy? I thought you were looking for a practical marriage."

Christy let out a trembling sigh. "I thought so, too. But somewhere along the line, it snuck up on me."

Jo could relate to that, all too easily. She felt her eyes fill and blinked quickly. Why did she have to get this phone call right now, when she was so emotionally wrung out herself? "What are you going to do?"

"I don't know. School's out and I'm at loose ends. I thought Pete and I would be getting engaged this summer, maybe take a trip together and get married in the fall. Funny, eh?"

Funny. She hadn't found too many things to laugh about lately, either. "I'm really sorry, Christy."

"Yeah, me, too. Maybe I'll go back to California. Any rich dudes on the horizon there?" The humor in her voice was forced.

"None that I know of." Hadn't the girl learned her lesson?

"How's your love life?"

"Nonexistent." She hoped she didn't sound as pathetic as her friend did.

"Maybe I should move near you. We could find us a couple of guys, have some fun and to hell with this love stuff. What do you say?"

That was about the last thing Jo wanted to do. Yet she felt disloyal not commiserating with her friend. "I'm not interested in looking for men, but I'd love to see you if you decide to come back."

"I'll think about it. Thanks for listening, Jo. I just...needed to talk with someone, you know?"

She knew that feeling, too, although she hadn't talked much since returning, except with her father. Her emotions were too raw to discuss with casual friends. "Sure. Let me know what you decide."

Jo hung up slowly, feeling more depressed than ever. Christy had sought a relationship, her eye on the man's bankbook, and lost out to love. She had fallen accidentally into a relationship that had led unexpectedly to love, and lost out to both of them refusing to compromise. Who, she wondered, was winning these days in the tricky game of love?

It was nearly dinnertime and she wasn't a bit hungry. Again. Two weeks and she still hadn't regained her appetite. Oh, well, you can never be too thin or too rich, she reminded herself as she walked through the house and into her bathroom. Without enthusiasm, she turned on the shower.

She still loved her home, the rooms she'd carefully decorated, the magnificent view. And her work was fun and fulfilling, making her feel as if she were making a difference in the lives of some children. Testing the water, she stepped under the spray.

Face it, though, the shine had disappeared. Where before she'd been alone, she hadn't been lonely. Now that, too, was a new problem. Grabbing her bath sponge and scented soap, she scrubbed her skin vigorously.

Yesterday, fighting a bout of self-pity, she'd dropped in on her father at his office and had him take her to lunch. By the time she'd picked her way through a spinach salad, she'd pretty much figured out where she'd gone wrong. Dad had listened to her edited and abbreviated version of her feelings about Michael and then told her what he thought. She'd learned something that had been a hard lesson to swallow.

Reaching for the shampoo, Jo lathered her hair. She'd interpreted her father's advice from years ago to her own liking. She'd found the man she wanted, plunged head over heels in love with him, then gone after him with a relentless campaign. But she'd left out an important consideration. Although she felt that Michael was right for her, perhaps she really wasn't right for him, as he'd painstakingly tried to point out to her.

Perhaps *pigheaded* described her as well. Love had to be earned, Dad had said, and perhaps, though she'd tried, she hadn't earned Michael's love and trust.

Stepping under the spray, she rinsed shampoo from her hair and soap from her limbs.

Maybe, in time, he'd revise his thinking and come around. Maybe he'd be willing to take another crack at trying to make it work. If he did show up, she'd try to compromise instead of ramroding him, wanting to change him, trying to loosen him up constantly. He was his own man, the one she'd fallen in love with. If only she could let him know that *she* had changed her thinking.

She had hoped to steer Michael gently into loving her. She'd known early on that he wanted her, just as she'd known that that alone would never be enough for her. She'd gambled that he would learn to care as deeply as she did.

Gamblers had to be prepared to lose. She hadn't been.

Jo turned off the water, stepped out and reached for a clean towel. She wrapped it around herself, then grabbed another and began to rub her hair dry. The hard lessons of life are the easiest to learn, her mother had always said. If you were smart. Jo considered herself fairly smart, most of the time. And she'd certainly learned this hard lesson quickly.

Never again would she offer her love to a man blindly, without making sure it was mutual. Never again would she lead with her heart in a developing friendship with a man. Never again. She paused, hanging up the damp towel. The trouble was she really didn't want to start over with another man as Christy seemed ready to do. She wanted Michael and only Michael.

Picking up her comb, she pulled it through her long hair, then opened the door to get the steam out of the bathroom. A one-man woman, wasn't that what Charlotte had called her? Oh, Lord, but she didn't want to wind up some pathetic old woman weeping over the love that could never be. Yet she was awfully afraid she was well on her way.

As she headed for her bedroom to get dressed, the doorbell rang. Jo debated whether to grab a robe, but decided she was well covered with the towel. Heinz was barking his own welcome. Shushing him, she opened the door a crack.

Shocked, Jo took a step back. Even Heinz stopped, staying at her side and growling.

Someone dressed as a droopy-eyed basset hound with long, floppy ears stood on her porch. He held one front paw behind his back. Surprise turned to hesitant pleasure as Jo got a hold of herself. "Yes?"

"Special delivery for Miss Jo Knight," the muffled voice from inside the dog outfit said. The hidden paw emerged holding a string with a big red balloon tied to the end. The message on the balloon read: I love you.

Hesitantly Jo took the balloon. Was he from one of those new outfits who do singing telegrams and the like? Or could the man inside the suit be—no! Had her mother been right? Had Michael woken up and come to her? "Is there a card?"

The dog shook his head, his sad eyes rolling around. Heinz, totally confused by the familiar scent of someone he knew who didn't look as he remembered, inched forward reluctantly. "It's okay, boy," Michael said, and whipped off his head covering.

His hair was wildly askew and his face damp. His eyes fastened on hers, famished for the sight of her. As hungry as his arms were to hold her. But first, a few things had to be said. "Would you invite a very warm dog in out of the afternoon heat?"

"Certainly." Holding her balloon, Jo stepped back.

"I knew you couldn't resist taking in a stray." He glanced at the couch and saw a blue-eyed Siamese curled up against a fat orange tabby, the two other cats Jo hadn't taken to Hawaii with her. In a corner cage was a bright green parakeet. Floppy was under the dining room table eyeing him sleepily, and Heinz, now that he recognized Michael, had moved inside to sit watching him, his head cocked.

"I do have a weakness for stray animals." His eyes on her were serious, she noted, as a pulse in her throat began to throb. "I should get dressed."

His paw touched her arm. "No, wait." He took a deep breath. "I came to thank you. I've been doing a lot of thinking, and I realize you did me a big favor."

He looked so adorable in the silly suit. She wanted to brush back his hair, to touch him. Instead she clung to the string of the balloon, needing to know the rest. "What favor was that?"

"You put me in touch with the child I'd buried deep inside me. I certainly struggled against it, I know. But that day at the school, I really got a kick out of seeing those kids' faces." He felt the tension mount as he noticed that her eyes were serious again.

"I'm glad, Mike." Of all the hopeful scenarios she'd pictured, this hadn't been like any of them. What about the message on the balloon? "But I wouldn't want to think you'd changed for me."

"No, not for you, although you showed me the way. I changed for me. And I've come to realize that I was afraid of marriage, and maybe I still am in a lot of ways. But I want to start over, Jo." He ran a hand through his damp hair. "I'm going about this all wrong. I'm not good at putting my feelings into words."

She was watching him very carefully and listening very hard. "Take a stab at it. Basic English, nothing fancy."

"It's just that I've never done this before, Jo."

"Done what?"

"Proposed. Will you marry me?" He put his doggie paws around her and pulled her against his hairy chest. "I love you, Jo, and I've never said that to another woman."

"Oh, Michael." Was she dreaming? Jo rose on tiptoe to kiss him. There it was, the fireworks she hadn't seen since leaving him. After a moment, she stepped back. "Will you take off this ridiculous outfit?"

Finding the tab, he pulled down the zipper and shrugged out of the suit, tossing it onto the floor where Heinz snarled at it cautiously.

He was wearing only briefs. Jo smiled. "Why, look at this. The proper Mr. Daye running around in his underwear." She could afford to joke now. He was back, here in her home, talking love.

Michael gathered her close to his warm body. "Yeah, I am. A lady I know told me I should loosen up. This loose enough for you, lady?"

Looking up at him, she nodded. "Now then, what were you saying?"

"About how I love you and want to marry you?"

"Yes, that part." She sighed, knowing she had a few things she needed to say, too. "I made some mistakes, Mike," she confessed. "I didn't want to change *you*. I love you the way you are. I wanted you to change your ideas about love and marriage. I wanted you to care enough to risk committing to me."

"I know." Leaning back, he smiled down into her incredible eyes. "I tried ignoring my feelings for you, Jo. I couldn't. Remember what I told you that my father said that long ago day he visited me in the hospital? It's about the only good advice he'd ever given me. 'Weigh things carefully and take a risk only if the price is worth the pain.' Jo, you're worth anything I might have to go through. I've been miserable without you."

The words she'd been longing to hear. "Me, too. I love you so much. I whispered those words to you once, then worried that I'd frightened you off."

"I heard it. And it did scare me. It still does. I don't know what kind of husband I'll make, Jo. Or what sort of father. I haven't witnessed any I'd like to imitate."

"Don't imitate anyone. Just be you, go with your instincts and you'll be fine."

Able to smile from the heart, he picked her up off the floor into a bone-crushing hug. "I was so worried you wouldn't let me in, that you didn't want me back."

Her feet back on the floor, Jo pressed herself to him suggestively. "Oh, I want you, all right."

His blood was heating quickly, but he wanted to tell her all of it. "I talked with Eric, my partner, about wanting to make some changes, do more work from home. We could live here ..."

"In my house?"

"If that's what you want, and keep my apartment, too. Until we build our own house, one that we design together. And when I need to travel, will you come with me? I don't believe in absentee marriages."

"Nor do I. And when I have an out-of-town commitment, will you travel with me?"

"Yes. The kids and I will sit out in the audience and applaud you. Unless, of course, I'm needed to fill in on stage."

Jo's eyes grew misty. "I'm not dreaming, am I, Mike? This is really happening?"

He kissed her again, bringing her body close so she could feel his desire for her. "Is that real enough for you?"

"I'm beginning to believe ..."

"You're dressed much too warmly for this weather." Stepping back, he pulled off her towel and tossed it aside, his eyes reacquainting him with her soft curves. Growing impatient, Michael picked her up into his arms. "Where's your bedroom? We have two long weeks to make up for."

Giddy with love, Jo smiled at him. "And a whole lifetime to do it in."

H A R L E Q U I N
American Romance®

American Romance's year-long celebration continues. Join your favorite authors as they celebrate love set against the special times each month throughout 1992.

Next month, recall those sweet memories of summer love, of long, hot days . . . and even hotter nights in:

AUGUST

S	M	T	W	T	F	S
						1
2			6	7	8	
9			13	1		
16	1					
		25	26			

**#449
OPPOSING CAMPS
by Judith Arnold**

Read all the Calendar of Romance titles, coming to you one per month, all year, only in American Romance.

JAYNE ANN KRENTZ

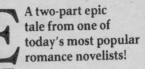

A two-part epic tale from one of today's most popular romance novelists!

Dreams
Parts One & Two

The warrior died at her feet, his blood running out of the cave entrance and mingling with the waterfall. With his last breath he cursed the woman— told her that her spirit would remain chained in the cave forever until a child was created and born there....

So goes the ancient legend of the Chained Lady and the curse that bound her throughout the ages—until destiny brought Diana Prentice and Colby Savager together under the influence of forces beyond their understanding. Suddenly they were both haunted by dreams that linked past and present, while their waking hours were filled with danger. Only when Colby, Diana's modern-day warrior, learned to love, could those dark forces be vanquished. Only then could Diana set the Chained Lady free....

Available in September wherever Harlequin books are sold.

Take 4 bestselling love stories FREE

Plus get a FREE surprise gift!

WELCOME TO

The quintessential small town where everyone knows everybody else!

Finally, books that capture the pleasure of tuning in to your favorite TV show!

GREAT READING...GREAT SAVINGS...AND A FABULOUS FREE GIFT!

Each book set in Tyler is a self-contained love story; together, the twelve novels stitch the fabric of the community. The covers honor the old American tradition of quilting; each cover depicts a patch of the large Tyler quilt.

With Tyler you can receive a fabulous gift ABSOLUTELY FREE by collecting proofs-of-purchase found in each Tyler book. And use our special Tyler coupons to save on your next TYLER book purchase.

Join your friends at Tyler for the sixth book, SUNSHINE by Pat Warren, available in August.

When Janice Eber becomes a widow, does her husband's friend David provide more than just friendship?

BIG SUMMER READ

Summer Reading
At Its Best

In July, Harlequin and Silhouette bring readers the Big Summer Read Program. Heat up your summer with these four exciting new novels by top Harlequin and Silhouette authors.

SOMEWHERE IN TIME by Barbara Bretton
YESTERDAY COMES TOMORROW by Rebecca Flanders
A DAY IN APRIL by Mary Lynn Baxter
LOVE CHILD by Patricia Coughlin

From time travel to fame and fortune, this program offers something for everyone.

Available at your favorite retail outlet.

BSR

**IF YOU THOUGHT
ROMANCE NOVELS WERE ALL
THE SAME...LOOK AGAIN!**

Our exciting new look
begins this September

And now, Harlequin American Romance is better than ever!
Starting this September, Harlequin invites you to
experience the *new* American Romance....
Bold, brash and exciting romantic adventures—where
anything is possible and dreams come true.

Also in September, look for our exciting new cover that will
whisk you into the world of fast-paced, romantic adventure.

**Watch for a sneak preview of
our new covers next month!**

HARLEQUIN AMERICAN ROMANCE—
Love was never so exciting!